Blinders Keepers

by

John Rachel

Published by
Literary Vagabond Books
Los Angeles • Osaka
literaryvagabond.com

LITERARY VAGABOND

Blinders Keepers
(Second Edition)
Copyright © 2015
by John D Rachel

Print Book ISBN #978-0-692-60213-3

Cover Art by Veronica Faulkner

Blinders Keepers

by

John Rachel

Collapse, chaos, confusion, rioting, looting.
And that's the good news!

America is coming apart and the President can do nothing to stop it.

Nonetheless, 23-year-old Noah Tass has his own problems. Stuck his entire life in the hayseed capital of the Bible Belt after his father abandoned him over 18 years ago, he has no future, all his friends are losers, his job is a dead end, his fashion-challenged mom is stark raving mad, his clueless sister a meth head stripper.

It was time to bail!

Yes, it was time for a new plan, a whole new direction, time to discover America, to kick start his life. Noah leaves Missouri and for a year truly experiences the adventure of a lifetime.

Noah soon discovers the country has become one big loony bin, as he is thrust into the puppet theater of contemporary American life, and the cast includes a deranged blundering president, brutal agents of the ATF, FBI and NSA — thugs who shoot first and ask questions later — and an underground of unkempt, wild and wacky but endearing freaks who are trying to overthrow the existing order.

How does that timeless expression go?

What doesn't kill you makes you all the stronger.

Hmm . . . . .

Acknowledgements

First, I'd wholeheartedly like to thank the fictional citizens of the fictional town of Pulnick for their unparalleled hospitality and valuable assistance during the writing of this book. For a place which doesn't exist and which therefore I've never been, I feel like I have lived there all my life and now have a second home to which I can comfortably return anytime.

I want to profoundly thank my wife, my best friend and constant companion, Masumi Nishida, for her encouragement and faith in me, and her magnificent role as teacher and guide in my discovering the wonders of Japan and Japanese culture.

For their inestimable contributions to my literary and intellectual development, as well as my fragile grip on reality, I too must express my appreciation and awe shucks to: Tom Robbins, Woody Allen, Kurt Vonnegut, Stanislaw Lem, Chuck Palahniuk, Christopher Moore, Charles Bukowski, Jerzy Kosinski, Bertrand Russell, Noam Chomsky, Ludwig Wittgenstein, Neil Postman, and Jared Diamond.

For their continuing friendship and support, I extend my sincere gratitude to Judy Rachel, Randy Calligan, Mickey Eres Finn, Travis Rood, Ron Ruiz, Gilly Adkins, Russ Swider, Nicholas Penrake, Jeff J. Brown, Randolph Winters, George Polley, and Alex Malherbe.

Lastly, it would be unconscionable and incredibly rude for me to fail to identify those individuals most responsible for my recent phenomenal success, and declare my heartfelt gratitude and indebtedness. I of course refer to the staff of my indefatigable publisher Literary Vagabond Books, every last one of you, but especially the svelte and droll head of that organization, Sybil Fairbanks, and my new editor there, Evelyn Ishimoto, who despite never having bothered to learn English has done a marvelous job on this challenging book. Both of you are studies in and witness to the irrepressible power of the human imagination.

Table of Contents

CHAPTER ONE

State of the Union

It was that time of year again. Last week of January.

The President was making his much anticipated State of the Union Address.

After the usual greetings and initial courtesies — thanking everyone for coming, acknowledging the important players in all branches of the government, and offering gracious regards for a few special invited guests, — the President delivered the type of crowd-pleasing line which has been the linchpin of State of the Union addresses for as long as anyone cared to remember.

> *"As I stand before this great body and look out at the faces of those who have dedicated themselves to this great nation, I can say with absolute confidence that America is on strong and certain footing."*

Then abruptly his expression changed, he shook his head and stopped speaking. Hands grasping the edges of the podium, he looked down at his feet and appeared to be lost in thought.

What followed was both unexpected and certainly unprecedented. He looked back up. Gone was the confident smile, the twinkle in his eye, the arched optimistic brow. He appeared somber, a touch sad, apologetic.

> *"Who am I trying to fool here? You, my respected Congressmen? Some of the finest legislators to ever hold public office? The excellent justices of the Supreme Court who preside over the greatest legal institution in history? Myself? No, I'm not here to try to fool anyone. These are times unlike any this nation has ever seen. So I'll tell you exactly what the state of our union is. It's a fucking mess!"*

A deathly silence filled the entire congressional chamber. If a pin had dropped, it would have been possible to know its exact size and just how many times it bounced. What wasn't entirely clear was if they had somehow missed what he just said, or if they had heard it, but it hadn't actually registered. Blank faces and unfocused eyes filled the chamber.

Then, as if being directed by some invisible conductor, or moved by an invisible resonant force field, everyone immediately stood up and began with thunderous applause, cheering, and raucous acclamation, to give him a huge standing ovation. This went on and on, for several minutes at least, never in the least waning in intensity. The President smiled and waved, basking in the adulation. Finally, he had enough and made it clear he had more that he wanted to say. Using a palm's down gesturing with his hands, he eventually got them to sit back down.

> *"So here's what we're gonna do. I want you all to look down at the floor. Now pull your pant legs up over your calves. What do you see? For those senators and congressman from Texas, this will be easy. You won't have to imagine. The rest of you, just look and see what I'm seeing. See those loops. Those are bootstraps. Yes, bootstraps. Okay. Now look back up at me."*

Dramatically the President held up high in front of him his two index fingers.

> *"See these? What we're gonna do is take these and insert them right in those bootstraps. Then all together, we're gonna lift. We're gonna lift like no one has ever lifted before. And we're gonna pick ourselves up. We're gonna pick ourselves up and we're gonna stay up. Do you know why? I'll tell you why. Because this is America. This is the greatest country that ever was or ever will be. And as we have demonstrated time and time again, as we have shown the naysayers and skeptics over and over, this is one country that can do it. We will do it! Yes! By God we will do it! Ladies and gentlemen, thanks to each and every one of you for your unselfish dedication, your unwavering patriotism, your honorable service to this great country. God bless America!"*

Everyone in the chamber, congressman, jurists, ushers, guards, special guests, select members of the press, again leaped to their feet. The response this time was totally over the top. It made the first ovation look like they had been standing graveside at a wake.

Suddenly and without warning, over the explosive din of the hysterical whooping and yelling, could be heard blasting from P.A. speakers hidden behind the long drapes at the rear of the gallery, the U.S. Army band playing *Happy Days Are Here Again*. This theatrical touch just added to the ongoing chain reaction, notching the hysteria up another two levels.

With climactic flair which rivaled the best Superbowl half-time shows, red, white and blue balloons then dropped from the ceiling. Like crazed, frenetic school children, the congressman start batting them around.

Maybe the country was going to hell in a hand basket. But darn it all, there was no reason to get all down in the mouth about it.

Bambi Meets Godzilla

The sun wasn't even up yet. Noah couldn't sleep. This was going to be a big day for him. By the end of the week, his whole life would change.

He slipped out of bed, made coffee, glanced out of the second story window of his miserable flat on the outskirts of town. Grey meets grey on a dull landscape that offered little and promised more of the same.

He poured some dry cat food in the dish beside the sink, then with a steaming cup of America's worst coffee in hand, sat down at his Acer desktop computer. As it booted up, his favorite fluffy kitty, Capri, jumped onto his lap. What an irresistible ball of fur! He rubbed behind her ears and under her chin, his petting skills fine-tuned to her hedonistic pleasures over the past two years. In his eyes, she was still the helpless little kitten he found two winters ago, shivering under the steps of his mothers house, abandoned and close to starving.

"Oh, Capri. Now don't you go telling Naomi you're the real love of my life."

The desktop photo of a Himalayan Sherpa came up on his monitor.

Perhaps sensing her time was up, Capri jumped down and went into the kitchen to eat the Purina pressed cardboard pellets in her dish.

Noah sipped his coffee and started his routine.

He looked at his email. All spam. Deleted.

He checked the headlines on USA Today Online. All rumors and garbage.

He then pulled up a video of *Bambi Meets Godzilla* on YouTube.

He loved this little film. How many times had he seen it? Fifty? A hundred?

Almost the entire length of the three-minute movie consisted of opening credits rolling over an idyllic animation of Bambi eating and frolicking in the forest. Gentle spring flute music playfully accompanied the chirping of birds. Finally the credits finish and to a thunderous, forest-shaking *kaboom!*, Godzilla's giant foot comes down and squashes the innocent little fawn. All we see is Godzilla's grizzly leg and Bambi's four tiny twig-like limbs sticking out from under the giant reptilian foot. The music and birds have stopped. Now as the *kaboom!* trails off in a long tail of reverb, **The End** fades up on the screen and the film is over.

As many times as he had watched it, it never failed to put him in a great mood. Of course, the first twenty or thirty times left him rolling helplessly on the floor in convulsions of laughter. Now it just left him pleasantly amused.

Naomi had gotten up and wandered sleepily into the room. She put her hands on Noah's shoulders, kissed the top of his head, and managed to get her lips functioning.

"Are you watching that again?"

"It's inspiring."

"Ugh! That's horrible! Seeing that poor, helpless little creature crushed inspires you?"

"It confirms my belief that the world is as screwed up as I think it is."

Now it was Naomi's turn for a hot beverage. She was a tea person. She went into the kitchen and started the kettle.

Noah shut down the computer and got ready for work.

"I'll see you at dinner. But the guys are doing a going-away thing for me tonight."

"I'm sure it'll be a night of thought-provoking conversation and ennobling sentiments."

Naomi was such a treasure. She had to be the only person within 1000 miles with anything resembling intelligence, wit, perspective. How was it possible for such a sexy creature to have such a remarkable mind and a maturity at age twenty, that people in this redneck wasteland never achieved over their entire lives? He and Naomi had been living together now for five months. Every day was a surprise and a source of discovery and wonder with her. She obviously loved, understood, accepted him in ways he never could have imagined, much less hoped for.

Was it really possible he was walking away from all of this?

Heavy Metal

Noah dutifully ambled into Building C and punched the clock for his last day at work — technically his last *half*-day, as he'd be leaving for good at lunch time.

Merkel Industries got the tin from China. Then they cut it, rolled it, pressed it, shaped it, twisted it, configuring it to the specifications of their customers. Mostly they produced corrugated panels and food cans. Those were the two big product lines, purely because that's what their three main customers needed — Hormel for their Spam and ham lines, Bartlett for everything from pears and walnuts to pork and beans, and United Sheet Metal Products for shipping containers, mobile homes, trucking enclosures, storage sheds big and small, and roofing.

The company had been started in a barn by Thadeus Merkel right there in Noah's home town of Pulnick. Thadeus was a blacksmith by trade who had the imagination and vision to conceive of how he could extend his simple metalworking skills to create a range of products useful for both the home and places of business — kitchen and bathroom, garage and barn, factory and farm.

The firm was the longstanding pride of the state of Missouri, which had celebrated for nearly a century its innovation and expansion. At its peak throughout World War II, followed by the business and building boom of the fifties, Merkel Industries sprawled over the center of Monroe County and employed over 8000, nearly a third of the region's population. Of course, in the past fifty years a lot had changed in America's manufacturing sector. Now cheap labor across the globe had gutted its industrial capacity, resulting in significant and steady reduction nationwide in the durable trades workforce.

To remain competitive and profitable, Merkel had gradually downsized and become the relatively small but solid company it currently was. The labor union was long gone. The region certainly didn't substantially depend on it any longer for its bread and butter. But it had its place, its own secure and respected position in the community and among its sustainable set of loyal customers. It was still at the top of the list for most desirable places to get a job, both for the school dropouts and for those who made it all the way through Calvin Coolidge Jr.-Sr. High School, who perhaps had rudimentary job skills, but were not in a position to go to junior college or a vocational school to obtain specialized job training. It was the factory equivalent of pumping gas, working at McDonalds, or clerking at one of the convenience stores in the area.

In his daily rounds, Noah came in visual contact with practically all of the four hundred plus employees who worked at Merkel, mostly those in the manufacturing area, since he was constantly carting pallets of raw galvanized sheet metal to them, where it was processed into the requisite final configurations. But he also became familiar with a number of the office staff, since he was the one assigned to go to the engineering office and pick up the new orders, spec sheets and blue prints.

Even so, he really spent 95% of his time side by side with just four other guys, all close to his own age — the Full Metal Jack Its, as they affectionately called themselves.

This mismatched, motley team manned the tractors, drove the fork lift trucks, maneuvered the hydraulic stackers, wielded the hand pallet movers, and operated the overhead cranes, to move hundreds of tons of metal every week across the thousands of square feet of factory floor space. They were renowned for their efficiency and effectiveness, but reviled for often being reckless and risky in the performance of their duties. Despite countless close calls, their track record was impeccable, unmarred by any embarrassing or potentially harmful accidents. Not that this offered any comfort to anyone else working there. Employees always scattered when one of the heavy-duty Cat Lift trucks or medium-size Raymond haulers came bearing down on them, usually carrying 40% more than the approved load capacity of the vehicle, engine whining as the huge stack of sheet metal or pallet of corrugated storage shed siding swayed like a circus clown's implausible stack of kitchen dishes.

Their antics had so entirely become the stuff of local legends that they had their own t-shirt. A young secretary in the front office with an artistic flair and a raging crush on one of the Jack Its, designed it and had a number of them printed up. The front displayed a lift truck with its forks high in the air and King Kong on top beating his chest like he had conquered the world. The rear of the shirt said *The FMJIs Forever!*

The four guys that Noah was teamed with had all been working at Merkel for some time, and among them had almost twenty years of seniority.

Tal "Blow Me" Caswell was the unofficial but undisputed leader of the pack. He was so nicknamed for the epithet which seemed to introduce or be somehow incorporated in his every utterance. Someone said that if Tal was orally serviced every time he used that particular phrase, by the end of a work shift, he'd be sucked so dry he would turn into a dusty, desiccated powder. *'Like blow me, dude. We gotta have five loads over to Bay 7 like ten minutes ago.'* *'Hey, blow me. You still owe me five bucks from yesterday.'* *'The Lakers? Right! Blow me. Their whory glory days have been over since Kobe got whacked for honey dipping that chick, you know, that Laker Girl.'*

Steve Toblinski was the strong silent type and a chain smoker. For a while the guys called him Mute, but since he never answered to it the nickname got dropped. A tall muscular facsimile of Heath Ledger, he could just sit in a restaurant or bar with a cigarette in his hand, never say a word, and within ten minutes have at least five girls competing for him. He never looked anyone directly in the eye, conducting the entirety of his human relationships in the periphery of his vision. He always appeared to be lost in thought, though no one was privy to the mysterious workings of his mind. He never laughed out loud. In his moments of wild abandon, his handsome face might brighten momentarily in a tempered grin.

Freddie "Fat Fuck" Stangler was short, fat and giddy. His nickname did not seem to bother him, in fact he seemed amused by it, maybe even pleased, since it generated a certain pride in the acceptance it connoted. "Fat Fuck" was usually replaced by "F" in mixed company or just out of laziness. Between pepperoni sticks, candy bars, and other handfuls of junk food, he told jokes — cumulatively thousands of jokes — never to anyone's recollection repeating a single one. He seemed to be a walking encyclopedia of gags, one-liners, quips, humorous quotes, and funny stories with groaner punch lines.

Samuel "Ghost" Leek was an albino. Every hair on his body was white and his skin was a purplish pink and highly sensitive to the sun. During the summer he could get a sunburn just running from his car into the factory, so he always wore a wide-brim hat when he was outside. Though his albinism implied a fragility or vulnerability, the fact was he was incredibly powerful and nearly indestructible. He often by himself did the real heavy lifting, or would be on one end of some huge load while three guys were on the other. He was understandable shy, since he looked like the photographic negative of a human being, but once engaged was the most personable and easy to get to know of the bunch. To add to the gasp-inducing first impression he made, Ghost had a scorpion tattooed across his face.

Noah had been spared being subjected to a nickname. A few were tried along the way but nothing really stuck. Maybe it was because he was hard to define. No one could read him. He was a Teflon enigma. He always was right there in the thick of conversations but often left everyone scratching their heads. Noah enjoyed propagating a moderately mirthful confusion. Not especially difficult with this particular crowd.

The five of them were all around the same age, within five years of one another. Noah at 23 was the youngest, Steve the oldest at 28. They had all gone to the same high school — since there wasn't an alternative, what local boy hadn't? — but none had been in the same class.

They worked together well. They were a good team. They got the job done, whatever it was, quickly and efficiently. While they constantly vilified management, the usual stuff — not getting paid enough, their working conditions, the cowpiss-in-a-cup the vending machine swill passed off as coffee, the line bosses generally having their heads up inside a dark orifice — they obviously took pride in their work and relished what occasional praise came their way. It wasn't uncommon to see them around town wearing their navy blue work shirts with the Merkel Industries logo, even on their days off.

Noah was easily accepted when he first came to Merkel. There was no requirement that he jump through hoops to earn his place on the team. Everyone got along well, both on the job and when they started inviting Noah to party with them. "Partying" could be anything — riding around, hitting a few bars, dropping in at some lame Pulnick party, going bowling or to a rodeo or some other local town event — but by unstated consent it always included two essential elements: drinking and looking at chicks. While these weren't the apogee in the soaring arc of human aspiration, Noah had no aversion either, so even if he was nowhere as aggressive a drinker or ogler as his workmates, he still fit right in. He felt a camaraderie, a male bonding. It felt good to have some guys to hang out with.

There was only one area which could have been a source of serious animosity. But by virtue of a silent pact of diplomacy, it was never discussed.

Noah was a Michael Jackson fan. The Full Metal Jack Its worshipped at the altar of heavy metal rock music.

Not even pop metal like Bon Jovi, Def Leppard or Guns N' Roses. That was wussy boy stuff. They liked the dark, dirty and demented. The stuff that would rip your brain out of your skull and tear your mind up into a thousand little pieces. Even Motley Crue, despite their appetite for wild orgies, sprees of random destruction, harrowing drug abuse, and near death drinking, were looked on as pathetic posers. More pussy rock for pimple-faced wannabees.

Basically, the original four Full Metal Jack Its loved the stuff that the religious right hated. The stuff that would send them on an express train to Hell. And paralleling their vehement vilification of those who condemned them, their love of death metal burned with a religious fervor that made evangelical Christians and the

Islamic jihadist mujahidin look like lethargic hobbyists.

One time during a cigarette break out behind Bldg #5, in a rare moment when he actually put together a verbal stream of more than two consecutive words, the usually silent Steve philosophized about metal and its place in their world.

With an interesting ontological leap — a Unified Field Theory for work and play — he carried on for several minutes, as if during the hundreds of hours of muteness which preceded his soliloquy, he had been constructing his new theory and now it was ready to be made public. Some highlights ...

"Think about the men working in the mines, the ore being loaded into box cars, the smelting factories, huge ships carrying the refined metal to ports, then it being brought here. Thousands of men across the world. Strong men. Moving the metal. Working the metal. Constructing buildings and bridges. We're part of that huge army. Soldiers of steel."

"Uh, Steve ... we're mainly doing tin here."

"Steel. I meant it as a symbol, asshole. And if you can shut the fuck up, it'll make sense. Because it's all just energy. Nothing is solid. In the Universe, there is more space than substance. Just like music. They say in music the notes that are not played are more important than the notes that are played. You know. Like the silences. Like the silence of outer space."

Noah had a little problem with that one. It seemed to him that heavy metal never let up. There was no silence. No space. Everyone played and screamed as much, as fast, and as loud as they could. It was like having a mountain dropped on you, with about as much "space" and wiggle room as you would have at the Earth's core. But he kept quiet.

"Music is vibration. Metal is the best conductor of vibration. Heavy metal music and real metal — I mean the stuff we handle every day — is like the perfect mating of everything in the world. It's the perfect mating of mass and energy. Like Einstein."

Fat Fuck lit up like he was getting it.

"Ah! Are you saying Einstein was a headbanger?"

"No, you dumb fuck! Heavy metal music wasn't even around then. But maybe ... yeah. If he was around now, he probably would have been. $E = mc^2$ says it all."

Noah might go along with that. The bands they really liked — Megadeath, Anthrax, Slayer, Venom, Motörhead, Sepultura — were about as subtle as a hydrogen bomb.

Tal, Steve, Fat Fuck, Ghost.

What could he say?

At least they weren't boring.

Suddenly out of nowhere, Tal came to a screeching halt within inches of Noah on the lift truck he was driving.

"Hey, sphincter lips. It's your last day. Let's do some damage."

Good-Bye and Good Luck

"Good-bye and good luck, young man. Hope your little adventure works out."

The HR rep, Frank Gladstone, looked to be in his early-fifties and had the air of someone who had been passed over many times before landing his current powerhouse position as an acting assistant manager of human resources in a sheet metal factory in the middle of nowhere.

Despite his best efforts to fake the smile of paternal encouragement, Gladstone couldn't hide his skepticism. Noah was obviously another young punk who'd have to learn the hard way. The HR director handed Noah a folder of de-assignment documents which would soon find their permanent home in the trash. Pigeons make poop. Corporate flunkies make paperwork.

Noah exited the admin office building with a sense of being 3,000 tons lighter.

He was smiling ear-to-ear as he headed for the last time to the employees parking lot of Merkel Industries.

As he approached his old but dependable Chevy Caprice, he couldn't help but hear the scream and rumble of a Slayer song — it sounded like *Blood Red* in the swirling muck of the distortion — filtering through the dusty air of the parking lot. As he got closer, he realized it was coming from the lunch wagon of choice for the Full Metal Jack Its, Tal's '72 Oldsmobile Delta 88 — truly a classic — fully tricked out with mag wheels and rear fender skirts, a fake air scoop on the engine hood, a racing-style spoiler on the trunk lid, and a tattered ill-fitting black vinyl bra across the front. It sat so low Noah doubted it could clear a pair of gym sneakers. Whether this was intentional or just the result of broken springs was anyone's guess. He had never bothered to ask.

It was lunch time and as was their daily custom, Tal, Steve, Freddie, and Ghost were using the 30 minutes to best advantage. At least their version of best.

As Noah walked up, the passenger side window of the Olds rolled down. A cloud of smoke billowed out like the seats were on fire. The volume of the music came down just enough for Noah to be heard.

"What's for lunch? Sushi and matzo balls?"

"Nutrition bar."

Freddie held up a king-size Snickers.

Tal leaned over from the drivers side and offered Noah a hit off a humungous joint.

"Brain enema?"

Noah smiled and politely waved it off.

Tal took a monstrous hit, holding it in with clenched teeth. He passed the cigar-size spliff to Steve in the back seat. Then with eyes fired up like a coal furnace and an expression like he was looking at Lindsey Lohan's tits, he launched into a half-mocking home-boy drawl.

"Noah Tass! Blow me, motherfucker! This is so fucked up! You're really splitting? Dude! You're going to miss out on all the fun!"

"I know. I know. What am I thinking?"

Ghost squeezed his face into the open window. It certainly was quite a face. Puffy pinkish-purplish skin adorned with tufts of cumulous cloud curly white hair and wispy white eyebrows. Then there was the tattoo. A scorpion the size of Nick Foles' hands.

"Tonight, motherfucker! Tonight we give you a Full Metal Jack Its send off you'll never remember."

Yeah. He'd miss these guys. Sort of. Maybe?

But would they miss him? Would they even remember him or would he dissolve after a few more cloudbursts of weed-fueled hilarity?

"Tonight, gentlemen!"

And that was that. No more job. No more Merkel Industries.

As he drove away, for some reason his beat-up old Chevy felt like a Rolls Royce.

It took about 35 minutes for Noah to pull up in front of Alliant Bank in Monroe City, where he had his savings account.

After a few courtesies and formalities — a print-out of his account history to date, a withdrawal of funds request in triplicate — the mousy teller, who looked like she might have been raised by ground hogs, only without that much fashion sense, was counting out his money.

"Eight thousand seven hundred, eight hundred, ten, twenty, thirty, forty, five, six, seven, and twenty nine cents. That's it. Are you sure you want to close out this account?"

"I'm opening a dental floss factory in Madagascar."

"Well, golly. Good luck with that. I try to floss every day."

"Awesome."

Almost nine thousand dollars richer, he climbed in his car to head back home.

As he left the city limits of Monroe, Noah felt like he had slipped into a sepia coma. He knew it was boring here. But he had never really noticed how dreary and drab it was. Grays and browns blended into browns and grays. The sky looked like a billowing mass of floating mucous. Norman Rockwell would have punched out and quit painting.

The drive back home was uneventful. In fact, it was less than uneventful. It was *anti*-eventful. Noah was certain that if anything *tried* to happen in this hopeless buttcrack of the Midwest, it would be sucked up by a cosmic energy sponge, stuffed into the infinite black hole of nothingness, and rendered null and void.

For 6 miles he got stuck behind a tractor. Finally, the jaw-dropping epiphany that his was not the only vehicle on the road broadsided the farmer. He eased onto the shoulder and let the forty-five cars behind him pass.

Cruising southwest on Highway 24 pointed Noah directly back to Pulnick.

The skyline loomed ahead like the diminutive mirage of an afterthought.

He pulled into town. What there was left of a town.

There was one main street. Reflecting an astonishing burst of creativity decades ago, it was called Main Street.

As he drove through, it struck him how forgiving he had been up till now. Without the prospect of escape he had always just accepted it for what it was, or more accurately, what it had become.

Maybe at some point, it had halcyon days of glory and splendor. But now Pulnick was a shambles. It had become a victim of big box collateral damage when a Walmart had opened in adjacent Ralls County. Pulnick's legacy stores, some that went back generations, were driven into the red and had no choice but to shutter their doors.

There had been a barber shop. The spinning candy-stripe pole sat idle. Now looking through the front windows, the place appeared to be storage space for a mattress company, which had no posted hours of business and never seemed to be open anyway.

The five-and-dime had become some sort of antique mall, which at least had the potential to offer an item-by-item flea market for the town's history. Unfortunately, the only real antiques were the five or six ladies who manned their booths full of worthless junk, hideous old clothes, and broken household appliances. Stuff that even the Salvation Army Store in nearby Fennersville wouldn't touch.

Three home-style restaurants had for years happily thrived. The most popular had been Fat City, a meat and fries place where in better days gastronomical gut bombs were consumed by the hundreds. Every spring it sponsored a pork-and-beef-barbecue street festival, which brought in people from five counties. They claimed the smoke from the barbecue pits drifted all the way to mainland China. The other two eateries were Gilda's Home-style Cooking and Mark Twain's Pudding & Pie, which despite the name had made the best fresh bread for counties around, seven days a week. Now all three were out of business.

A hardware store, a walk-in vet clinic, two beauty salons, a sewing supplies and yarn shop, a Bible book store, a collectibles consignment shop, and a genuine country-style haberdasher, were all likewise out of business. Several still had their last words of apologies and regret posted in their now empty and unattended storefront windows.

The only exception was Fuller's Apothecary. Mr. Fuller mysteriously seemed content running his business at a loss, or had some unknown source of income which kept the place afloat. Whichever it was, the old-fashion drugstore held its own and opened its doors at 312 North Main, 7 am till 6 pm every day except Sunday. Fuller had expanded beyond medicinal needs and did a fairly brisk business in candies and frozen treats, though hardly enough to compensate for the loss of his entire prescription business to the mega-drugstore contained inside Walmart.

Even with Fuller's still in business, what charm the town might at one time have claimed had steadily eroded, as all along Main Street the paint pealed, the signs faded, the limestone discolored and dissolved, and the building bricks became dark and dingy with dirt and decay. The store front windows were either boarded up, unwashed and dusty, or randomly pitted as targets for occasional drive-by slingshot practice.

Pathetic.

Noah didn't even get out of his car. It was a drive-thru farewell.

He had one last stop before going home.

This he was truly not looking forward to.

He needed to say good-bye to his mom. Which required him trying to get her to comprehend that he was leaving. Much easier said than done.

When Noah pulled up to the house, his mom was on the front porch dressed as she always was. Trailer park chic. It was what Lady Gaga would look like at 60 if she fell on hard times and had garden variety dementia.

Today his mom was wearing a dark green track suit which had been accessorized with shiny sequins, jewels, and strips of fake rabbit fur. It was inexplicably cut out in back and showed the top of her leathery ass crack. She had a black vinyl New York Mets baseball cap sideways on her head, and additionally wore a thin woven leather headband which she might have gotten from a *Last of the Mohicans* memorabilia catalog. Instead of running shoes, she shuffled around tentatively on black plastic platforms, embossed with white Chinese characters.

She had a hose in her hand and was watering the lawn — in winter. Actually, she was watering a gravel parking area next to the porch where nothing ever grew even in summer.

"Hi, mom."

"Global warming. It's killing everything. I give up."

She put the hose away and they went into the house.

For the next hour, they talked. They talked the way they always talked. Noah would say something. His mother would reply like she was channeling King George III.

"Mom, I'm leaving."

"I have a new doctor. He's Mexican. Dr. Rajesh Gupta."

"Mom. That's an Indian name. From India. Like Gandhi."

"Same difference. I can't understand a word he says. When he talks he sounds like his mouth is full of guacamole."

"This shepherd's pie is good."

"That's pumpkin bread. I didn't have any flour, so I used ground beef."

"Mom, I'm leaving Pulnick for a while. I need to—"

"Why do you hate your sister? She's a nice girl."

"Mom, I don't hate Gretchen. I just don't know her anymore."

"You don't know your own sister? I thought I introduced you."

So it went.

Failing to accomplish his mission, he gave up and decided to leave.

His mom followed him out the door onto the porch.

"Can't you stay for a little longer? You can say hi to your father when he gets home."

"Mom. Dad left in '96. He hasn't lived here for eighteen years."

"Has it been that long?"

Noah gave her a long deep hug.

He had to fight the urge to cry.

Maybe she was crazy.

But she was his mom.

Motorcycles

What was it about motorcycles?

Maybe the psychologists were right. Perhaps in the greater scheme, the motorcycle was a perfect throbbing, lunging, testosterone-fueled, mechanized penile substitute. Strapping more than 1200 CCs and 150 horsepower of roaring metal between your legs, a charged vibrating bullet-like projectile capable of over 160 MPH in a quarter mile and able to leap school buses full of hot lusty high school cheerleaders, does have the suggestive strands, the titillating tinges of erotic thrills and carnal adventure.

Psychologists could think whatever they wanted.

Noah just thought they were cool.

He hadn't ridden since his accident nine months ago, the one that laid him up for almost two months. He didn't even have a bike, unless the twisted pile of scrap metal his Kawasaki Ninja 250R now was, somehow factored in.

But he thought about them often. In fact, all of the time. He was sure that when the time was right, he'd start riding again. In the meantime, he decided to live vicariously.

He had only gone to a few motorcycle events since he had started riding five or so years ago. A couple of local weekend barbecue and beer bashes had been put together by Hilltop Cycles, the shop in Hannibal where he did all his business. They were pretty feeble, with more little kids and grandparents chomping down hot dogs and hamburgers than serious riders making the scene.

But he liked the guys at Hilltop. He bought both of his bikes there, as well as all of the accessories that go with the territory — helmets, gloves, leathers, boots. They kept his machines tuned and lubed, or on the rare occasion he had some serious mechanical difficulties, did the troubleshooting and the heavy lifting to get him back on the road.

That was all history. His riding days were on hold. At least for now.

But here was the plan.

There were some shows and a number of motorcycle rallies he could attend in various parts of the country. It would give him an excuse for visiting these particular areas. He could scope out some of the road bikes and travel gear that was available for serious road tripping. By the time the weather started to warm up, he would be able to make an educated decision as to what he should buy. There was no hurry. For now, he would just cruise around, enjoy life, visit different cities and states, check out the scenery. He'd enjoy life as it happened. What could be better?

He found several he thought looked interesting. The first was coming up soon in Fort Wayne, Indiana. Not easy or cost-effective to fly there, but he could take a bus.

He was really excited. This was the missing piece of the puzzle.

Noah was still on the computer when Naomi got home from work. Not looking at *Bambi Meets Godzilla* this time. Rather, he was downloading some fliers and maps from the internet.

She glanced over at him but didn't say anything.

There on the floor next to the door was his backpack, ready to go.

Noah didn't have to guess. He knew what she was feeling.

But there was nothing to say. Nothing more anyway.

They'd been over and over this. She understood. But that didn't make it any easier. Not for either of them.

Noah really loved her. But not nearly as much as she loved him. And certainly not in the final, possessive way that drives a person to abandon their dreams.

He had been obsessed with getting out of this godforsaken wasteland of a town for too long to let himself get bogged down with a girl, no matter how much she cared for him, no matter how good the sex, no matter how perfect they were for one another.

If they truly were perfect, they could pick up where they left off once he figured out his life — once he got something resembling a life!

"So you're leaving."

"You know I have to."

"What are you looking for?"

"I don't know. I really don't know. It's nowhere in Missouri, that's for sure."

"That's for sure."

Usually he loved her keen sense of irony.

This time it slashed him like a razor, laying bare sharp pangs of guilt.

Noah stood up and gently gathered her into his arms.

"Come on, Naomi. I don't mean you. I've given this shithole 23 years of my life. It's given me nothing in return."

She broke free from his embrace and turned around. Was she crying? If she was, she was doing a good job of covering it up.

"I still don't understand what you're looking for, Noah."

"I'll know it when I see it. It's not here. It's the opposite of here. I'm dying in this town. I need to find some way to give meaning to my life."

She picked up one of the fliers he had just printed out.

"You're looking for the meaning of life at a motorcycle rally?"

"It's not entirely random."

"Sometimes random is good. In fact, in this case random might be preferable."

"It's not a mindless orgy."

"No. It's a mindless motorcycle rally."

"I like motorcycles."

"And I like whipped cream. But I'm not going halfway across the country to look at creampuffs and sundae toppings."

She went into the kitchen, then came back out with two glasses of cranberry juice.

"When?"

"Day after tomorrow. I'm taking the Greyhound to Indianapolis."

"You need a ride to the station?"

"You're too good to me."

"You're right. I am."

Man Up!

Noah was sure that his buddies meant well, he appreciated the gesture. But from what he could tell, tonight would just be another excuse to get shitfaced and raise hell — the Full Metal Jack Its singular idea of a good time.

It took them two-and-a-half hours to drive to the *Man Up!* It was right across the state line in East St. Louis, Illinois. A giant sign with the neon outline of a two-story high naked girl standing astride it, announced their wares: *All Nude - The Hottest Sexiest Girls In The World!!*

The bouncer at the door was as wide as the door. He checked them for weapons and eyed them warily, but he probably eyed everyone warily. They each paid the $10 cover and stepped inside.

The entire club glistened with mirrors and chrome, had brilliant rock-concert lighting all around, a pumping pulsing sound system better than any he had ever heard, and two high-tech bars presided over by scantily-dressed, breathtakingly beautiful female bartenders, whose smiles alone could send a man reeling in lubricated vortices of sexual fantasy.

As they swept past the bar, Tal ordered a round on the fly, and dragged Noah right to the 'firing line', as it was called. This was the area right at the perimeter of the dance stage itself. There were seats one next to the other, and a narrow counter which wrapped around the entire stage, there for the guys to set their drinks on. This also provided a convenient surface to put their elbows for leaning in to get a better look. The girls would sometimes park one foot or stand on this surface so that they could get right in a guy's face with that sweet part of their bodies that held the most fascination.

The drink of the evening was Buttery Nipples. Damn good drink when you're looking at a girl's shaved crotch. Round after round came and went in a sticky blur of sweet melon liqueur, butterscotch schnapps, and Bailey's® Irish Cream. It was a concoction that destroyed the liver, abused the pancreas, and disabled the brain.

Noah usually drank in moderation. If at the end of the evening he couldn't precisely nail the official benchmark for Designated Driver, he was always the most *designatible* driver.

But tonight even drinking in moderation only went so far. He sat there for almost three hours, moving little more than his eyeballs, bringing his dominant hand up just enough to dribble between his lips his overpriced drink. Not exactly burning a lot of calories. The alcohol level in his blood was definitely building up.

The girls came and went. The money just went.

The club had three stages. There were maybe twenty strippers on duty. They rotated on a pre-programmed schedule. The Full Metal Jack Its had been sitting at the main stage, but off in the corners of the club were two others, a little smaller but set up the same, with the firing line counter around three sides. They had fewer chairs and provided a slightly more intimate dance experience. Like the main stage, by now all of the seats were filled.

The girls danced three-song sets. At the beginning of each set, a live DJ — he must be somewhere in the club though Noah never spotted him — would announce the dancers.

> On stage three, to make your mouth water we have Ariel. On stage two you can fly to Heaven with Angel. And on the main stage, making her international debut in the performing arts, we have now from heartland of America itself, from the flatlands of Monroe County, Missouri, where women are women and sheep are sheep and the men can't tell them apart, the lovely and enchanting Lady Tata.

Noah's head felt very heavy and hung down on his chest as she mounted the stage. Lady Tata was well into her first song before he looked up ...

... and saw who it was.

Oh wonderful! Just wonderful!

Tal was sitting next to him and leaned over.

"Just look at this scaggy bitch. What a sorry-ass pair of tits!"

"That's Gretchen. She's a meth head."

"You know her?"

"That's my sister."

What followed was perhaps the longest nine minutes of Noah's life. Whether she was so high she didn't know it was him or just blocked him out, she showed no reaction. But Noah was still more uncomfortable than he could have ever imagined possible. Was there anything weirder than having his kid sister parading her shaved vagina at eye level back and forth in front of him? Especially in a club full of drooling bone monkeys? Long before she had removed every article of what little clothing she had started with, he just couldn't look at her.

20

He put some dollar bills on the counter and stared at his feet.

Mercifully, the third song ended, she collected the contributions from the generous benefactors of her wonderful new career, and picked up the tiny scraps of her costume scattered all around her. Then Gretchen quickly turned to leave.

Not that he thought she would care, Noah figured maybe he should mention to his sister he was leaving, and say good-bye.

After she climbed off the stage, he followed her toward the backstage dressing area. She was still ignoring him, but that was hardly unusual or unprecedented in their twenty-year relationship.

Gretchen reached the velour curtain draped over the doorway to the dressing room. A bouncer stood next to the door. He eyed Noah suspiciously as he saw him approach.

"Gretchen."

She kept going.

"Hey, Gretchen."

The bouncer moved between Noah and his sister as she went through the door.

"Listen. That last dancer. Could I talk to her?"

"If she wants to talk to you, she'll come out."

"No. Really! I need to talk to—"

"Right. You guys all need to talk to her. If I asked every motherfucker in this joint, they'd all say they need to talk to her. Back off."

The bouncer pushed his chest out and positioned himself directly in front of Noah. He was huge and his bulk pretty much filled the entire doorway to the dressing room for the girls. But there was a slight gap between the curtain and the door jamb, so Noah stood on his tiptoes and leaned to one side to get a look.

"Gretchen! Gretchen! It's—"

There seemed to be no transition. One second Noah was standing there. The next he was flat on his face on the floor in an arm lock. The pain was excruciating.

Then he was on his feet. Not through any effort of his own. The bouncer lifted Noah like he was a small sack of groceries and was now carrying him toward the exit. Three more burly bouncers appeared out of nowhere and were right behind them.

Tal, Steve and Ghost saw what was happening and jumped up. Freddie was just coming back from the lavatory and joined them. Tal tried to apply some diplomatic charm.

"Hi guys! What's going on? This is my friend. Hey! Come on. He's harmless."

One of the Ten Commandments of bar bouncers declared that troublemakers traveled in packs. Tal, F, Steve and Ghost had just established the precise membership of the pack that Noah belonged to. Two more bouncers appeared. Were these guys dropping out of the ceiling? No one had noticed that a small army of buffalo-shaped guys in black pants and white shirts were there in the club when they walked in. The boys were a bit distracted at the time by a lot of skin.

The Full Metal Jack Its were all now being escorted to the parking lot.

Keep those eyes in their sockets, gentlemen. On stage three, we've got a sexy young thing who'll put a bulge in your trousers and make your girlfriend or wife look

like a mangy old dog, if she doesn't already. Oh my,
it's the delicious and talented ...

Wow!
What a going-away party!
It was the kind that definitely made a guy want to ...
Go away.

CHAPTER TWO

Planes, Boats and Trains

Every day started with a real bang. And clank. Some squeals. Quite a few booms. There were explosions, fires, bucklings, collapses, crumblings. It was gravity yanking away, tugging and pulling down on things, often accompanied by plumes of dust or smoke oppositely rising into the sky to add some symmetry to the drama.

February 24 (UPI) – Camden, NJ: Residents watched helplessly as their apartment building burned to the ground this evening. As soon as the blaze started, firemen were called to the scene. Conveniently the fire station was only four blocks from the fire. But the main ladder truck stalled in the driveway of the station, effectively blocking all other emergency vehicles. A fireman, who refused to be identified, later claimed that because of budget cuts they were not able to perform a long overdue tune-up on the vehicle.

February 26 (CNN) – Chicago, IL: An Amtrak train from Milwaukee bound for Chicago, derailed about four miles outside of Sturtevant, Wisconsin. No one was killed and only nineteen people injured, though authorities said it could have been much worse. The passenger train jumped the tracks and one passenger compartment came skidding to a stop just feet short of a truck hauling a full tank of heating fuel. Crumbling track foundations and a lack of proper maintenance were said to be responsible for the derailment.

February 27 (NBC40.net) – Two ambulances collided head on at a busy intersection in Atlantic City. Both drivers were pronounced dead at the scene. Two paramedics are still in critical condition. The two vehicles were both on their way to Shore Memorial Hospital in Somers Point, leaving police puzzled as to why they were heading in opposite directions. One ambulance was carrying a 73-year-old cardiac arrest victim and the other a pedestrian who had been run down by a hit-and-run driver outside of Trump Taj Mahal Casino. A faulty traffic light was held at least in part to blame for the tragic accident. But also factored into the catastrophe were driving conditions. A water main had burst and flooded a two block stretch of street, including the intersection where the accident occurred.

March 1 (Seattle Times) – On its regular run between the West Seattle suburb of Fauntleroy and nearby Vashon Island, a Washington State Department of Transportation ferry mysteriously, and with no warning, started to take on water and then sank, as employees for the ferry shuttle service and passengers queued for the return trip watched from shore. Hundreds of personal items were floating about and dozens of individuals were trying to swim to dry land as the vessel went down. No figures are yet available on the number of persons who may have drowned in this horrible incident.

March 2 (CNN) – Sewer mains exploded in the Central Business District of Cincinnati late last night. Several fires broke out and spread to stores and commercial buildings in the area. Authorities are guessing that either natural gas from ruptured adjacent gas pipelines, or more likely, methane generated by accumulated organic debris in plugged adjoining feeds may have caused the explosions. Firefighters brought most of the raging fires under control by mid morning. A four-square block area has been cordoned off and no one is permitted entry until the remaining fires have been extinguished and the structural integrity of the buildings has been confirmed. Initial estimates of the damage are upwards of $650 million.

March 4 (Reuters) – Making a scheduled stop in Phoenix, AZ this morning, a Southwest Airlines plane from Albuquerque, NM ultimately bound for Reno, NV crashed mid-air into a US Airways jet arriving from Los Angeles. Flight controllers at the Phoenix Sky Harbor Airport reported that neither plane appeared on the radar. It appears they were still separately given permission to land by two different individuals working the tower that morning. It has just been discovered that the control tower was short two regular senior air traffic controllers at the time, who had refused to come to work because over the past several days the radar had repeatedly malfunctioned. Work was scheduled to be performed on the system later the following week. The crews and all of the passengers on both planes were killed in the crash but the exact number of fatalities is unknown. The computer network providing access to final passenger logs had been down for several hours but estimates put the total at around 350.

Leave the Driving to Us

Fort Wayne, Indiana.

Noah was heading to the Fort Wayne Cyclefest, being held at the Memorial Coliseum there in town. Admission for the entire event only was $10. A bargain! There would be an opening ceremony, featuring a ride-in to the arena where presumably riders could show off how great they looked sitting on a motorcycle going the speed of a baby carriage, followed by a competition show in a number of different categories based on size and horsepower, an ongoing swap meet, vendors, music, cotton candy.

Frankly, it sounded pretty hokey. But it was a start. Noah had never thought about going to Indiana. In fact, he had never even heard of Fort Wayne. But what the hell. Why not? Just go! Maybe it's the Garden of Paradise. Maybe it's Hell. It didn't really matter. Most likely he'd just be there a couple days, then move on.

A few days after this underwhelming extravaganza, there was an event called Boston Mike's Custom Bike Night at the Shovel Head Lounge in Longwood, Florida. Florida! The weather would probably be outstanding, even though it was still winter. Don't people in Florida keep their tans a lovely leathery brown all year? It seemed like he recalled seeing photos on the internet of these old people on the beach there, with skin that looked like rawhide riding chaps.

Or instead of traveling 1100 miles, he could kill some time in Indiana — wasn't Gary, Indiana where Michael Jackson and his brothers got their start? — maybe check out Illinois, Michigan, Ohio, then head south a bit where in just a couple weeks the U.S. Biker Parties Association was holding their annual bash in Pea Ridge, Tennessee.

Pea Ridge! Ha ha ha. Where the hell was Pea Ridge?

He had to admit, this one really looked stupid. It was being held at some sleazy bar called The Sawmill and promised an evening of cheap beer, cheap women, greasy food, and a wet t-shirt contest — as if anyone would want more anatomical detail on the hideously fat women pictured on the website. Noah would probably skip this particular extravaganza. It looked like it was more about bikers than bikes, an excuse for a bunch of pot-bellied Harley-driving Hell's Angels wannabees to get drunk and puke on whatever bimbo they could wrestle onto their laps.

Regardless, the more Noah looked into it, the more he realized he could hop from one place to another indefinitely. There were literally thousands of such events each year dedicated to motorcycles. Especially moving into spring with the weather starting to improve, there were more shows, rallies, conventions, competitions, bashes and brawls than he could attend in a lifetime. He would start with Fort Wayne and just play it by ear.

Naomi dropped Noah in downtown St. Louis to board the bus for the first leg of his journey. There were kisses, tears, more kisses, more tears.

He was going to miss her.

He stepped into the terminal a little before 11 am. Plenty of time, since his bus was leaving at 11:30. The trip to Indianapolis was only 5 hours 30 minutes. A nice straight shot. And a great connection. He would change buses and be on his way to Fort Wayne a mere 25 minutes later.

But that's when things got dicey.

Though on a map, Fort Wayne was only about half the distance he would be traveling from St. Louis to Indianapolis, this next leg of the journey would take 11 hours. This second bus would make stops in Lafayette, Gary and Hammond, Indiana and keep going basically in the wrong direction all the way to Chicago, Illinois. There Noah would have to transfer to yet another bus. That bus would then go back through Gary, slog on through the featureless Midwestern countryside, stopping in South Bend, Elkhart and Angola, then finally arrive in Fort Wayne.

Travel time for the entire ordeal was over 16 hours — 16 hours and 25 minutes to be exact.

He would get there at 4:25 am. Wonderful. Then he could wait 3½ hours to watch the sun come up, catch some breakfast before parking himself outside the Coliseum for four more hours until the gates finally opened for the show.

Whatever. He had all the time in the world. It would be an adventure!

He heard the announcement. Now boarding for Indianapolis. He decided to make a quick dash over to a concession stand to buy some soda, maybe a Twinkee and a bag of potato chips.

By the time he was back in the loading bay of the terminal, everyone else had already queued up and were putting luggage in the undercarriage compartment, then getting on the bus. He was the last in line. Looked like a full load. From what he could tell, it was a rather nondescript cross-section of humanity, all looking pretty typical. He'd fit right in.

This was going to be a long trip. Noah wondered who he would be sitting next to. Hopefully not some guy who would fall asleep and slump over onto his shoulder. He wasn't homophobic but at the same time not partial to having some strange guy drool all over him.

Noah started to throw his big duffel into the undercarriage compartment, then decided against it. Carrying both his bags, he climbed aboard.

Seats were not assigned.

Noah looked down the length of the bus and it became immediately clear that luck was clearly not on his side today. In fact, luck was being a real prick.

There was one seat left. Actually, it was only half a seat. The bulk of the man already in the seat beside it drooped well over the armrest, like a huge sack of cattle feed ready to burst. The enormous protoplasmic lump who had staked a claim on the window seat, had on blue overalls which if poled and staked could shelter a family of five. Under the overalls was a red-and-black plaid shirt with the sleeves partly rolled up to expose two tree trunks carved into the approximation of forearms. Sitting on top of this mountain of flesh, tipped back with its tiny bill pointed straight up, was a filthy old wool cap, bunched up and comically too small for the anthropomorphic pumpkin — a fleshy orange ball pantomiming as a human head — wedged between the hillocks of the man's shoulders.

Noah sat down. It became immediately apparent that the guy was the social type. He grinned, stretching his already thin lips into long slivers of hot dog casing.

"Yup. Ahm a pig fahmer."

Really? You're not America's next male supermodel?

Right then it hit him. An odor unlike anything Noah had ever encountered, having never exhumed a person from a grave or stuck his head inside the bloated anus of a cow that had been rotting in the sun for several weeks.

Noah's respiratory equipment went into a code blue lock down. Instantly it felt like he was in the advanced stages of trismus shock.

The pig farmer was determined to take their budding friendship to the next level.

"Muh name's Tildon. Gots me a pig fahm. Rights down da road foam Inee-appliss. Shore nice a meetin' ya all!"

There was no way Noah could reply. Talking would require him to open his mouth and if the stench simultaneously entered both his nostrils and his eating-talking orifice, it was certain to induce projectile vomiting which would swamp at minimum the three rows of seats in front of him. There was no room for error. He compressed his mouth like a drowning victim.

Noah nodded and tried to smile, then focused on looking very interested in a magazine left on his seat by the previous passenger. *Us* with a picture on the cover of Bruce Willis getting out of a limo with some bimbo on his arm.

This was unbelievable. But it wasn't that there was an option. He had to sit next to the guy. It was the last seat available, obviously for good reason. Everyone else had let their gag reflex do the talking and taken a pass on sitting there.

How long was this trip? Five and a half hours!

Noah lost track of how many times he threw up in his mouth and swallowed it. All he could think of as he watched the mile markers on the highway crawl by was getting off the bus. If it weren't going over 60 MPH, he might consider just diving out the window and taking his chances with a Hollywood stunt man body roll. Anything to escape!

After what seemed like centuries, they pulled into the main bus terminal in Indianapolis. Noah bolted to his feet, grabbed his bags from the overhead luggage rack, raced to the exit door just as it was swinging open, and leaped from the bus. A few feet from the vehicle he inhaled a deep, much welcome lungful of breathable air, while continuing his dash to the terminal building. He wasn't sure if he should immediately make a beeline for the restroom and attempt a peristaltic purge of the accumulated noxious off-gassing of the pig farmer, or first buy several bottles of vending machine soda pop in order to wash from his throat the second-hand stench which had set his gag reflex into a St. Vitus dance. He should probably do both, then check into a local detox hospice for a couple months.

He managed several more long strides, putting him halfway to the *Welcome to the Indy City* banner which hung above the swinging doors to the main lobby. Suddenly an explosion sent him hurling forward in a spectacular if involuntary triple somersault. The shockwave immediately shattered all of the windows of the terminal facing the bus loading area. Noah's end-over-end tumbling stopped and he skidded a few more feet, curled in a fetal position. He straightened out and struggled to get himself upright to a sitting position. His ears were ringing and everything sounded like his head was squashed between two pillows. But that was the least of his concerns. When he looked back he could see the bus he had just gotten off was silhouetted by a gigantic ball of fire. The vehicle was then shaken by another explosion which sent chunks of metal, flaming upholstery, handbags, clothing and body parts arcing in every direction.

With more presence of mind than seemed possible under the circumstances, he noticed that he was still gripping his bags, his overstuffed duffel bag in one hand, and the more modest-size backpack in the other. Though a little wobbly, he managed to get to his feet. Then he just started running. Running as fast and hard as he could.

The next couple minutes were a blur, for him and everyone there. People were screaming in horror, filling the cavernous bay with cries of desperation, anguish and unbearable pain. Movement seemed random and chaotic, as bodies scrambled in every direction, some toward him, some away, some momentarily joining him in his determination to get as far from the heat and noise as possible.

For Noah, it was pure reflexes. It was survival. It was pure adrenalin and the protective terror of self-preservation.

When the feverish scrim of fright-and-flight eventually dissolved, he found himself sitting on a curb, head between his knees, panting and shaking. It felt as if he were waking from a dream, but one which he could remember in every vivid detail. His ears were still ringing but he could hear the muted shriek of sirens in the background. When he looked over his shoulder, he saw several police cars and emergency vehicles.

He decided he would not go back. There was nothing he could do to help. Nothing he could later say that would make a difference. All of those people, even the disgusting pig farmer, had to be history. Based on what he saw, no one survived.

Except him. A Missouri boy with a mouth full of vomit.

The numb paralysis started to lift and he stood up.

Noah had no idea what he looked like.

No clue as to his ripped clothing, singed hair, soot-smeared face.

He got a hint when after walking several blocks, he managed to hail a cab.

"No offense, buddy. But before I take you anywhere, I need to see some green."

It didn't quite compute. But maybe this was a normal request here. Or maybe this driver had been ripped off more times than he wanted to think about. Noah pulled a wad of twenties from his money belt.

"A hotel. Any hotel."

"You got it, Son of Sam."

Apparently to avoid tarnishing his professional image, the taxi driver pulled up to the curb across the street from the hotel property, rather than use the actual passenger zone where there stood a hospitality greeter dressed like one of King Arthur's knights. Noah paid. The taxi sped off before Noah could even close the passenger door.

As he entered the lobby, several people went in some rather wide circles to avoid getting anywhere near him. A bellhop rather than offering to take his bags, turned away, then just stood there, whistling and looking at something on the ceiling.

The receptionist, a young man who had hair that looked like patent leather and the skin of a Japanese school girl, alternated between meticulously examining Noah's identification and credit card, and stealing glances at Noah himself. He maintained an air of cool but pleasant professionalism which would have made Donald Trump proud, and completed the check-in process without betraying any overt hostility or repressed panic. When he handed Noah the electronic key to his room, he quickly withdrew his hand, as if flesh-eating bacteria might leap onto him and destroy his exquisite manicure. The receptionist gave Noah a final head-to-toe appraisal, then formally bowed and with a toothy smile festooned with a sincerity that he must have learned from watching hours of self-hypnosis videos, extended the corporately crafted official welcome.

"Enjoy your stay here at the world-renowned Conrad Hotel, Mr. Tass. If there is anything we can do to make your time with us more comfortable, please don't hesitate to ask."

As soon as Noah entered his room and caught his reflection in the mirror, he understood the reaction he was getting. He looked like he had just crawled out of the rubble after the collapse of the Twin Towers.

After a long hot shower, he keeled over onto the king-sized bed, and fell into a near coma before his head hit the pillow. His dreams were deep space silent movies.

Twelve hours later, Noah crawled out of bed, made some instant coffee, and turned on the television. A local news anchor was updating the story that monopolized every station in America.

> *"Michelle Carradine, a 28 year old mother of three was here at the bus station tonight, waiting for her mother, Sarah Schmidt to arrive from Tulsa. Because of family issues, they hadn't seen one another for almost eight years. Michelle's mom had never seen her three grand children. Michelle was so excited and was videoing the arrival of the bus with her hand held camera, planning to catch her mom as she stepped off the vehicle. You are now looking at the actual footage of this horrible incident."*

And there was Noah, front and center, running toward the camera with the bus in flames behind him.

> *"The Indianapolis Metro police, and we are now told the FBI, are looking for this young man. They believe he is from Missouri and is now a prime suspect in this wanton carnage, a merciless terrorist attack that claimed the lives of 53 innocent people. This is Steve Stephens and you're watching WTHR. We'll be back after this commercial break, with more on this story."*

Noah's worst suspicions were confirmed. Everyone, including the driver, had been killed.

Except one.

One young man not only survived but was filmed as he bolted from the doomed vehicle. He looked desperate, obviously in a very big hurry.

Sure enough, over and over, they were running the 11 seconds of video showing Noah as he ran toward the terminal, then was thrown to the pavement as the bus exploded in a giant ball of flame. The image was slightly unsteady at first, then all over the map, as the person doing the filming was also knocked off her feet. But she got back up and kept her camera running just as Noah ran past. There was no mistaking it. It was him all the way.

It was gruesome, bone-chilling, stomach-turning video. Screams, desperate cries for help, horrible lamenting wails, and the deep-throated torment of whoever was filming it, provided the soundtrack for the immolation and nearly instantaneous death of over fifty people. For a brief instant, the flailing anguished silhouettes of two of the passengers on the bus could be seen reaching zombie-like through blown-out windows on the near side of the bus, before falling out and collapsing into bubbling cinder cones of flesh.

It was obvious that they were pinning the explosion on him.

Noah knew exactly what he had to do.

Paranoia Runs Deep

Maybe in more sane times, he could have gone to the authorities and by telling his side of the story, could have convinced them of his innocence.

But those days were long past. Now everyone was guilty until proven innocent. There were even accusations floated every day that certain members of Congress were members of jihadist terrorist organizations. Even the President. Especially the President!

The level of paranoia in the popular mind and the atmosphere of fear perpetrated by politicians in the name of the War on Terror, made the McCarthy era hearings seem like a selection committee to choose a prom queen.

Noah went online — he was able to obtain a computer from room service — and ordered from a local theatrical supply house a number of items. Soon it all arrived. Several hats, including a rip-snorter of a Texas rodeo-style classic Stetson, a wool beret, and a leather bush hat à la the land down under. A set of brass bling teeth caps which would have made Houston rapper Paul Wall cream in his jeans. And most important of all, since his own was pathetically thin and almost pre-pubescent, he bought various configurations of facial hair. He got the Freddie Mercury mustache, an Abe Lincoln beard, sideburns long, medium and short, a set of ZZ Top whiskers also convenient for polishing furniture, and even three sets of eyebrows which were billed as 'babe magnets'. The eyebrows looked ridiculous, so he immediately threw them away. But he kept everything else for whenever he had to go out in public.

Over the next 48 hours, Noah never left his room. He got to know the room service menu by heart. When the food was delivered, he only opened the door a crack and threw a $5 tip into the air. While the room service attendant scrambled for the money, Noah reached around, pulled the serving cart inside and immediately slammed the door shut. No one got a glimpse of him. The staff probably thought it was the reincarnation of Howard Hughes staying there.

He continued to follow the news. CNN already had a theme song and special graphics for the incident. Each segment started with a blast of the patriotic anthem and the American flag superimposed with flaming letters: *Dog Days of Doom Bus Bombing*.

In one special news flash, it was revealed that a fanatical leftist fringe organization based in Boston, Americans For Personal Autonomy, had claimed credit for the explosive device on board the bus in a statement published on their internet website, before it was taken down by the Department of Homeland Security cyber police:

> *We celebrate this historic event as the day the revolution begins.*
> *America, wake up! You have become slaves. The corporate state*
> *has declared war on the individual and intends to subjugate each*
> *and every one of you to serve its endless pursuit of profit and the*
> *consolidation of wealth in the hands of a few selfish individuals.*
> *We are Americans for Personal Autonomy and we intend to*
> *do to all symbols of corporate power what we just did in*
> *Indianapolis. This is just the start. Revolution now!*
> *No fear! No Surrender! Liberty forever!*

Whatever relief Noah might have felt, given this announcement and reasonably concluding that the pressure was off him, was immediately dispelled. In the follow-up segment they interviewed the Department of Homeland Security official handling the investigation:

CNN: *You originally thought that a young man from a small town in Missouri was responsible. That's his picture on the screen, for you viewers. Twenty-three year old Noah Tass, originally suspected of being the Greyhound Bus Bomber.*

DHS: *That's correct, ma'am. And he's still a suspect. These terrorists travel in packs like wild dogs. We're still figuring out exactly who was responsible.*

CNN: *Do you have any information as to his whereabouts?*

DHS: *If he's still in this country, we'll find him. Members of the public having any information leading to the arrest of this individual can call our 24-hour* *hotline. There is a $250,000 reward.*

CNN: *But what if he's innocent?*

DHS: *We have the photo of him running from the bus. In our view, this is very suspicious behavior, running in a zone where people normally walk. We are keeping him at a counterespionage status SCC, level Yellow+.*

CNN: *SCC? Yellow +? What does that mean?*

DHS: *Search, confine and capture — suspect armed, unstable, dangerous.*

CNN: *Thanks, Mr. Okrutny for taking time to be here with us today. There you have it. The homeland security forces at work to keep us safe and secure. Next up. Heather Spring on the latest in anti-aging cosmetology. Injecting kangaroo pituitary gland extract for a more youthful you.*

Great! Running from a bus to escape a bloated bag of unwashed hillbilly offal made him a threat to the national security. Things were going to be strange for a while.

One other thing he knew for sure.

He'd better get moving. He didn't know where. But he couldn't just sit here and wait for them to show up at his door.

What time was it? 8:39 pm. Good. It was better to move by cover of night.

Noah packed his bags — it took all of four minutes — then decked himself out as a cross between Wild Bill Hickok and the cowboy in the Village People. He looked like he was on his way to an audition for Brokeback Mountain II.

Stetson in place, he headed down to the reception desk to check out. It was now a little before 10 pm.

Everything went smoothly. He was especially grateful it was a different person behind the counter, this time an affable young lady who looked like Kirsten Dunst. She seemed pleasantly amused at his getup.

His bill was astronomical but he had expected that. Just as he started to step away, the desk clerk halted him.

"Mr. Tass. I'm sorry. I almost overlooked it. This came for you today. Someone should have let you know."

It was an envelope, addressed to him, handwritten, as was the note inside. He took it and sat down in the corner of the lobby to read it.

> *It's not like you to blow up buses. Be careful of the company you keep. Stay away from pig farmers, even if they make good mules.*
>
> *Wyatt Grayson Tass*

Noah's mind would not have been more thoroughly blown if he had just received a letter from Jesus Christ or Adolph Hitler.

His father.

His father!

The man who walked out on his family 18 years ago, never to be seen again.

Who was this man? Noah had no idea what he even looked like.

18 years.

Not a letter, not a Christmas card, not a birthday gift, not even a phone call.

18 years.

Now this weird, off-the-wall, completely insane note.

Why now? What did he want?

Noah felt like he had been hit by a wrecking ball.

But his shock quickly turned to anger.

Wyatt Grayson Tass.

What a pretentious asshole. Who signs their name in full?

What kind of man is he? What kind of father …

Noah didn't have any impression of the man at all. His mom had left those pages blank while he was growing up. She'd only say, "He's very smart, Noah."

Smart maybe. But an irresponsible heartless fucker. He had abandoned them when Noah was five, his sister Gretchen only two.

Well …

Maybe not completely irresponsible.

He knew his mom got checks every month in the mail, which was how they had been able to survive.

Maybe not completely heartless.

It's not like his mom was any gem. In fact, she was a complete fruitcake. As Noah got older, he began to think that maybe her mental instability was the reason his father flew the coop. Maybe the man couldn't stand being in the same house with a total hypochondriac who dressed like Zsa Zsa Gabor on a bag lady budget. Trailer park chic. Originals by Bozo the Clown.

It had to be embarrassing.

At the same time, Noah recalled that his mom hadn't always been that way. Hadn't her eccentricity started *when* his old man left, then gradually blossomed into the full-blown if harmless wackiness Noah endured through his adolescent years?

Actually, what difference did it make anyway why his father left? It was water over the dam. Water that had gone far downstream and evaporated into an irretrievable mist, and was now lost in the vast homogenous clouds of the forgotten past.

What Noah really wanted to know was what was going on right now. Why now? Why after all these years had this man showed up in his life? And what was next on the agenda? Was this some kind of a joke? Or did it represent some real threat to the fragile equilibrium Noah was trying to achieve in his life?

And how the hell had Wyatt Grayson Tass found him?

He knew about the bus. Even the pig farmer. Well, it made sense he knew about the bus. Everyone knew, thanks to the saturation of if-it-bleeds-it-leads television. But how could he possibly have known about stinking pile of pig dung in the next seat? Then again if he did, maybe there were others who knew why Noah was beating a hasty retreat from the bus before it exploded.

Noah's head was swimming.

Pig farmers? Mules? Why would a pig farmer make a good mule? Like mating them? Mating *with* them? This was so screwed up! Now of all times when he needed a sharp eye and a clear head, no extraneous tension, no diversions, no distractions, this completely baffling note landed on him like a ten-ton pterodactyl turd.

Noah felt drained. Incapable of moving. He just sat there.

People walking through the lobby must have thought he was a Wild West sculpture.

He sat motionless for over a half an hour.

Thinking. Thinking. Thinking.

Wyatt Grayson Tass.

18 years.

Scene of the Crime

Finally, Noah bolted upright, grabbed his duffel bag, backpack, then half-walked half-ran to the lobby door. He left his father's note on the chair he'd been sitting in.

A taxi was waiting outside the entrance of the hotel.

"Airport, please. Can you hurry? I'm late."

They needed to get on the freeway, but the route to the closest ramp took them right past the bus station.

As they approached, Noah could see that the entire building was cordoned off. There was so much police tape it made the structure look like it had been gift wrapped. Cadres of security guards everywhere, local and military police swarmed the sidewalk.

"Let me out here."

"I wouldn't go there. It's not a tourist attraction, you know. They got it completely locked down. No buses running."

The light turned red and the taxi had to stop.

Noah threw a $10 bill over the seat and jumped out onto the sidewalk.

This put him on the opposite side of the wide boulevard from the bus station itself, where he encountered a completely unexpected and rather astonishing scene.

A demonstration. At least fifty people, mostly young, looking like they had been transported there in a time machine from the 60s, were standing, sitting, milling around. Some held up signs, others were leaning on them or had laid them down next to them as they sat in small groups and talked excitedly. A few strummed guitars. Noah thought he caught a whiff or two of marijuana in the cool evening air.

The protest signs lacked a coherent plot but told the story.

Down with corporations!

Truth is the H-bomb to tyranny.

People want jobs, not empty promises.

End the class wars! Put an end to corruption.

Bombs and bullets will break the bonds of bullshit.

Fuck the rich ... be sure to use a condom!

Power to the people! Right on!

Blow it up, start over!

There was no political philosophy here. Just rage and a celebration of violence.

Apparently those here were a small but vocal body of political activists who found the bombing of the bus as a kind of flash point, a cause célèbre which would provide a powerful platform for them to vent their frustrations and try to garner public support. They were out in sufficient numbers to slow traffic along this major thoroughfare and cause the police on the other side of the street a lot of anxiety. *This will make people pay attention.* That was the theory anyway.

Noah noticed back in the shadows to one side of the bus depot reception area, what appeared to be a platoon of officers in full riot gear, ready to spring into action. That certainly spelled trouble.

A girl, maybe 18 or 19, with long dreadlocks and a pretty face, came up beside him.

"Love the disguise. Are they shooting a western here or did you fall off your horse on your way to the OK Corral?"

His first reaction, which was the hot flush of complete humiliation, quickly melted away when Noah turned to look at her. From the incredibly innocent, warm smile he was seeing, he could tell she wasn't making fun of him. She was just being cordial. She had that quality that conveyed the feeling they were old friends, the kind of friends that could dish out a good ribbing.

"If I told you, I'd have to kill you."

"I can keep a secret."

"I'm hiding."

"No shit, Sherlock."

"Really, I am." He nodded toward the police lined up across the street.

"Parking tickets are badges of honor here. You're among friends."

She took him by the arm and led him to an old Chevy van which was parked at the edge of the gathering. It was all white, except for a huge black peace sign painted on the side. On the way over, she introduced herself.

"By the way, I'm Tetra."

"As in tetracycline?"

"Tetra, as in theater of the absurd. Don't ask me to explain. I can't."

Sitting in the passenger seat of the van was a young guy working on a laptop. As they approached he glanced at them, started to type again, then did a double-take on Noah, giving him a thorough once-over from top to bottom. Shaking his head.

"What have we here? Are you kinky or confused?"

"My mother buys all my clothes."

"Listen. If you're a friend of Rick Perry, you've come to the wrong place."

"I'm from Missouri."

"Well, our women are safe then. And we don't have any sheep. So I guess we're alright. Hey! Missouri. Like the guy the cops are looking for. Do you know him?"

"I am that guy."

"Holy fuck! You? You?! Whoa! You are in deep shit, my friend. Welcome aboard. Fucking fantastic, by the way. I'm Tyson.

"But I didn't actually—"

"This is truly awesome. So what now, Mr. Top-Ten-Terrorist?"

"Noah. I'm Noah. Yes. What now? I have no idea. I'm new at this."

"Tell you what! This is great. Like it or not, you have been recruited. You are in, baby! And tomorrow, Tetracycline here and me and some of the others are on our way to the desert."

"I thought that was my joke."

"Going to a desert is a joke. What's funny about that?"

"Nothing … never mind."

"Dude, I get it. I really do. You need to stay under the radar. This is it. This will be the perfect place. Perfect! I guarantee, there is *no way* anyone will find you there."

"There? There being …"

"Area 51!"

Chaos and Confusion

It was the Rachel Maddow evening news show on MSNBC.

She looked even more serious tonight than usual.

> *"We all know the numbers. Unemployment is officially reported at 7%. Many experts think that this is just wishful thinking, that the real unemployment rate is over 25%. Last year more than 12 million homes were foreclosed on. Almost 50 million people are living on food stamps. That's 16% of the American population! One out of five children go to bed hungry every night. But most people don't need statistics to see how bad things are. So for three days now, there have been massive demonstrations in Washington DC. We go now to the scene in front of the White House. Reporter Phil Johannes is there live."*

As the livecam shot fills the screen, it's total bedlam at the entrance to the south lawn of the White House. People are shouting, chanting slogans. Canisters of tear gas are being fired by the police, then lobbed back at them by the crowd. Protesters are carrying an effigy of the President with a noose around its neck.

The reporter, Phil Johannes, has a handkerchief to his mouth and can barely open his eyes. He's obviously in a lot of agony.

He yells to be heard above the din.

> *"The violence has not let up now for more than 48 hours, Rachel. The police just attacked the crowd again. I can barely breathe, the tear gas is so thick."*

Suddenly a protester jumps on camera and grabs the microphone. He looks crazed.

> *"They want our blood. They won't stop till they get every last drop. They're the vampire squid. The free market? I'll tell you about the free market. It's free alright. Free of concern for decent people. Free of compassion. Free of hope. Capitalists are just a bunch of greedy pigs. Oink oink! Oink oink!"*

They cut back to Rachel Maddow in the studio.

"You know, things don't look good in this country. People are tired of empty promises. They're tired of the rich just getting more and more, them getting less and less. I'm sure this story is far from over. We'll keep you up to date as it continues to develop."

CHAPTER THREE

Area 51

A trip that at most should have taken three days ended up taking five.

Noah recognized that every person was a unique blend of talents and shortcomings. What was astounding was that he was in a vehicle averaging 65 MPH generally headed in a westerly direction with four people who shared identical cerebral impairments.

None had a sense of direction, none could make a reasonable judge of distance, and none was capable of reading a map. These four could get lost on a Ferris wheel.

On the plus side, he didn't have to be any particular place by any certain time, underscored by the fact that he had no idea where he was heading in the first place.

There also was a pride factor in play. They wanted to impress him. Especially Tyson. Imagine that. Regardless of all the disclaimers Noah offered, Tyson and the others following his lead, considered Noah some sort of heroic figure in the struggle to upend the established order. In their star-struck view, he apparently ranked somewhere between Bob Dylan and Timothy McVeigh, the lunatic who blew up the Federal Building in downtown Oklahoma back in the mid 90s. As a result of this misplaced hero-worship, they wouldn't let him even look at the highway map, insisting that they had it covered. He should just sit back and enjoy the ride.

Tyson did most of the driving. Tetra sat up front with him and Noah assumed they were an item, till he eventually noticed there was no chemistry or any physical contact between them.

The other two were guys who had been at the bus station rally, who came along for the ride. They were mere foot soldiers in the revolution, pretty much willing to go wherever something interesting might be happening, but personally not informed or sharp enough to discuss political issues or wrestle with the complexities of the related controversies. They were affable, harmless, likeable and made no impression. Noah still couldn't remember their names though they were crammed together in the back of a Chevy van for five days, as it serpentined across America.

To say the ride was uncomfortable would be a vast understatement. It was a cargo van, meaning there were no seats in back and Noah was forced to sit on the floor sandwiched between crates and road cases of who knew what. Electronic equipment? Assault weapons? Survival gear? Much to his relief when he eventually found out, it all turned out to be video recorders and related accessories. Tyson was making a documentary about the secret activities of the Federal government, particularly those of the military and the CIA, which many believed were putting America on a collision course with the rest of humanity, activities which Tyson was personally convinced threatened the very survival of the human race.

There was one highly guarded complex of research facilities where it was suspected many of the most nefarious activities were taking place. That was where they were now headed.

"Area 51 is where it's really happening, man. The government won't talk about it. In fact, they won't even admit that it exists. You can't find it on a map."

Of course, these guys couldn't find North America on a map.

"They've got the remains of an alien there and his space ship. It crashed in the 1950s and they talked to the alien till he died. They still have his space ship but it's so advanced, they can't figure it out. Now they're building their own flying saucers."

Tetra seemed to know what Tyson was talking about.

"Didn't they develop the U-2 and some advanced supersonic titanium plane that crashed? Then they turned it into the SR-71 spy plane. I heard it could go over 2000 MPH!"

"Yeah. But that's the harmless stuff. Now they are working on technology that causes earthquakes. And holograms so they can fake an invasion of the earth and control everyone on the planet."

Even Billy X put in his two cents.

"There's a laser that can cut the moon in half!"

All Noah could think was how amazing it was what you could learn from people who were completely educated by reading comic books.

They arrived in a town called Rachel, Nevada, population 98. It was as close to a ghost town as you could get, except the ghosts had all moved out. It consisted of a handful of buildings on Hwy 375, nicknamed "The Extraterrestrial Highway". Rachel sat right outside of the entrance gates of Area 51, that proximity being the foundation of the town's tourist trade, which had to run into the tens of dollars in a good year.

They pulled up to the Little A'Le'Inn, one of the four businesses in Rachel.

"Little A'Le'Inn. Little *alien*. Get it, Noah? Ha ha ha."

Noah got it.

After checking in and getting some exciting travel tips from the owner, Pat, who had somehow survived this town for the past 20 years, they filed into the adjoining restaurant where they waited for their contact to arrive and brief them. Retired Colonel Brett Kerr came bursting through the door 25 minutes late, which gave each of them ample time to finish a second helping of the specialty of the house, apple pie with vanilla ice cream.

The Colonel was tall and skinny, tent-pole erect. Despite being in his early seventies, he was energetic and moved with quickness and certainty. He was fiercely earnest and looked like he had forgotten how to smile, if he ever knew in the first place. He wore a pared down version of his military uniform. His words came spitting out in harsh bursts.

"Tyson. Good to see you again." He looked suspiciously at everyone else at the table. "Who are these people? Has everyone here been vetted?"

"They're cool, Colonel. This is Billy X, Heath. You know Tetra. And this is Noah. He blows up buses."

"Okay. Fine. Can't take any chances. You got here just in time, Tyson. Things're about to break wide open."

The colonel opened his briefcase and took out a thick envelope. He pulled out at least 200 photos and spread them out on the table. They were aerial shots, probably taken from earth orbit. Noah looked at about half of them. They were all identical. The only barely detectable variations were a passing cloud, slightly different exposure or subtle difference in hue.

38

"Can you believe this? It's fucking outrageous."

"What makes you say that?"

"Tune your sensibilities, boy! Look at these photos. Can't you see the writing on the wall? Something big is in the works. Apocalyptic. All their energies are being diverted. Nature abhors a vacuum. This is how it always is. The eye of the hurricane. You know it's really going to blow when things are this quiet."

Noah studied the colonel for a moment, then casually asked.

"How long has it been quiet like this?"

The colonel took it as an affront.

"How long? Is that what you want to know, young man? Is that your question? Well, lemme tell you. Give or take … about 12 years."

So *because* the corpses in a cemetery have been quiet for decades *is* the reason we should expect them to claw their way to the surface and start dancing.

They waved good-bye to Pat, then all piled into the van. Colonel Kerr road shotgun, so Noah had the pleasure of Tetra practically sitting on his lap in the back.

Though he couldn't see anything — there being no windows in the back of the van — Noah could tell that they were going up. The road was paved at first but then became a gravel service drive and they bounced around quite a bit. After parking, they hiked for maybe 45 minutes and came to the end of a trail at the top of Tikaboo Peak. This was the highest point in the Pahranagat Mountain Range, a long series of escarpments which ran parallel to the eastern perimeter of the Area 51 Restricted Airspace.

The colonel handed his binoculars to Tyson, who passed them along to Noah. All Noah could see behind the shimmering thermals and obscuring haze were some grey characterless buildings sitting on a sprawling plane of desert dust.

The colonel's paranoia and excitement wasn't dampened by the torpor of the dusty still life they strained to pull into focus.

"Those fuckers think they can pull this shit right under our noses. Well, they better guess again! That's all I gotta say."

The next four days had to rank as the most boring of Noah's life. He learned to tune out the ranting and conspiratorial indignation of the colonel. But he couldn't shut out the choking silence and oppressive ennui of Area 51 itself. While Tyson and the colonel could spend hours looking at nothing, Noah and the others quickly grew restless, then frantic to do something, anything other than stand on the summit of Tikaboo Peak in the breech of abysmal boredom.

Tetra interceded using her feminine guile. Next morning, she convinced Tyson that she needed to go into Las Vegas, which was only a few hours away, to pick up some personal supplies related to her gender and the lunar cycle. She apparently had a way with him, because as unlikely as it seemed to Noah, she managed to get use of the van for the trip into town. The colonel could make the journey with his support team to the Area 51 mountaintop reconnaissance perch in the 1972 Mercedes coupe he usually left parked everyday at the A'Le'Inn.

Noah jumped right into the van next to Tetra. The other two guys, Billy X and Heath also were apparently wanting to take a day off and head into the city.

"Hey, got room for me?"

"I'll go too."

Besides being bored out of their minds, neither of them had ever seen Vegas and though the idea certainly had a counter-revolutionary stench about it, they didn't want to miss out on the opportunity to visit the landmark famous Strip, experience the legendary decadence first hand, and maybe even try their luck on some slots.

Tyson immediately shot that idea out of the water.

"You two! You're staying right here. We've got work to do."

Tyson would let Noah go along so Tetra wouldn't have to deal with all the crazies in Vegas by herself. But he couldn't compromise the mission any further.

The colonel emphasized the urgency of the task at hand.

"Damn straight! We need to look sharp, gentlemen. We got 'em with their dicks hangin' out." He started shaking his fist in the general direction of the Area 51 base. "Fuck you, motherfuckers! You're goin' down!"

Noah wasn't sure exactly what was being done that a weather vane or a scarecrow couldn't do just as well. But he sure wasn't going to argue. He was beyond grateful he was leaving, if only for a day. The others would have to fend for themselves.

Before Tyson could change his mind, he and Tetra were on their way to the city that made Wayne Newton more famous than fig newton.

It was a fairly uneventful day in most respects. They had a few laughs, enjoyed some great practically free food, experienced that sense of wonder and awe that everyone experiences when they see the fantasy world of affluent splendor and tackiness that is Vegas. But neither of them were, for entirely different personal reasons, particularly sensitive to or impressed by such hyperbolic excess. Tetra came from a very wealthy family, and had been to many luxurious and genuinely lavish locations around the world. To her, Vegas looked like a cheap papier-mâché forgery. Noah grew up where anything beyond a more efficient way to shear a sheep or milk a cow was considered silly and impractical. To him Vegas was both frivolous and ugly.

They shared one amazing moment watching a guy they called Daddy Long Legs — a name which described his appearance perfectly — lose over $80,000 at a craps table. He was completely unfazed and laughed it off like he had misplaced a cufflink. He had attracted quite a crowd and Noah overheard someone say that the day before, the unshaven stick figure had won over a quarter million. All in a day's work.

They ended up staying a little longer than they had initially planned. It was just before 9 pm when they pulled up to the Inn.

Something was wrong. All the lights were out. There seemed to be no one around.

Noah jumped out of the van and headed toward the office. Tetra ran to her room.

Sure enough. Noah looked in the reception area, the restaurant, came back out and started to head around the building.

But Tetra was already back.

"What are you waiting for? Get your shit, man. We're leaving!"

Noah found everything as he had left it. He quickly packed.

He stepped out of his room just as Tetra was pulling the van around. He jumped in on the roll.

"What are we going?"

"Away. As quickly as possible."

"What about your stuff?"

"They took everything."

"Who? The space aliens?"

She practically did a wheelie out of the parking lot.

After Noah recovered from the whiplash and they were a couple miles down the road, he looked over at Tetra. It was obvious from her expression, this was not a joke.

"Who are we running from?"

"You have to ask?"

"I'm so confused. I mean, what—"

"I'll be alright. I can pull privilege. My dad is well connected. You're a whole other story. We should've never come here."

"So what's next? Are you sure—"

"You, bomber boy, are going to Casper, Wyoming."

Notes from the Underground

They were on a little-traveled secondary road.

Noah was confused.

"This is it?"

"This is the drop point."

"Says who?"

They had just pulled up in front of a dilapidated building on the outskirts of Casper, that had definitely seen better days. The sign out front said: *The Friendly Ghost.*

Friendly Ghost. Casper. Clever.

Noah grabbed his bags and got out.

"Good luck, Noah."

She sped off like she was late for a dinner date.

Calling this place dodgy would be flattery. Why anyone would ever choose to stay here was beyond his comprehension. Did they ever give out negative stars to a motel?

He walked to the small office at one end of the structure that appeared to be the reception area. When he opened the outside door, it creaked, then the screen fell out.

There was a grizzled old man behind the counter, incredibly fat, chewing tobacco, playing solitaire. He looked up, irked at the audacity of someone interrupting his game.

Noah paid for a single night — he certainly hoped he wouldn't be here any longer than that, though he had no idea — and went to his room. It smelled musty, everything was covered with a layer of dust. If he had to venture a guess, it had last been cleaned when Bill Clinton was president.

He turned on the television. It was disaster after disaster, a disheartening stream of hopelessness.

Noah found it fascinating. He had never seen a black-and-white TV before.

After more bad news than he could handle for a night — but at least encouraged by the absence of anything about the bus bombing — he decided to try to call Naomi. Amazingly, the dial phone actually worked.

Naomi apparently had purchased an answering machine. The outgoing message was very personalized:

41

If this is the fucking CIA,
hang up now, you dickweeds!
Noah! My life is hell. I miss you
but ... my phone is tapped and my
email hacked. There is a black SUV
with tinted windows sitting across the
street 24 hours a day. This is not good!!
I wouldn't leave a message unless you
promise to visit me in Guantanamo.
I don't think you blew up the bus.
But then again I couldn't blame
you if you did. They usually
smell like bum's pee. Bye
for now. I do love you.

If you wish to leave a message ...
Nice work, Noah. Just wonderful! Missouri boy spreads the love. Another innocent victim. Poor Naomi!

On the other hand, he was an innocent victim too. How the hell did he end up in this mess? He just wanted to watch some Midwestern rubes ride around an arena on their motorcycles and he ended up here, Casper, Wyoming of all places. On his way to God knows where.

Casper, Wyoming. The café at the end of the void.

Just before he dialed the phone Noah had a feeling he shouldn't try to call Naomi. But he was suddenly possessed by a urgent need to talk to her. It had been three weeks. He felt so isolated. Nothing made any sense. He had no control over his life. Everything seemed so totally random. It was Kafkaesque. Only not that funny.

Next morning, he went down to the reception area, bought a Snickers bar from the vending machine. It had been manufactured before they started putting expiration dates on wrappers, and had the consistency of asphalt. After eating it, he was grateful he still had teeth.

This time there was a grizzled old woman behind the counter. She was fat, chewing tobacco, and bore an uncanny resemblance to the grizzled old man who was there when he checked in.

"Did anyone call? Ask for me?"

She stared at him like he was crazy.

He paid for another night and bought a pack of cigarettes.

He went back to his room. Turned the TV on. Turned the TV off.

Then he stood in front of his room and gazed at the highway that ran past in front. Though it was middle of the afternoon, there was virtually no traffic.

Noah tried to smoke a cigarette. He choked and threw the pack away.

He went back in his room, laid down on the bed, couldn't sleep, couldn't think, couldn't ...

"Screw this."

Noah quickly packed. Bags in hand, he went to the office and turned in his key. The grizzled old lady took it, spit in the wastebasket next to her, then pointed at the vending machine.

"Want another Snickers?"

"Thanks. But I'm trying to maintain my svelte, new millennium figure."

As Noah walked out to the highway, the grizzled old man came running after him.

"Hey boy! This came for you."

He handed Noah an envelope. Noah immediately recognized the handwriting. The note inside said ...

Hey, Son. Let me know if you run into this guy. I hear he's in a heap of trouble.

Wyatt Grayson Tass

Attached was a photocopy of an artist's sketch. An artist's sketch of Noah.

However, it was not Noah as he normally appeared. It was him in his 10-gallon cowboy hat and his ZZ Top beard.

Was his father a stalker? Some kind of incestuous psychopath? How did he ever come up with this sketch?

Baffled as he was, it soon passed. Shock and awe quickly morphed into anger.

He crumbled it all into a tight sphere and fastballed it across the parking lot.

Noah then stepped onto the shoulder of the highway and started walking.

Brain Drain

The President was in a small conference room talking to a select group of creative advisers. They were all young, nerdy, unpolished, and allegedly out-of-the-box thinkers, who would bring fresh perspective and ideas. It was a very special monthly meeting called the Brain Drain session, in theory a brainstorming free-for-all in its most intense form, where everyone was supposed to "empty their heads" by literally saying anything that came to mind, regardless of how outrageous or extreme. Not that anyone did. This was after all the President of the United States and who wants to look like a complete idiot in front of the most powerful man in the world.

The President was holding up a copy of the National Inquirer. The headline read: *Famous Psychic Predicts End of the World.*

"What's with this anyway? Someone's always talking about how the world is going to end."

Carl was the least shy and usually first to speak out.

"Astrophysicists actually do say that in about 4 billion years—"

"I'm not talking about 4 billion years from now, you numbskull! I'm talking about right now. There's a lot of weirdness out there. Maybe we can use this."

Felicia was from Princeton and looked like her mom raised her in a tree house.

"Use what, Mr. President?"

"The end of the world!"

Tomas' skin was so bad, he could have been turned inside out and he would've looked the same.

"Are we for it or against it? The end of the world, I mean."

The President was getting visibly impatient.

"Well, why don't you set up a focus group and poll the general sentiments of the voting public on whether the world should end or not? Maybe we can corner the doomsday vote. What morons! I'm just brainstorming here. That's what these meetings are for, aren't they? Come on, people! Give me some ideas here!"

A matronly lady poked her head in the door.

"Excuse me for interrupting, Mr. President. But we're getting tight here. In four minutes, you have a photo op and formal lunch with Dr. Machivenyika Mapuranga, the ambassador from Zimbabwe."

"Well, I certainly don't want to miss that. Did he bring me a zebra head for my desk?"

Everyone in the room started to laugh but stifled it when the President snapped back around and gave them his serious business look.

"Listen up, people! We have a little PR problem here in the White House. The country is falling apart. At the rate we're going, I'll be asking the ambassador from Zimbabwe, Dr. Macarena or whatever the hell his name is, to start giving *us* foreign aid. And I'm taking the heat for this goddamn mess. Let's get those dormant lumps of grey matter between your ears working. The end of the world. It's big. It's bold. It's sexy. It's fucking scary! There must be some way we can put it to use. Like was famously said and oft quoted, 'There is nothing that greatness can't turn to its own advantage.' Words we should try to live by here, eh?"

Carl, trying to redeem himself, immediately jumped in.

"What a great quote! Who said that, Mr. President?"

"I did, you freak. In my inaugural address!"

With that, today's Brain Drain session adjourned.

Some of My Best Animals are Friends

Did anyone ever hitchhike any more?

Apparently not. After leaving the Friendly Ghost Motel, Noah walked about six miles with his thumb out and no one even slowed down to check him out or yell random expletives at him.

It was closing in on 5:30 pm and the sun was low on the horizon.

The temperature would soon be plunging. He was beginning to question the wisdom of his impulsive decision to move on.

Suddenly a vehicle pulled up next to him. The passenger side window rolled down.

The guy looked like Leon Trotsky.

"Hey, asshole. The next town is forty miles. Have a nice day."

The car peeled off.

But when the car got about 75 yards, it came to a screeching halt, then peeled back to where Noah was standing.

"Just yankin' your chain, bomber boy. Get in."

Noah started to climb in. At first he thought the back seat was empty. But as soon as he opened the door, he could see someone laying down asleep. It was a girl with a shaved head and an Iron Maiden tattoo on her scalp. The driver turned around and shook her roughly.

"Wake up, you stupid cunt! We've got celebrity cargo."

He was as charming to look at as he sounded. He could have passed for Steven Segal wearing one of Tina Turner's wigs. He reached back and shook her again. The girl bolted upright.

"Don't ever talk to me like that again or I'll cut off your balls and stuff them up your ass!"

Whoa! A little PC would go a long way here.

"Hi. I'm Noah—"

"We know who the fuck you are. You're the guy who blew up the bus! That's why we picked you up, dork." Trotsky reached over and started knocking on Noah's head. "Hello! Anyone home?"

The driver offered milder abuse.

"Why the fuck did you leave the Friendly Ghost? You're just lucky we found you."

"Well. I think I'm being followed."

The driver started mocking him, whining like a little kid.

"I think I'm being followed."

Trotsky shook his head.

"What a dipshit!"

The girl in the back seat rallied to Noah's defense.

"You guys are a couple of fucking barbarians. It's not counter-revolutionary to have some plain old fashioned good manners, you know." She slid over so that Noah could get in the car, then turned to him. "I'm Francine."

The car peeled away. No one said anything for a while.

Then Trotsky reached in the glove compartment and pulled out a pipe. He lit up a bowl of weed, then handed it to the driver who took in about 700 cubic feet of smoke and handed it back.

Trotsky offered. Noah waved it off. Trotsky reached over the seat and waved it in the Francine's face.

"How about you, Miss Magic Eight Ball?"

She just ignored him. The driver just sneered.

"You know Miss Purity and Bean Sprouts won't touch it."

"Right. Dry mouth. She can't have that swamp living inside her face dry up and turn into a desert. Where would the one-eyed trouser eels live?"

"Did you say one-eye trouser *eels*?"

That brought peals of whooping hilarity from the front seat. Two hallucinating hyenas on a helium high.

They calmed down a bit, kept passing the pipe back and forth.

Night had fallen. They went another twenty miles or so with no one saying anything.

The car was really old. Noah couldn't be sure but he guessed it was a mid-to-late 70s Dodge or Plymouth. It didn't have a cassette player and certainly nothing to play CDs. And unless you wanted to listen to bible-thumpers or rodeo music on AM, the radio was worthless.

Trotsky kept sharing the pipe with the driver. The only sound was the two of them with their for-maximum-effect inhaling and exhaling. Noah started to feel lightheaded. Was this what everyone referred to as a contact high?

Trotsky reloaded the pipe. Good grief! How much dope could they smoke?

Ten more miles. This was going to be a long night.

The driver finally broke the silence.

"Hey Francine. Why don't you suck his dick? You haven't had any dick yet today, have you?" He turned to Trotsky. "Has she had any dick today?"

Trotsky was busy cleaning his wire-rim glasses. As wasted as he was, it was hard to fathom he could still see.

"Nope. Can't imagine she has. Hey Francine, show our revolutionary hero here your stuff."

Francine apparently was used to this abuse. She took it in stride, and replied rather calmly under her breath.

"What a couple losers. Total ass breath losers."

She then closed her eyes and went to sleep.

Maybe an hour passed.

Suddenly, Francine woke up and started staring at Noah's stomach.

"Oh God! This is so wrong! So terribly wrong!"

She turned, grabbed him and wrestled his belt loose, then reached down and pulled off his shoes. Before he knew what was happening, she rolled down the window, and threw them out. As soon as she got the window back up, she closed her eyes and went back to sleep.

The belt he could probably live without. But his shoes! What about his shoes?

Nobody said a word. The driver and Trotsky acted like nothing particularly unusual had happened. Were these people completely nuts?

"My feet are cold."

This provoked another barrage of raucous guffaws from the front seat.

Noah was getting perturbed. His patience was running thin. He didn't mean to but he ended up yelling.

"DO YOU GUYS HAVE NAMES?"

They didn't seem to notice his testiness.

Driver: "You can call me Al."

"Got it. Al."

Trotsky: "Leon."

Leon? He's got to be kidding.

"Has anybody ever mentioned ... uh—"

"That I look like Leon Russell? Yeah, I get that all the time."

"Who's Leon Russell?"

More guffaws.

"She threw away my shoes. My belt. My shoes and my belt."

Leon was filling the bowl of the pipe again.

"Did it ever occur to you that the cow you stole them from, maybe wasn't done with them?"

Okay. If there were any doubts before, Noah was certain now. These two guys, maybe the girl too, were clinically insane.

"Have you seen our ad in front of the cave? You've see it, right? Where the bear comes out and this hunter just ignores it?"

"Ad? Ad for what?"

"Our PETA ad! You haven't seen our PETA ads? There's about twenty of them running right now. Everybody's throwing a fucking conniption. They're saying it's pornography! Fuck 'em with their porno. I'll tell you what's pornographic. Stripping the hide off of an animal is pornographic. What the fuck's an animal supposed to do? Go to The Gap and pick up a new one?"

PETA. PETA. Noah had seen the acronym but had never actually tuned into it.

Ah! He suddenly remembered a couple of weird posters. And some news item about naked people running around and protesting something. Dare he ask? He didn't want to appear stupid. Unfortunately, it was too late. Leon noticed the bewildered look on his face.

"Save your breath, Al. Unabomber here hasn't the faintest idea what you're talking about."

"PETA …"

Leon turned all the way around and looked at Noah like he was talking to a child. A child with Down's Syndrome.

"PETA. People for the Ethical Treatment of Animals. Can you remember that?"

Ah! It was like the sun had just risen. They were animal rights activists. He *did* remember seeing one of their ads. There was a lot of sexuality in it and it indeed had stirred a lot of controversy. All about promoting human sensitivity to other species.

But what assholes these two guys were. The jury was still out on Francine. But without a doubt, Al and Leon were total … *animals!* Actually that was probably an insult to the animal kingdom.

"I belong to a … a kind of a similar organization. It's called PHTS. People for the Humane Treatment of Strangers. Can you remember that?"

Leon shook his head. Al just rolled his eyes and turned to Leon.

"He made a funny. Should we laugh? Or skin him alive and turn him into a belt."

"He'd make a nice pair of shoes."

Francine had woken up.

"Why don't you losers shut the fuck up?" She turned to Noah. "I was in the video with Bill Clinton and Alicia Silverstone. People keep saying it looked like we were having a threesome. What is wrong with everyone?"

Al couldn't let that go by.

"But I'll bet Clinton stuck a cigar in your twat right afterwards."

She turned away in disgust.

"You have no clue how pathetic you are. Both of you. Pathetic fucking creeps!"

Surprisingly, there was no rejoinder from the front seat. Leon had freshened the pipe and they were intently involved in sharing another bowl. Francine just sat with her arms folded and watched the dark featureless landscape roll by.

Noah decided she was okay. Weird but okay. He couldn't figure out what she was doing with Al and Leon. Certainly now that there was some peace and quiet in the cramped vehicle, he wasn't going to probe the matter.

The second-hand smoke made him drowsy. He dozed on and off. When a bump in the road woke him up, he glanced out the window. There was nothing to look at. They were traveling through vast stretches of plain and pastureland. There were virtually no lights, and only a few nondescript towns along the route. Even the bland countryside of Monroe County, Missouri was more interesting than this.

It was close to midnight when they pulled into Pierre, South Dakota. Noah pitched in his $7.00 for the room they shared. Apparently being a celebrity terrorist didn't come with many special privileges. He slept curled up in the bathtub.

He woke up to see Al standing two feet away taking a piss.

"You sure sleep a lot Mr. Bus Bomber. Everybody has been in here. I had to stop Francine from taking a shit on your head. She's such a fucking pervert."

From the other room.

"Fucktard! Don't listen to anyone with a gummy worm for a dick."

Noah stood up, splashed some water on his face, and stepped out to see what was going on.

"Are we leaving soon?"

"Just waiting for you, Sleeping Beauty."

"Should we get something to eat?"

"No time. Take one of these."

Al handed him a small white pill.

"Brain fuel. It'll pop those blood shot eyes open and you won't feel like eating."

"Nah. Not for me. But thanks. What is it?"

"It won't hurt you. It's modafinil. Don't be a hoser. It's subtle but it'll give you a leg up. Genius pill. It's all natural."

Francine was pulling a bright red t-shirt on over her head that said …

Hey you!
What part of
'Eat shit and die'
don't you understand?

"All natural my ass. Uranium is all natural but you don't see people sprinkling it on their cereal in the morning. Don't take that crap, Noah. You'll end up as crazy as these two wackos."

Al just shrugged.

Noah stepped outside. It was chilly, but otherwise an incredibly beautiful day. Except for some wispy high-altitude clouds hovering above the eastern horizon, the sky was crystal clear.

Leon was sitting in lotus position close to the door. He had a camping knife in one hand. Blood was running down the opposite forearm. He caught Noah staring.

"Hey, dude. You're a sleeping machine."

He seemed pretty calm for someone who appeared to be bleeding to death.

"Are you alright? What's going on?"

Leon reached for a motel towel, already heavily soaked with blood, and wiped his arm. There were thick scars which formed letters. The last letter was more a cluster of fresh bleeding cuts than scar tissue. So far it read:

Cruelty to anim

"I been working on this forever. Getting these scars to thicken up like this takes a long time. You got to cut each one four maybe five times. It's gonna say 'Cruelty to animals is a crime.' Or 'a fucking crime.' What do you think? I don't want to alienate people. You know?"

Absolutely. No one will be put off by your carving human flesh into a grotesque billboard. The "F word" is what crosses the line here.

48

"You mean little old ladies. Pastors and priests. Dweebs. The PC police!"

"There are a lot of pussies out there. And we need everybody on board about this cruelty thing. The world is a slaughterhouse."

"It's a bloodbath."

"Right on, bro'."

"But I'm thinking for your arm, maybe drop the 'fucking crime' approach. You can use that someplace else. Maybe a t-shirt."

"We could sell t-shirts. Great idea!"

Francine could be seen running around grabbing things, sloppily stuffing them in her hand bag. Leon tipped his head toward the inside of the room.

"Do you believe *that* t-shirt she's wearing? That is one fucked-up chick!"

Leon tapped on his temple to drive home the point.

Yep. That Francine. One fucked-up chick. Coming from a clear-thinking guy with expertise in deep-tissue meat calligraphy like Leon, that was something you could take to the bank.

Al and Francine came bursting through the door. They headed straight for the car.

"If you guys are coming, time to get your asses in gear. We're behind schedule."

Schedule? There was a schedule?

Noah and Leon rushed back in, quickly collected their bags, and they were on their way. Leon kept the motel towel on his arm till the bleeding stopped. He threw it out the window as they passed the Morningside Cemetery outside of Ree Heights. Thoughtful.

They drove for almost another hour passing through several blink-and-you'll-miss-them towns, then pulled over to the side of the road. Middle of nowhere seemed to best describe the spot.

Francine jumped out of the car, then went around to the trunk and pulled out a suitcase and a backpack.

Everyone got out. Francine ignored the other two and turned to Noah.

"I know what I believe in but I don't try to convince others. People have to figure things out for themselves. Then they become truly convinced and do the right thing."

Sounded plausible. Noah just nodded.

"I have what I call the Paul McCartney test. In any situation, I just ask myself, 'What would Paul McCartney do?' It works."

Noah didn't know what to say. It was probably good advice if he could figure out what it meant. He started to mumble something generic but Al interrupted.

"Now that's really brilliant. 'What would Paul McCartney do?' What? Pull out a bass guitar and start singing 'Band on the Run'?"

She walked away pulling the suitcase, her free hand held high in a middle finger salute.

"Where is she going?"

"Francine's got some business to take care of."

Business? In the middle of Buttbarf, South Dakota?

"Get in. We're looking at maybe five more hours and we can drop you off."

They kept heading east and after passing through Watertown, jumped on I-29, the first major highway they had traveled so far for the entire ordeal. Now heading directly north, Noah noticed that Al kept the speedometer right on the speed limit. He also noted the absence of dope for this leg of the journey. Maybe it was purely a night time activity, or more likely, they were concerned about being nailed by the highway patrol. This was a red state to its 19th Century core and the local population viewed marijuana as another form of heroin, a sure sign of moral degeneracy and total personal corruption.

They drove for another 3½ hours, cruising across the North Dakota state line, zipping by Fargo and arriving in Grand Forks. They had lunch at the Loaf 'n Jug, a convenience store right off the freeway. Nothing like kielbasa the consistency of a night stick with some orange Fanta to pick a guy up. Noah wanted to vomit but figured his depleted body needed whatever nutrition might still be in the sausage after five days in the countertop rotisserie.

They headed west, skirting the edge of Grand Forks AFB. In just under an hour they arrived in Petersburg. Al pulled the car to the front of the post office and stopped.

"We're here, bomber boy."

Noah grabbed his bags and got out.

"Thanks for the lift. Al. Leon. You're my kind of guys."

Al looked at Noah's feet.

"You might want to buy some warmer shoes. Those tennies definitely aren't going to cut it. It gets down to 70 below here at night."

Leon flashed the victory sign and yelled back at Noah as the car pulled away.

"Keep your dick moist and your fuses dry."

And Justice for All

It was so dark, Francine could barely see her hand in front of her face.

The battery on her tiny penlight was getting weak, so she'd have to work quickly.

She pulled bulky wire cutters out of her backpack and went to work on the chain link fence which surrounded the compound. After making a hole big enough for her small frame, she slipped through.

Quickly, keeping low, she traversed the forty yards to the main building.

Luck was with her! Either they never did or someone forgot to lock the thick steel entry door, though it was fitted with no less than three heavy-duty dead bolts.

She propped it wide open using the hinged metal stop mounted on the bottom, and went in.

As soon as she entered she heard them. They stirred, flitted, and made scratching sounds. Some were just curious, but others had become agitated and frenzied by the presence of an unfamiliar intruder.

Minks. Hundreds of pure bred minks. Some of the most prized minks in the world, perfected over decades by meticulous breeding to produce the most precious of all furs.

Francine moved like a sped-up action figure.

She raced up and down the rows and aisles, unlatching the tiny doors, slamming the side of each cage loudly with the palm of her hand to panic every single one of the priceless creatures into bolting.

Out they leapt, onto the cement floor, and out the door.

In less than seven minutes, 434 of the frenetic little critters had been set free to live in the wilds and do whatever frenetic little critters did out there.

50

Francine followed them in their flight, her fearful scurrying and express desire to get away not unlike theirs.

As she made her way back through the hole in the fence, there were no alarms or any other indications that she had been detected.

She breathed a sigh of relief.

The perfect crime!

Or ... act of civil disobedience, as she preferred to think of it.

With the last faint flickerings of her pen light, Francine managed to find her way to the pre-agreed meeting spot.

Al and Leon were waiting.

She jumped in.

"How did it go?"

"Smoother than vanilla pudding on a summer day."

Al slipped the car in gear and they slowly pulled away, with only their parking lights on, and Janis Joplin singing "Me and Bobby McGee" on the radio.

> "Freedom's just another word
> For nothing left to lose ..."

Francine was still a bit paranoid from her little escapade.

"Hey, Al. Maybe you should cut the radio till we get out of here."

"We're cool."

Slowly, they crept along. The main road was only a few minutes away.

Suddenly, in the darkness ahead, headlights pointed directly at them all came on in the very same instant. There were four vehicles side-by-side blocking the road.

Ten men step out from behind the darkness. They were in full combat gear and held heavy armor-piercing assault weapons.

A command was given and the commandos started firing, instantly unleashing an earthshaking barrage of bullets into the little car Francine, Al and Leon were trapped in. It shuddered, shook, pitched, as if in an earthquake. The weapons kept firing without mercy or pause. Francine, Leon, and Al were tossed about like sock puppets.

When the fusillade finally ended, their bodies looked like they had been run through a meat grinder.

A few days later when interviewed, Major Horatio Spaulding, the ATF officer who had headed up the enforcement team, explained:

"They were armed to the teeth and put up a good fight. We did what we had to do."

CHAPTER FOUR

Got MLK?

Over the next few months, while many common items usually taken for granted came up short — gasoline, coffee, anything made out of aluminum, toilet paper, automobile tires, house paint, marshmallows — there would be no shortage of bad news.

The only good news about the bad news — if you could overlook the tragedy, even horror that was being personally visited on many individuals — was that it was often rather interesting. It was often as bizarre as it was abundant.

A man smoking a cigarette in Scranton, Pennsylvania turned on his tap to fill a tea kettle. The water caught on fire and a giant ball of flame took off the guy's beard and eyebrows, leaving his head looking like a peach that had fallen into a barbecue pit. He was in fairly good humor when CNN interviewed him in the hospital but still said in no uncertain terms he "was going to sue someone's ass till the only thing they'll be grabbin' in their pockets will be their balls. Or maybe I should take a blow torch to their [bleep] heads and see how they like it."

A freeway overpass in Little Rock, Arkansas collapsed under the weight of a tractor-trailer, ironically hauling massive steel components for building freeway overpasses. The driver was in critical condition but was expected to live. Unfortunately, six motorists were killed who were underneath at the time it buckled and fell. The structure was long overdue for periodic maintenance and reinforcement.

A massive explosion in a sewer main running along Broadway in New York City rocketed hundreds of manhole covers into the air. The crashing clattering of the resulting hailstorm of steel was followed by thousands of rats scurrying in every direction from the conflagration. City engineers soon reported that the blast was so powerful, it had collapsed the subway tunnels running adjacent to the sewer, shutting down surface streets and huge sections of the subway system itself. Numbers of those injured and killed had not been determined but were thought to be in the hundreds.

A power outage, which cut electricity to almost 25,000,000 residents in five southwestern states for three days, was blamed on grazing goats. Rumors were adamantly denied that the actual cause for the outage was the simultaneous malfunctioning of nuclear power reactors at Palo Verde, Arizona and Diablo Canyon, California, which had forced them to be taken off the grid. Department of the Interior officers armed with rifles were dispatched to "selectively thin" the bothersome herds of wild goats in the areas where the problem was alleged to have originated.

The Andy Warhol Bridge in Pittsburgh collapsed at rush hour dumping dozens of vehicles into the Allegheny River. Cars, trucks and at least one city bus were briefly seen floating on the surface until they sank and disappeared. Rescue efforts got immediately under way but mostly ended up recovering the bodies of those trapped and drowned in their vehicles. Several pedestrians and at least one bicyclist were killed as well. The Andy Warhol was one of three nearly identical suspension bridges in downtown Pittsburgh, raising concerns about the integrity of the other two. Citizens were demanding thorough inspections to identify potential structural problems but the city's safety engineers were laid off a year ago due to budget cuts.

The apparent crumbling of America's infrastructure really hit home with a piece that stole the media spotlight in the middle of spring.

> April 30 (Reuters) – Twenty six people plunged to their death inside the Washington Monument. Apparently broken cabling and the failure of the emergency braking system on the state-of-the-art passenger elevator was responsible for the tragedy. In his comments before boarding Air Force One for his trip to the G-10 economic summit in Mumbai, India, the President extended his heartfelt condolences to the grieving relatives and added this: "Perhaps the families can take some comfort knowing the stock price of the manufacturer of the elevator has plummeted. The free market has spoken. America does not reward incompetence."

In light of all of these disasters, who would have thought that an ad promoting milk would set off riots in every major city across the nation?

The advertising campaign was called 'Got MLK?', and was created on behalf of the American Dairy Association. It was launched in a massive media blitz, along the lines of hundreds of similar ones that had been running for many years.

It featured the most famous portrait photo of the great civil rights leader, Martin Luther King, Photoshopped with a white mustache of fresh milk on his upper lip. This remarkable work of advertising genius — a public relations faux pas guaranteed to consign to death row the careers of the entire ad team that created it — was everywhere. Billboards, internet ads, television spots, magazines and newspapers.

The right wing went nuts. It was bad enough having Beyonce or Shaquille O'Neal staring back at you in these obnoxious ads with the milk mustache. But to have to look at a proven commie pinko turncoat like that Martin Luther King SOB, a rabble-rousing enemy of good patriotic Americans, those big lips grinning that know-it-all shit-eating grin while making it look like he'd be drinking anything other than cheap wine or Sterno, was an outrage. Everybody knew all these Negro types were lactose intolerant anyway. What a pile of lefty propaganda! What a total pile of crap!

Fox News led the harangue practically non-stop, then of course the other media outlets not to be outdone, followed suit. Soon the fever pitch of hysterical commentary boiled like a crockpot which had been welded to a stove which couldn't be turned off. A never-ending stream of self-righteous acrimony and disdainful disbelief bubbled over and spewed out of suit-and-tie talking heads and bouffanted bubble brains. 'Got MLK?' was a total field day for the freaks of the far right.

The left wing also went ballistic. A non-stop harangue condemning the virulent racism and unbridled bigotry of the right thundered away on MSNBC, and raged on over hundreds of progressive internet web sites, podcasts, and ad hoc interview shows, taking left wing whining and opining to new dizzying heights of pre-menstrual hysteria. Their quiet brothers in spirit, that special class of self-effacing latte-sipping liberals who normally only considered such matters in peer-reviewed journals and never raised their voices above a gentile whimper, were likewise so incensed they joined the fray. They were so indignant that the image of a great man had been crudely and boorishly desecrated, that commercial exploitation had stooped to such crass levels, they publicly *pouted* before buying a nice bottle of 1989 Cabernet to anesthetize their bleeding hearts and try to make the icky ad go away. It was bone chilling to see.

Not surprisingly, it was the African-American community, especially those living in urban ghettos which had been the main beneficiary of just about everything that was going wrong in America, who pumped up the volume of public outrage to a whole new level.

From New Orleans to New York, Minneapolis to Miami, Houston to Detroit, Philadelphia to San Francisco, from the black ghettos of DC to the black ghettos of Los Angeles, and every place in between where African-Americans constituted a significant chunk of the population, the streets were filled with infuriated marchers. A few of the demonstrations were peaceful, more resembling a street dance than a political uprising. The majority, however, rapidly evolved into full out insurrection, with piles of rubbish, automobiles and buses set ablaze. Windows were smashed, stores looted, and unpopular owners of local convenience stores dragged into the streets and beaten. Several ordinary citizens with rifles were observed standing on rooftops shooting at whatever and whoever passed on the streets below. In seven major cities, sundown to sunrise curfews were imposed and the National Guard called in to try to restore order.

One incident which occurred right on the National Mall in Washington DC dominated the news media for three days and truly polarized the nation. Tensions were higher than at any time since the riots in Los Angeles in 1992 over the police beating of Rodney King.

Two officers in a patrol car noticed suspicious activity occurring at the base of the Lincoln Memorial and on the statue itself. They called for backup and shortly five black adolescents, age 17 to 19 were arrested and taken in to be booked for defacement of public property. But not before they had completed the job they had come to do.

They had just painted a big mustache in white enamel house paint on Abraham Lincoln and hung a huge sign on the chest of the historic figure. It was what was on the sign that caused most of the controversy.

> Yeah, he's got milk...
> All the milk he can drink.
> That's because he's white.
> Us niggas can't afford it.

Local officials and politicos were so outraged that they demanded the young men be additionally charged with acts of terrorism, in violation of the Patriot Acts I and II. And because of unfounded rumors unleashed on the floor of the House of Representatives in a speech by a fanatic congressman from Mississippi, they were also being investigated for possible connections to blacklisted Muslim terrorist cells in Yemen and the Philippines.

Viewers of ABC's *This Week*, one of the more popular Sunday morning news talk shows, sipped coffee and nodded their tacit approval over an exchange between George Will and the show's host and regular anchor, Christian Amanpour, about the incident.

"I really don't know where they're going with that. Meaning the Homeland Security people. Maybe they know something we don't. But from what I can tell, these are just punks from right there in DC who took a break from pimping or pushing drugs or whatever other insidious things they've got going on, to disparage one of our greatest presidents."

"I completely agree. I don't get the symbolism here. It seems contradictory. I mean, Abraham Lincoln was the man who gave them their freedom."

"Well, one of the more articulate gangbangers, one that could at least speak some English I could understand, said something to the effect that, yes, they should be free now but that's not the way things have worked out. They are still being oppressed by the white man."

"That's gratitude for you."

The follow-up ad campaign by the team that came up with the original *'Got MLK?'* idea was put on hold. It was called *'MLK ... it does a body good!'* and featured Martin Luther King's head Photoshopped on the body of Denzel Washington muscle-posing in a Speedo.

Life in a Nuclear Honeycomb

Noah lost track of how many hours he sat in front of the post office in Petersburg, North Dakota. All he knew for sure was that he almost froze to death, and it had to be pushing midnight when a white Porsche 911 GT3 came tooling up and dramatically screeched to a stop, there to finally take him where he was going. Wherever that was.

"Looking for some hot action? We've got girls that'll make your yam bag blow up like the Hindenburg."

The driver was maybe 19 or 20, baby-face handsome, bursting with enthusiasm.

Noah threw his bags behind the seat and got in.

He would have said something but he was suffering from cryogenic lockjaw. It was a moot point anyway, because the driver never gave him a chance.

"You gotta to be more careful, dude. People die in this cold. This is like Antarctica. Can you believe this place? What a joke! North Dakota is the land that time forgot. I'm telling you, these people ..."

And so it went, for the next twenty minutes, as Joe — at some point along the way the guy remembered to introduce himself — carried on like a magpie on amphetamines.

Finally, they pulled up to an enormous, rather dilapidated, old farm house. There was junk piled everywhere around it. The paint was peeling, the wood steps and the porch they led to, broken and full of holes.

Joe didn't seem fazed by the cosmetics of the place.

"You're gonna dig this."

They entered a scene that was right out of Haight-Ashbury in the 60s.

55

Holding court to maybe a dozen neo-hippies in his spacious living room was the titular head of the crashpad safe house, a holding tank for every shape and size of anarchist, nihilist, insurrectionist, and social misfit that came his way. He was an archetypal 60s burn-out hippie, a gnarly old guy named Jim 'Quicksilver' Quant, who got his nickname from having been a roadie for the San Francisco psychedelic band Quicksilver Messenger Service, heyday contemporaries of Jefferson Airplane and the Grateful Dead. It wasn't entirely clear whether his providing a safe refuge for the hunted enemies of the state like Noah was born out of political conviction, or his desire to recreate the summer of love hippie days of Haight-Ashbury, with their open doors and communal living.

Quicksilver was a slam-dunk argument against using drugs, if there ever was one. He looked worse than the tobacco screen for the hookah he was constantly toking from, an object of pragmatic devotion he probably hadn't cleaned since he bought it at a head shop in 1965. Half of his teeth had fallen out. What hair he had left, grew in a band around his head in long stringy gray filaments that looked like moldy furniture stuffing. He had clusters of raisin-shaped age spots on every exposed surface of skin. He was given to staring at a person long after they had stopped speaking, as if he was privy to some silent stream of words no one else could hear. He was annoyingly cheerful, unable to grasp or insensitive to the things that bothered other people. Sometimes he just laughed for no apparent reason.

One intriguing thing about the farm itself was its location, a geopolitical fact which was providing grist for the lively exchange that was going on as Joe and Noah entered.

Petersburg was dead center in the middle of one of five major missile fields in America, built to counter the Soviet military threat during the Cold War.

Quicksilver was pointing at a large map which hung over the fireplace.

"Just look at the map."

Hippie punk #1: "Yeah. So what?"

"That peace symbol in the center is us. This farm. All those dots? That's how it all ends, baby!"

As the map showed, within a hundred miles in every direction, there were over 160 missile silos for the launching of Intercontinental Ballistic Missiles carrying nuclear warheads of enormous destructive power. When they were at full capacity, the missiles launched from this field alone could destroy the world 50 times over. Of course, with the new treaties, some of the silos had been decommissioned and were either disabled or empty. No one knew exactly how many were still active and ready for deployment. Estimates were they could only destroy the world 25 times over. Pathetic. We were becoming girlie-boys.

Hippie punk #2: "I get it. But why do we even have ICBMs now that the cold war is over?"

"'Cuz we're livin' la vida loca, that's why! You got women drowning their babies in the bathtub. People shooting up post offices and schools. The polar caps are melting and tap water catches on fire. Don't you see a problem here?"

Hippie punk #3: "That's why we've got to fuck some people up and soon! We've got to stop the insane motherfuckers before it's too late!"

"Wrong! Violence begets violence, my hyper-thyroidal soldier of misfortune. Love is the answer."

Quicksilver wandered over to a very young girl — 15-years-old tops — dressed like Selena Gomez channeling Grace Slick. The girl was giddy and shy, and inching back to try to hide behind a mangy stuffed chair. Quicksilver started gyrating his crotch only inches from her face, as she giggled and covered her eyes.

"And how would you like an hour of flower power, sweetheart?"

They weren't going to wait to see how that worked out.

Joe led Noah up the stairs. Noah threw his stuff in one of the bedrooms and staked a claim on one of the mildewy mattresses scattered around on the floor. Then he looked out the window at the vast, seemingly endless landscape.

The farm sat on a flat 50 acres of fallow land. There were only a couple trees and the sky stretched to horizons which seemed at the edge of the Earth itself. If there were an exchange of nuclear-tipped missiles, Noah had to admit: This was a perfect place to watch the fireworks.

When he and Joe went back downstairs, Jimi Hendrix was blasting from the stereo. Quicksilver was trying to get everyone up dancing.

After a monotonous hour of this silliness, Joe turned to Noah.

"We better get some sleep. We're waking the rooster. Lots of road to cover."

They went back upstairs. Despite the blaring music and constant ruckus from the quasi-party going on downstairs, Noah had no trouble falling asleep.

Next morning Noah sat in the kitchen sipping terrible coffee. The clock on the wall said 10:35 am. The kitchen was a disgusting mess, people straggling in and out, making toast and Tang, scrambling eggs, never bothering to clean up after themselves.

Finally, Joe staggered in with a serious case of bedhead.

He tried to pour coffee but most of it ended up on the countertop. While he was trying to sop it up with a dish towel, the 15-year-old girl came up behind him, wrapped her arms around his torso, and licked his ear. Then she wandered back out.

"Good morning, Joe. The school bus stopped out front and waited. I guess that shoots her perfect attendance record at Petersburg Elementary."

"Give me a break, bombs away. She told me she's eighteen."

"And if I told you I was head of Richard Branson's Virgin Galactic and could fly you to the moon, would you believe that?"

"If it was convenient."

Joe managed to get some acceptable amount of coffee in his mug and sat down across from Noah. He looked up and saw Noah's ironic grin.

"What?"

"Nothing important. Just thinking."

"Thinking what?"

"I'm sure glad we got an early start. Lots of road to cover."

"Our particular approach to life requires flexibility."

Apparently a lot of flexibility. They ended up staying three more weeks. They wouldn't be covering all of that road until Joe finally got tired of bonking Miss Jail Bait.

Noah's time there was uneventful, if in some twisted way instructional.

Nothing happened. Noah slept twelve hours a day. He kept to himself, bided his time, and became a fly on the wall.

The first night turned out to be fairly representative.

Quicksilver was always around leading seemingly endless discussions that started

57

nowhere and ended nowhere. The guy never slept or ran out of things to rant about.

He would hold court day and night, his audience captive, but surprisingly attentive. Quicksilver was an encyclopedia of facts, figures, anecdotes, and mocking commentary. He made it all bearable — in fact, enjoyable — by being self-effacing and just plain funny. No matter how intense he got, no matter how profound the topic, the old hippie never seemed to take anything very seriously. He was a one-man National Lampoon.

Nothing remotely useful ever came from anyone else in the room. Whatever they said was never very illuminating or interesting. If it wasn't some clichéd bit of hearsay, it was uninformed fulmination or a bit of pseudo-philosophical posturing, trite on its face, ridiculous at its core.

It was hardly unexpected. The place by and large was a flophouse for drifters, a shelter for drop-outs who liked to think of themselves as domestic political refugees. A lot of them had dropped out to avoid doing the hard work of knowing anything.

Noah counted forty-six people coming and going during his three weeks there. Though the farm house was huge — as in seven bedrooms — there were sleeping bags and back packs strewn about everywhere. The kitchen was filthy and constantly a mess. It was a major undertaking to go to the bathroom and he only managed two baths the entire time. He dried himself with his socks.

There were eco-protesters from the state of Washington on the lam for blowing up a lumber mill. A platoon of militia men from Michigan out on some random maneuvers. Some stoners from Texas who barely escaped being caught in a raid on their industrial size marijuana plantation. Two nerdy-looking bomb makers from Minnesota who never spoke to Noah but must have winked at him about 900 times in the three days they were there. Two lesbians from a sustainable living commune in New Mexico which had come under an assault by the ATF, convinced it was an kamikaze cult of baby killers. There was an AWOL army corporal who had leaked a treasure trove of classified documents to the underground media. Three anarchists from upstate New York who never smiled and just glared spitefully at everybody.

They just kept coming and going. With some notable exceptions they were basically nice kids, but without question, most of them would be a glove fit for the legal definition of domestic terrorists.

What must the Petersburg post office think? Over the course of a week, there had to be more strangers waiting out front by the drop box than there were people living in the town. It made no sense. Petersburg had no tourist attractions. It had no appeal whatsoever. It was the kind of town which was dying all over America, where the children left as soon as they turned eighteen and never came back.

To say the least, the strangers coming and going were some very strange strangers. Quite a contrast to the buzz-cut, straight-laced military types which were regularly seen cruising the roads in the area in jeeps and humvees.

And what did the locals make of Quicksilver Quant? This strange new immigrant from the West Coast, around which orbited this constellation of youthful outcasts.

Noah couldn't imagine, and quickly lost interest trying.

By the end of the second week, he couldn't wait to get out of there.

He was at Joe's mercy, therefore was ecstatic when he got the word.

"I ran out of lollipops. Time to hit the road."

"So there's no wedding. I was hoping to be your best man."

Next morning, they did get up with the rooster, threw their bags into the Porsche, and were ready to do some serious driving.

In spite of the cold, Quicksilver was out front to see them off. He flirted with hypothermia by appearing in just sandals and a paisley kurta, presumably no underwear. He danced around, throwing flowers at Joe and Noah, then sprinkled petals on the car, all while chanting some nonsensical mantra.

Noah grabbed him as he flitted by and possessed by an inexplicable impulse, gave the old man a big hug. There was something fatherly about Quicksilver, though he would be the father typically no one would talk about.

"Thanks for everything, Quicksilver. This has been very … uh … well, interesting. Mind if I ask you something?"

"My soul is an open book."

"I can see you're a man of peace. So I've been wondering. Why would you want to live in the midst of all these weapons of mass destruction? All these ICBMs?"

Quicksilver let out a big whooping laugh.

"So I can feel the love, my man! So I can feel the love!"

As they pulled away, Noah looked back.

Quicksilver was still dancing like there was no tomorrow.

Hammer Time

Joe started talking his usual shit as soon as they got on the highway.

"Alright! Dude! Let's save the world. By the way, Noah. Where's your ark?"

Wow! Clever guy.

"Ark's history. Hit an iceberg on a freeway in Lauderdale. Since I was behind in my child support payments, I just ran. Damn thing was falling apart anyway. Never buy pressboard from the Chinese."

"Ha ha ha! You're funny, man. But I won't hold your looks against you. Do you know what we're doing here? Like, why you're with me?"

"You're supposed to teach me to skateboard. Then if I'm not mistaken, we're meeting with the Dalai Lama."

"Wow! So incredibly close, it's scary. Actually, they have big plans for you."

"They? I have no idea who or what you're talking about."

"I'm supposed to look out for your sorry ass. We gotta keep you under wraps. We've been losing way too many lately."

"Too many what?"

"Guys like you. Yahoos who know the boom boom stuff. Myself, I don't need the glory. Unless it's a glory hole! Ha ha ha."

"I'm not what you … what *they* think."

"They told me you'd say that. Name. Rank. Serial number. That's cool."

It was like that commercial: *This is your brain on drugs.*

"Do you do drugs?"

"Never! Absolutely not! No way. No fucking way! Got any? Ha ha ha. Man, I'm hungry. Are you hungry?"

"No, I filled up on bread mold before we left the farm."

Joe pulled off the next freeway ramp, scofflawed the stop sign, and aimed his sports car at a 7-11 a short distance ahead. He slammed on the brakes as soon as he saw the drama unfolding there.

"Whoa! What the fuck?"

There were at least nine police cars barricading the parking lot, with officers armed with shotguns and rifles crouched behind them. They were in the middle of a lively exchange of gunfire with whoever was blasting away at them through the shattered windows of the convenience store.

"Damn! I just wanted a bag of corn nuts."

Joe almost stood the vehicle up on two wheels as he made a u-turn and headed back to the freeway.

A record-breaking three minutes of silence passed before Joe's motor mouth rebooted.

"So, Noah. Do you want to hear the plan?"

"There's a plan?"

"Habitat For Humanity. See, I'm like a professional do-gooder."

"Does it pay well?"

"You like my wheels?"

"I thought Avon gave out pink Cadillacs."

"It's educational funding, my friend. Institutions of higher learning are facilitating my personal development."

"Education is a beautiful thing."

Welcome to the world of Joseph Dzyzynski, a 20-year-old half-Lithuanian half-Polish vagabond born and raised in Providence, Rhode Island. Here he sat, behind the wheel of a 2013 Porsche 911 GT3, an automobile he was obviously very proud of.

As Noah certainly knew by now, Joe talked non-stop and had no secrets. His father was a corporate lackey for Textron, his mother an executive assistant to the manager of a restaurant chain. He had two older sisters. Sylvia was 26 and had cerebral palsy. Donna was 29 and was a slut who had been married three times and now lived with some loser who worked odd jobs when he wasn't incapacitated by dope. Both his parents were alcoholics in denial. Joe didn't drink or do drugs. But he intended to bang every good looking girl in America. Senior year he was a halfback on his high school football team. It was excellent! There was only one cheerleader he didn't manage to skronk. She was a lesbian, so it didn't count.

"It's like this, Mr. Boom Boom. I live on student loans. And I learn by doing. I'm getting a real education. Fuck college!"

"Student loans?"

"I check in with my university every three months, register for classes, then the day after they start I drop them. The university refunds the course fees to my bank account and here I am driving us to the deep South, famous for hominy grits and lynching colored folks."

"Won't you have to pay the money back? I mean, they are loans."

"You aren't very imaginative, are you? The one thing I have learned by not sitting in a box listening to some bearded blowhard, is how to think outside the box. Yes. In theory, I will have to pay the loans back. But that is built on a lot of hypotheticals."

"Hypotheticals like?"

"Look around you! We are on the short end of a short fuse, my friend. You think there will be banks? You think there will be an economy? We're going to be a bunch of hunter-gatherers, man! They're not going to try to collect my loan. They're going to be collecting berries for their next meal. Ha ha ha!"

"They're at least going to want your berries."

"I thought you would be cleverer. Maybe building bombs is a pretty narrow specialty."

"It is. But I can fix clocks now. And bicycles."

"I've learned so much these past two years. So much, dude! The world isn't at all what they want you to think it is. Text books are just propaganda for small minds."

"Especially the calculus texts."

"See. Smart answer for everything. But that doesn't mean you're smart. I can tell you haven't lived. Where did you grow up? Some ant farm in the Midwest?"

"Missouri. Pulnick, Missouri. You've never heard of it. I wish I hadn't."

"Listen to me! Don't take offense. I'm not coming down on your case. It's never too late. I'm just saying, that's all. Just saying. And the really great thing is we're starting right now."

"Starting what?"

"Your education, my friend. Your education. Yo baby, It's hammer time!"

Crazy is the New Desperate

Ed Schultz, the liberal MSNBC journalist was already famous for chiding pundits and politicians for ludicrous and irrational pronouncements and policies. Now he had just added a brand new segment to his nightly news program. It was called "We Aren't Making This Up!" and it became an instant hit.

The news items covered were not so much political as they were social, personal. They were the things going on in America, symptomatic of systemic breakdown and individual desperation.

Ed kicked off the first show by interviewing a man who was selling himself as a punching bag. For $5 you could hit him in the stomach. For $10 you could hit him in the face. If you were willing to ante up $20, you could kick him in the balls. The guy looked like he had been hit by a bus, whipped with chains, then stomped on by cage-fighting Thai kickboxers. His face was bruised and swollen, crisscrossed with cuts and stitches, his eyes were black and blue, his nose twisted like a maple cream cruller.

Ed: "Why are you doing this?"

Man: "I'm broke. I need the money."

Ed moved on, next looking at a posting on eBay under Home and Garden - Major Appliances:

> I love my kids but credit collectors are at my door. Two adorable children, boy 7 and girl 5. Sell as a pair or separately. Low maintenance if you have cable TV. Father from Cuba and mother from Dominican Republic. Cuddly. Cute. Happy smiles. Bidding starts at $600 each or $1000 for both.

Ed: "People selling their children? What's this country coming to? And $1000 for two kids? Sounds kinda cheap to me. Now we go to Portland, Oregon where a retired stage director for children's theater has apparently put some unusual items on the market to raise some cash. This is Marty Kordakis."

Marty: "I got a lot of duplicates, you know. I figure I only need one. So let others put 'em to good use."

Ed: "Duplicates? I'm not following you. Duplicates of what exactly?"

Marty: "I got two lungs, two kidneys, two testicles, two ears. Hell, I really only need one arm."

Ed: "You're selling your body parts?"

Marty: "Don't act so surprised. Women have been selling their bodies for centuries. It's pretty much the same thing."

Ed: "Well, not quite. But I'm not here to argue. I guess you do what you have to do."

Over the coming weeks, there certainly were no shortages for Ed's new segment.

In a form of performance art for pay, a teenage girl offered to hold her bare hand in a fire for as long as the money lasted. She charged $50 for each ten seconds. Ed railed at whatever adults had allowed this attempt to make a buck. It had not ended well. The girl's arm had to be amputated, even though the person who had hired her for the cruel stunt had disappeared and not paid a single penny.

Another evening Ed talked about strange new services that were popping up in print ads and on internet sites like Craig's List and Backpage. There was one listing which left little room for doubt as to the nature of the person's expertise:

Professional Arsonist. Get out from under those big mortgage payments and collect the insurance. We will burn down your house for you. 100% satisfaction guaranteed. Proven methods. They'll never know it was you. Call for a free estimate. Dial or text us now! 888-367-3473. 888-FOR-FIRE!

There was an unsavory ad which touted the effectiveness of blackmail.

FIRE YOUR BOSS! Just send us three photos of your boss (cell phone pics are fine) and let the magic of Photoshop do the rest. We'll send back pics of him or her like no one has ever seen them before. Sex with animals, nude with prostitutes, gay canoodling, shooting up drugs, pole dancing naked, meeting with terrorists. Get that raise you know you deserve or just fire the SOB, it's up to you. Reply to #GS-454.

With such new fires of entrepreneurship ablaze, more and more people saw the hot embers of opportunity glowing and joined the action. In what was dubiously dubbed copycat capitalism, all sorts of bizarre enterprises were soon underway.

In the new economy, money is time and everything is for sale.

The Ultimate Status Symbol. Living sculpture! Why settle for boring bronze or marble. Fill your garden or living space with real humans. Me and my friends will stand, sit or lay in whatever poses you want in whatever clothes you choose. Nude okay too. Both short and long term. Prices you can afford. By the hour, day, week or month. Email is best: juicylucystatues@hotmail.com

Another guy had a lot of time on his hands and more than his share of confusion.

Prison time? Don't know how this would work but I'll serve your time for you. I need a place to stay and three squares a day. Call it even! Contact ASAP. Reply to ad #HX-993.

Need a hit man — or more politically correct, a hit person?

Snuff Is Us. Is something or someone bothering you? We make problems go away. Ad #TL-113.

There was also the increasing popularity in new forms of recycling for profit. As one Craig's List ad offered:

Take my wife. Please! 42 years young. She ain't no beauty but she's a damn good cook. Irons, cleans house, smart shopper. Gives great head when she's drunk. $1000 and she's yours.

An unemployed lumberjack from Oregon decided to skip the middle man:

Man 4 sale. Unemployment has run out. I'm big. I'm strong. I'm obedient. I'm housebroken. Put me in the barn next to the cow. No problem. Why rent when you can own? Make me an offer. No real estate fees. Original owner.

One derelict-looking guy posted a video on YouTube of himself sitting with a handgun held to the head of his dog. He threatened to shoot the animal if people didn't send him money. Apparently no one took him seriously. They should have. Two weeks later the tragic sequel appeared. It was a wobbly hand-held video camshot of the dog laying on the floor with a pool of blood spreading from under its head, or what was left of its head, with the man screaming, "You cheap motherfuckers! Look what you make me do!"

After a while, Ed Schultz settled on what became his trademark closing.

"There you have it. And no, folks, we aren't making this up. We wish we were. But we're not. That's all for tonight's segment. It's all I can handle."

School of Hard Knocks

Noah and Joe shared the driving. Each drove four or five hours while the other slept. Joe was behind the wheel when they went through Kansas City and headed east across Missouri on I-70. It was dark and Noah slept most of the way but woke up at one point and realized where he was. A single simple reaction poked through his drowsy semi-consciousness: *Ugh!* He instantly fell back asleep.

With a generous number of rest stops, at least two hours for beef burgers, buffalo wings and beer in Nebraska City at a sports bar called the End Zone, and a lard-based breakfast precisely at sunrise in Gilmore, Tennessee featuring deep fried pork belly, it took them just under 26 hours to get where they were going.

They pulled up to the main headquarters of Habitat For Humanity, Tuscaloosa, Alabama. The offices took up the first floor of a regal old house on the southeast side of town, just down the street from the Salvation Army Thrift Store.

Tuscaloosa wasn't that unlike cities of its size all across America — the most recent census put the population at just under 100,000. It had the same problems, just more of them. Its 11.3% unemployment rate was substantially higher than the national average. One in four children lived in poverty. Its schools were falling apart, as funds for education got cut, then cut again many times over.

The city's greatest notoriety came from the frequent tornadoes that visited the area. They were still recovering from one that cut a swath of devastation back in April 2011.

Noah stepped out of the car and realized that for a change he wouldn't need a coat. It was 62 degrees and the sun was shining. Both he and Joe had gotten enough sleep along the way, were wide awake and extremely stoked about being there. They grabbed some lunch, met the staff and crew, then went to work.

Noah knew right off he was going to like this.

And he did.

For the next six weeks he immersed himself in major repairs on two homes which were being refurbished top to bottom, inside and out; also doing minor maintenance and touch-ups on several others occupied by poor families in town and the surrounding area; but in the main, helping to build from the ground up a bungalow for Clarence and Grace Lee Wills and their two pre-school age children.

Clarence was the foreman and project leader for Habitat. He was a big strapping fellow, African-American, in his late 40s, charming, funny, handsome to a fault, but with the rough-hewn and burly presence of a man who worked with his hands. This was his second time around at marriage. His first wife had died of ovarian cancer but not before all of their savings and the equity of their home were eaten up by medical bills. His new wife was twenty years younger than him and though they were starting from scratch, he was determined to make a good life and a bright future for his new family.

Clarence was required by Habitat's build-to-own program to invest his own "sweat equity" in the construction. He not only contributed his time but oversaw every aspect of the project, and most importantly, acted as a tutor to guys like Noah who had good intentions but little expertise and no experience. He was a master carpenter who simply couldn't find work in an economy that wasn't building much of anything. Now he was putting his talent into a labor of love, building the house that would be his future home.

Noah spent a lot of time with Clarence, learning the tricks of the trade, getting a generous dose of ribbing every time he smashed his thumb with a poorly directed hammer. For Noah, it was a phenomenal education getting to know someone whose life was so completely different from his.

Rural Alabama was like rural Missouri in many respects. A cultural wasteland. A quicksand pit that swallowed whole lives and generations of pitiful people. Boring to anyone with measurable brain wave activity. Full of religious, superstitious people who were timid but ornery. People suspicious of book-learnin' and slick city ways. People who embraced the Bible as the great eternal book of brotherly love, yet had no problem taking a shotgun to anyone who didn't see eye-to-eye with them.

But the similarities were superficial. Somehow viewed through the eyes of a black man in many ways turned the whole picture on its head.

For one thing, Clarence by himself laughed more in one day, than everybody combined did in an entire year in Monroe County, Missouri. He had hundreds of stories about life in the South, and always right on the tip of his tongue some figure of speech or turn of phrase for every conceivable situation.

Good times: "We ain't had so much fun since the hogs ate grandma."

Existential confusion: "I was happier than a dead dog in the sunshine."

White trash: "Them folks go bare feet in the pig barn."

Black trash: "An aristocrat to them niggers is someone with a bathtub."

Sex with an ugly woman: "Tough titty said the kitty but the milk sure tastes good."

Stupidity: "That guy's so dumb he can't pour piss out of a boot with the directions on the bottom."

Everybody loved working with Clarence. The girls were like groupies. The guys his adopted sons.

One evening, work on Clarence's new house ran way over the regular schedule. They were laying up some dry wall and sealing it. It only made sense to use up all the finishing compound they had made up, so five volunteers including Noah kept on working by portable lamps until 9:30 pm. For their extra work, Clarence took them out for beers at a local tavern.

Everybody was yakking away about the usual stuff. Women. Sports. Cars. Women. Men. Then a 22-year-old kid who had just arrived earlier in the week, a bright-eyed idealistic fellow named Robert from somewhere in northern California, brought up the civil rights movement. He was showing off a bit, trying to let everyone know how much he knew about the 60s and all of the horrible things that had happened to those on the front lines of the protests in Montgomery and Selma, Alabama, and other hot spots of racial discord in the South. Finally, he engaged Clarence directly.

"It must feel good to see some progress down here. I'll bet things used to be pretty awful, eh?"

Clarence raised his glass of Rye Squared Imperial Ale and smiled.

"You are so right, young man. Progress. It's a damn good thing."

Everyone detected something a little off about the way he said it. It wasn't like Clarence to be clever or ironic. Certainly never sarcastic. But there was a strange edge to this last comment. And a look in his eye that spoke of a secret torment.

"Robert. That's right, isn't it? Robert from California. What you were sayin', Robert, is true. Absolutely true. I can speak from my own experience. See back then, the white folk woulda hung me from a tree till the life drained out through my boots. But because of all the progress that's been made, they only done this."

Clarence stood up and in one motion pulled his shirt over his head. Then he turned around. His broad bare back showed the ugly and horribly painful scars of a cattle brand. The branding in bold letters read:

Not a human.
This here is
a nigger!

Just like Joe had promised.

Noah was getting an education.

CHAPTER FIVE

Visions of Joanna

One exceptionally sunny day, Noah was working beside Joe, on top of a house that was being framed. They were pounding nails to set the 2x10 support joists for the roof.

"Hammer time."

"I always tell it like it is."

"And I take it, this is your idea of fun?"

"Noah. Wake up and smell the coffee. I get laid more on these gigs than Charlie Sheen with a suitcase of roofies."

Just then, a tall, thin, very striking female volunteer pushing a wheelbarrow, passed alongside the house right beneath them. She looked up and smiled at Noah.

"Aha! That one right there. She's definitely checking you out."

"You're whack."

Noah had noticed her before. How could he not? She was sinfully good looking. If he had to compare her to a movie star, it would have been Charlize Theron. Blond hair, blue eyes, at least 5'9" tall, slender. She was feminine but sure in her movements. She somehow made pushing a wheelbarrow one of the sexiest things he'd ever seen.

Noah hadn't talked to her. But he found out her name was Joanna and came from Maryland, had attended Princeton.

From what he had gathered, Joanna was so intelligent it was scary. Noah had never met a smart female. Truth be told, this wasn't considered remotely possible by either the guys or girls he grew up with back home. It just wasn't in the cards. Guys assumed girls would be dumb. Girls wanted to be dumb to please guys. It was a pitiful pact which promoted the lowest expectations and never disappointed.

They finished up. The day in the sun had done him in. He wasn't used to such intense physical work. Plus listening to Joe all day would take down the best Olympic decathlon champion. Between the sawing and hammering, jawing and yammering, he was totally exhausted. He had just returned to his room from showering and was getting ready to go to bed, when he heard a knock on the door.

"Come in, Joe."

Joanna walked in carrying a bottle of wine and two glasses. Noah scrambled to put on some pants.

"Don't bother. I grew up with three older brothers. You're Joe's friend, eh? Are you trying to screw every girl here as well?"

"I don't think Joe has to try. He already has."

"Not every one. I've been saving myself."

"Saving yourself?"

That was how it started. That was how it continued for the next several weeks. Usually twice, sometimes three times a week. He could always smell a faint whiff of wine on her breath and taste the tart sweetness of a merlot or rosé on her lips. He didn't mind. She always brought the bottle and they shared a glass. He had never had wine before but was definitely developing a taste for it.

They made love from the first like they had been together for a very long time. It was as if they instinctively knew the nuances of one another's desires and individual hot buttons. Noah had nothing to do with this. He was by every measure a novice. But Joanna knew her way around his body like she had drawn up the blueprints, and had a way of teaching him the map of hers so that he felt like he had a PhD in the art of lovemaking.

It was the first time he had ever been with an older woman. It was the first time he had even considered it. Older? She was 31. When he initially thought about it, eight years had seemed like a lot at his age. It still did. But in a positive light. If it took eight years for someone to grow beyond the silliness, inhibitions, cluelessness, coyness, and dollhouse pretend games that seem to plague younger girls, he was all for it.

Joanna loved sex. Everything about it. Sucking. Licking. Caressing. Kissing.

What was incredibly cool was when it was over, it was over. Some girls had to play the sex card constantly. Why? What were they trying to say? 'I am sexy 24/7, baby! You can't get enough of me because I am a full-on full-time lovelust machine. I am 100% sex appeal all of the time.' What? Nobody is 100% anything all of the time. Men aren't even men 100% of the time. Or women women.

It must be insecurity. And one thing Joanna wasn't was insecure.

She had no reason to be.

Noah decided that, male or female, Joanna might be the most competent human being on Earth. Certainly by light years the most competent person he personally had ever encountered. Or imagined possible.

Which is what in the end made her so sexy.

She *was* sexy 100% of the time.

Because she wasn't.

The Gold Standard

It came out of nowhere.

In a move that surprised everyone, and certainly baffled economists of every ilk and color, the administration put America back on the Gold Standard.

The announcement came from perhaps the man most unsuited for public life in the entire history of the nation, the sheepish and cowering Secretary of the Treasury. He tried to clear his throat before speaking, but in doing so spewed an a large oyster-grey phlegm ball onto the lapel of his ill-fitting pinstripe jacket. The lump of mucous sat there quivering as he delivered a prepared statement.

> *"As advocates for and servants of the people of this nation, we are charged with doing all in our power to keep the U.S. on a sure footing. With this in mind, the policy we are announcing today is a natural and proper next step. Retroactive to midnight yesterday, the full faith and credit of the United States of America will be assured by tying all currency instruments to the value of gold, fixed at $2500 per ounce. Moreover, the personal or private ownership of gold by any*

individual, business entity, trust or corporation is deemed illegal. All citizens who have ownership or control over any asset containing more than 20% gold are required within 30 days to bring any and all such assets to government agents responsible for the retrieval and accumulation of the nation's gold supply. There will be special booths set up in all of the major banks and public financial institutions. The possessors of such gold will be fully compensated, and moreover be recognized for doing their patriotic duty, by receiving a special embossed Certificate of Appreciation, automatically signed by the President's own personal signature imprinter. We thank you in advance for your loyalty and cooperation in this great national endeavor."

So all of the gold would be collected, melted down, and held in reserve by the government to shore up confidence across the globe in the value of the dollar, and faith that America would pull itself out of its current economic crisis. We were putting our money where our mouth was. Or more accurately, we were putting gold where our money was. We would walk the walk and it would be down the yellow brick road. That road would be paved in everyone's jewelry and gold fillings.

Before the initial gasps of shock and bewilderment had completed their whispery journey into the zeitgeist, the pernicious effects of this ill-conceived about-face reared up in terrifying Mephistophelean wonder.

No one was safe. In their homes, walking down the street, driving their cars. If they were suspected of having gold, they became targets for enterprising thieves and burglars, who were more than happy to relieve them of the precious metal and turn it in at $2500 an ounce.

No one was smiling. Especially anyone with gold fillings. At least not in public. Reports were becoming more common of persons being dragged into alleys and having their teeth removed, usually with a pair of pliers or vice-grips, certainly without the benefit of an anesthetic or the comforting smile of a pretty young dental assistant.

But these were tiny inconveniences next to what followed the 30 day confiscation period. For as soon as the gold was locked up and safely behind the thick vault walls of federal depositories, the speculators took over.

$2500 per ounce was widely heralded as a very generous price tag. But now that gold within the U.S. borders was no longer subject to the forces of the free market, gold futures on international exchanges shot through the roof. Actually through the roof, the closest cloud cover well into Earth orbit. Soon gold was trading at $12,500 per ounce and rising.

And the value of the dollar plummeted. It fell and fell and fell.

To put into perspective the effect this had on the common citizen, Fox News did a piece on a lady shopping at Walmart. She was in her mid-30s, married, and had three kids. The reporter stood at the check-out counter with her as her groceries were being tallied. Finally the bagger handed her a small bag, barely half full. The LED read-out on the cash register read $457.22, as the lady shaking her head looked into the bag in disbelief. She dejectedly handed the cashier a huge wad of bills.

Nearly in tears, she dragged herself toward the exit. The reporter tagged along and stuck his microphone in her face. She just rambled on to no one in particular.

"I can't believe it! $450 for this? That's a whole week's pay, for chrissakes. A loaf of Wonder Bread $44.95! How am I supposed to feed my family?"

The news report cut back to the bubble blond celebrity host in the Fox News studio. Behind her was a graphic of the President dressed as King Midas, rubbing his hands together, gleefully looking at a huge trunk overflowing with jewelry and gold ingots.

> *"Yes. 'How am I supposed to feed my family?' That's the question a lot of people are asking as the price of everything spirals out of control. We have reports that gasoline in California just topped $57 per gallon. Recently I spoke with a White House insider who chose to remain anonymous. But he told me quote, 'Everybody here is scrambling to come up with some way to address this crisis. But don't hold your breath.' Unquote. Well, with this administration, I don't think people are holding their breath. I think they're holding their noses."*

Invisible Man

The six weeks working on the Habitat for Humanity projects in Tuscaloosa, Alabama seemed to just fly by. There was an interesting variety of work and an even more interesting variety of people.

Everybody stayed in one of two large dorm houses. Some people shared a bedroom. Noah had his own on the third floor of a huge old colonial-style house. It was more of a large closet than an actual bedroom but it afforded him privacy and a comfortable place to sleep.

Both houses had spacious common areas, living and dining rooms which had been adapted for use and provided the typical conveniences itinerant volunteers appreciated. They were set up very much like youth hostels. Each had music and DVD players, a decent enough television monitor with a satellite hook-up, a snack bar including coffee, tea, light snacks, a microwave oven, and a desktop computer with a high-speed internet connection.

Noah spent relatively little time on the computer. He didn't do any leisurely surfing, mainly out of courtesy to the several others who he shared the communal PC with. On average he spent maybe 10 to 15 minutes a day, either before starting work early in the morning or in the evening after dinner. He sampled enough of the news on the web to see that he had not come up at all since his initial 5 minutes of fame right after the bus bombing in Indianapolis. This was not sufficient in itself enough to think that he was no longer being sought after by the authorities. It just meant the media had moved on. And there was certainly a lot to move on to. The country seemed to be falling apart, the population up in arms, the President and Congress clueless and paralyzed, all of which was a reflection of the larger picture of the rest of the world. Chaos and frustration were in abundant supply, harsh ingredients in the grey soup of despair and languor constantly fed to a public starving for the nourishment of hope, hungering for any news item which promised an improvement in anything.

For sure Noah had his own problems. But relatively speaking, he was better off than most people. Rather than immerse himself in the misery of others, he immersed himself in books. There was between the two dorm houses a phenomenal library of classics, literature which Noah had never been particularly inclined to read in the past. At the urging of those around him, including Clarence who demonstrated a scholar's familiarity with the great literary works of both America and Europe, Noah read Plato, Aristotle, Melville, Hemingway, Dickens, Tolstoy, Bronte, Wilde, Lawrence, Faulkner and Fitzgerald. He was constantly adding to his list for future reading, which already included Huxley, Orwell, Bellow, Robbins, Balzac, and Norman Mailer.

An unanticipated bonus from this immersion in literature was how much it gave him in common with the other volunteers. He spent many late evenings in engrossing conversations, himself mostly listening since he was a bit shy and rather tentative about the value of his own ideas. He couldn't help but feel he had up till now been missing out on a lot in life — an awful lot! But as Joe had said at the beginning of the drive here, it wasn't too late and he was starting right now.

One evening, he was sitting in the ground floor lounge area across from Joanna, reading *On The Road* by Jack Kerouac. One of the computers became available, so he sat down, planning to merely check his email and quickly browse the day's headlines.

As soon as he signed on to his Yahoo account, the Instant Message window popped open.

> *WGT says:*
> How r things there in Tuscaloosa?

> *Me:*
> Who is this?

> *WGT says:*
> What's wrong with u, boy? Don't know yur own flesh and blood? And I thought we were becoming good buddies.

Was it possible? Noah was in shock. What should he do?

> *WGT says:*
> Cat got your tongue? Listen, my confused rebel without a cause. Every fugitive isn't a hero.

> *Me:*
> WTF do you want?

> *WGT says:*
> You could show some gratitude. I'm keeping you alive, you know.

Noah hastily closed the chat window and signed off.

His head was a cyclone of possibilities, questions, confusion. Anger was the thread that fused it all together into a self-destructive assault on his sense of well-being.

He had been getting too comfortable. He thought no one was on his trail.

What a rude awakening.

Of course, this was his father. Or the sperm donor that technically counted as his father. But how could he have found Noah? And what was the point?

When he sat down again in the easy chair, Joanna looked up from her book.

"Are you okay?"

"Do I look okay?"

"No."

"I guess that sums it up pretty well."

Joe the plumber … and carpenter … and …

Crazy talking Joe.

Noah was especially surprised to see Joe quite often late at night in one of the common areas slumped in one of the stuffed chairs with his nose deep in a book.

He had to confess. At first he wasn't impressed. Initially Joe struck him as an incredibly immature, flighty party animal, just looking for the best way to avoid responsibility and get laid as often as possible. But first impressions can be misleading and in this instance, they were pretty much dead wrong.

As the days rolled by, Noah frequently got to work alongside Joe. Clarence Wills effectively was the foreman over everything that Habitat was working on at the time, because of his many years as a master carpenter. But when Clarence couldn't be two places at once, more often than not, it was Joe he leaned on for basic supervision and oversight. As young as Joe was, he handled it well. He was knowledgeable and patient. No bloated ego. Just seemed glad to be there to help. As time went on, Noah's understanding and respect for the guy steadily grew.

Not that he was a Clarence wannabe by any stretch of the imagination.

If Clarence was the wise old man full of sage wisdom and southern humor, Joe was the young wise guy full of piss and vinegar, hormones and irreverence. But everybody loved him. He never stopped talking and most of the time those around him never stopped laughing.

It was humbling to think that Joe was Noah's junior by three years. If Noah was keeping score — and he really wasn't — he came in at a distant second in just about everything they did. Noah wasn't merely running a bad race. He wasn't even on the same track. Joe was a phenomenon. With talent pouring out of his hands and enthusiasm rippling through every cell in his body, he was able to do at least three times as much as Noah, whatever it was. Doors hung, walls painted, windows framed, tiles laid, electrical outlets wired, pipes installed, the number of bank shots sunk in a game of eight ball, girls boinked. In this last arena of manly prowess, there was definitely no competition. It was 12 to 1. It might however be said in Noah's defense, the 1 boinking for him was more than a one-off wam-bam-thank-you-ma'am incident, in sharp contrast to the hit-and-run vagina derby that Joe pursued with the fervor and ADD of 13-year-old boy hiding out in the sheik's harem.

Noah was not threatened or intimidated by any of this. If anything he was awed and amused. If as Joe predicted we all again became hunter-gatherers, there was no doubt in Noah's mind that whenever Joe was around, there would be nothing left to hunt or gather. Over the course of the six weeks, he developed a deep admiration for him — his energy, his expertise, his passion, his twisted world view, his love of the opposite sex.

He was definitely one-of-a-kind, which was probably for the best.

How many guys living on student loans could the world handle?

Red Clay and Catfish

There was one thing Noah could say about life in the deep South.

They kept it real and they kept it simple.

Of course he was seeing it through the eyes of those who had never had the luxury of living any other way. People who were a long way down on the social ladder from the airs and pretenses of old southern wealth, outside the opulent manors the aristocratic oligarchy built on the backs of the slaves, the ancestors of people just like Clarence.

Clarence was Noah's window to this fascinating new world. He was the first black man Noah could say he had the pleasure of knowing. Really knowing. But never entirely knowing. There were always surprises. Most of them pleasant and endearing.

Clarence was always generous in his praise of the work of the volunteers, keenly aware that their energies were going into building the house he and his new wife would someday make their home. He often came up with additional little ways of expressing his gratitude for their hard work.

It was into the fifth week since Noah had arrived. The crew had just worked nine days without a break, sometimes going well into the evening, having to eat dinner late just before turning in for the night. Clarence decided they all deserved to have some fun.

They broke off in the middle of the afternoon and got themselves ready for a night out on the town, some good southern style cooking, and an evening of the music that had the characteristic stamp of Alabama in its heyday on the pop music scene.

Muscle Shoals was one of a cluster of towns situated on the south side of the Tennessee River across from Florence, Alabama. This northernmost region of the state sat on the border with Tennessee about 2½ hours south of Nashville, and was famous for its rich red clay, the pay dirt for fecund farms and thick lush flora which flourished in the bright carmine soil.

While Nashville was and remained the intergalactic capital of country music, during the 60s and 70s Muscle Shoals itself had once been famous for its unique blend of southern rock, R&B, gospel, soul and blues. Acts arrived from all over the world to take advantage of the profusion of great studio musicians, two top-notch recording studios, and that magic something which could always be identified with productions originating there. A tight group of elite musicians formed the core of the Muscle Shoals Sound Rhythm Section, and a handful of brass instrumentalists offered their legendary skills as the Muscle Shoals Horns. Artists as diverse as Wilson Pickett, Aretha Franklin, Staple Singers, the Rolling Stones, Elton John, Dire Straits, Boz Scaggs, Willie Nelson, Paul Simon, Bob Dylan, Lynyrd Skynyrd, the Allman Brothers, Rod Stewart, and Julian Lennon pumped the hits out of Fame Studios and

Muscle Shoals Sound, and for a decade it was hard to turn on the radio without hearing the amazing music that had some of that Muscle Shoals red clay on its boots.

Those days were now long gone. The studios and record labels had closed. All those original rock musicians were either in rocking chairs or underground buffet for the local cemetery's worms. Muscle Shoals' venerate and legendary place in the pop music scene now only resided in fading memories of a golden age four decades past. The hip night clubs in the area rarely hosted live bands, and certainly wouldn't consider playing the old timers stuff that had put Muscles Shoals on the world map so long ago. The whole scene had been transformed by electronics and lasers, light shows and break dancers, rappers and DJs. Places like Trancers and Surrender brought in star power mixmasters from Miami and New York, who pumped out thunderous dance beats over monstrous 1000 watt stacks of speakers. The clubs featured all of the latest big hits, electronically massaged, cross faded in a continuous screaming surge of synthesized sound and sampled rhythms, orchestrated to create the pounding pulse of a night of dancing and partying, often preludes to sunrise carnal coupling.

But that was the beauty of pop music. It was always reinventing itself. Out with the old. In with the new. Every generation had its own music so that the next generation had something to look down their noses and laugh at.

There was among the area night clubs and bars, however, one exception to this inevitable romancing of the latest fad and fashion. There was still one place a person could go and hear those good old songs, that dated but somehow timeless old sound — those old licks, kicks, and musical tricks — produced by the ancient masters of the Muscle Shoals music scene.

That's where Clarence was taking them tonight.

The Red Clay Tavern.

Fifteen of them, all but three of the volunteer staff, piled into three cars and pointed directly north for the 2½ hour drive — six girls and nine fellows, plus Clarence.

Clarence drove one vehicle, Joe another, and Noah the third with Joanna next to him, her skillful hand discretely comforting the inside of his thigh like a purring cat.

They got there at 8:30 pm, a good hour before the band would fire up. Clarence insisted they try the house special for dinner — grill-blackened catfish, cornbread with cotton thistle honey, paprika-and-pepper peas, and spicy deep fried butter-dipped fries on the side.

Catfish is an ugly mutant of the common carp, itself an ugly mutant. Regardless, when Tillis 'Shanty Town' Tubbs, Red Clay's cook in good standing for the past thirty odd years, got done with it, the dull-witted bottom dweller with whiskers and a constant angry frown was transformed into a delicacy of the highest order. At the end of the meal, Noah himself looked like a cat licking every last greasy molecule of the stuff off his oily fingers.

They finished their meal and ordered another round of suds in a pitcher, some generic brand of southern brew which mystifyingly tasted like the elixir of the gods.

What a fantastic idea! Clarence should be the ambassador to the United Nations. The man certainly had the magic touch. As was the case when they were sweating away at the business of building and repairing houses, tonight all eyes were on him. Not only was he naturally charismatic, he was thoroughly entertaining, funny and engaging, with a depth of character and humility born in both the pain and joy of living.

The house band, Mr. and Mrs. Bojangles, fronted by a couple of old timers right out of Grant Wood's *American Gothic*, had come on stage and was tuning up for their 10 billionth nightly performance. Despite the dreary persona of the lead singers, they were legendary for their high-energy and faithful renditions of the great songs that had poured out of this humble little town in its heyday. The Red Clay Tavern was literally packed every single night by devoted fans and people drawn from counties all around to savor the sound of the 60s and 70s, Muscle Shoal style. It was barely 9:30 this evening and it was already standing room only.

Noah was having problems figuring out the crowd. A lot of the men wore cowboy hats, but had the long stringy unwashed hair and wild unkempt beards of hard-core bikers or the Charles Manson School of hippie burnouts. They were 60s leftovers but definitely not of the flower power ilk. They had that annoying shitkicker arrogance, a dangerous combination of laid-back and lethal — the type who would casually pick their teeth with a toothpick while blowing your brains out with a large bore Winchester. The women weren't much better. They dressed like square dancers but their hair was teased like they were going to a Guns 'n Roses concert. Their makeup looked like it had been applied with a spackling knife for the remake of Fellini's *Satiricon*. Noah was surprised there weren't bingo cards on the tables. To call them white trash might be an insult to white trash. He knew if he struck up a conversation, they would definitely not be discussing the effect of green house gases on the world's climate. They might talk about the countless ways rebar could be used as a disciplinary tool for child rearing.

When Clarence and company had walked in, the entire Habitat contingent got a lot of looks and stares. In part it might have come from the fact that they were twenty to forty years younger than anyone else in the bar. But most of it was because Clarence was the only black man in sight. And he had arrived with at least six of the prettiest young white girls seen in the place since it had opened its doors back in 1977.

None of the regulars in the crowd did anything or said anything. Noah decided — at least hoped — it was just very local people wondering who these new faces were and what they were doing in a place like this. Apart from Clarence, the Habitat volunteers were more of the age to be popping ecstasy and doing the disco thing over in Florence than to be slumming in a rundown establishment that was more museum than night club.

The band launched into "Sweet Home Alabama". Electricity filled the air as the guitars thrashed and whined and the vocal harmonies soared in a sweet drawling tribute to southern pride and lazy celebration.

Before the intro of the song had segued into the verse, Clarence was on the dance floor. First one on — and as it turned out — last to leave. On his way, he deftly grabbed Joanna and dragged her rather willingly to join him, to get out there and shake a leg. This set the tone for the entire evening. While the Habitat males, Noah certainly included, were a bit shy, Clarence single-handedly kept the girls in rotation, not in any suggestive or flirtatious way, but just to show them a good time.

After Clarence kicked it off, it became evident to everyone in the place that the party had started. More and more people drifted onto the dance floor, and very quickly it was packed with revelers who, regardless of their individual dancing skills, all had a good time.

Clarence was a great dancer. His dance floor technique was a gymnastic meld of swing and jitterbug. Being big and strong as an ox, he was able to hurl the girls around with confident ease and grace. They knew they were in good hands and certainly never felt the fear normally associated with being tossed and twirled like life-size cabbage patch dolls.

His performance drew a lot of stares and glares. Of course he was black and all of the Habitat girls were white.

This didn't sit well with everyone in the bar. But as he had pointed out, things had improved. Where not that long ago they would have just dragged him out back and beaten him to death with a tire iron, now they had to settle for sipping on their beers and only fantasizing about unloading both barrels of a shotgun in the nigger's mouth.

Again, nothing was said or done, at least within the tight premises of the tavern. But there was a tension that could be felt. Stepping mentally for a moment out of the fervor and fever of the festivity, sensing the overall vibe ... yes. It could be felt.

Noah had the time of his life. He had always been too self-conscious to even attempt dancing. But eventually the contagion of the good old down home good time overwhelmed his immunity — and certainly the generic southern beer played its part. The jubilant music and visceral energy of the dancing infected him with an out-of-body experience. Immersed in a cool and confident rapture, he spent the last two hours of the evening soaking his clothes in the aerobic froth of his own wild personal celebration of hillbilly rock. By the end he was thinking in a southern drawl.

They left the tavern as a group just after 1:00 am and headed to their cars. Joe had a young local sleaze on his arm, who looked like a cross between Daisy Mae and Slim Pickens in drag.

As they made their way through the dozens of vehicles packed into the lot, Noah was first to spot them.

They all stopped in their tracks, and stood there, shocked, stunned, very afraid.

There stood five pot-bellied rednecks, armed with crowbars and a chain saw.

They grinned at Clarence, then began to demolish his car. They smashed the hood, windows, rear deck. The guy with the chainsaw went to work on the interior. When they finished, it still had the general shape of a car but one that had been forced into retirement after years of service in a demolition derby.

The five rednecks then marched in single file past Clarence and the volunteers. The last in line saluted Clarence with the chainsaw.

"Have a nice day, nigger."

Joe wanted to go after them and they had to hold him back. His sleazy pickup chick had wandered off in the fray.

Amazingly, the car still ran.

But it was a somber drive back from an evening that had started out so brilliantly.

Clarence was characteristically stoic. At some point, he just smiled his big warm Clarence Wills smile.

"Didn't I tell ya? That's the best damn catfish this side of the Savannah."

CHAPTER SIX

Three's a Crowd

In a speech televised to the nation, the President gave what was billed as a major policy address, to an elite assembly of his most devoted supporters and generous campaign donors. It was held at the Kennedy Center in Washington DC.

The camera followed him as he stepped up onto the stage. The room filled with near deafening applause, as the President shook hands and gave a big hug to Senator Dianne Feinstein from California, who was acting as master of ceremonies.

The President stepped up to the podium, winking and acknowledging various people in the audience, waving from one side of the reception hall to the other in grand style, not wanting to leave anyone out.

The applause finally subsided, and the President began his address.

> *"My fellow Americans. I know times are tough. I feel your pain. I hear you. That's my job. Listening. Then doing something about it. Right now, things may be difficult. But America is the greatest country in the world. We are a 'can do' nation of 'can doers'. We're gonna put our noses to the grindstone. We'll hit the ground running. We'll be all that we can be. You see, the buck stops here. I know where the rubber meets the road. As each day begins and I see the new dawn illuminate the American flag as it's raised in the White House gardens, I look in the mirror and say, 'Good morning, Mr. President. This is the first day of the rest of your life. Just do it! Ladies and gentlemen. Girls and boys. Be proud. Stand strong. Keep your groove. Have a nice day. And God bless America."*

Again, the applause quickly built to a deafening roar. The President waved to the audience, then bid farewell to the handful of VIPs who were sitting at the rear of the stage during his speech. He headed off the stage, and out of the door.

The cheering and clapping again trailed off, as the live broadcast came to a close.

Had anyone happened to look, they would have noticed that the rise and fall of the audience's ovation for the President, aligned perfectly with the increase and decrease of one particular fader by the sound man on his audio mixing board.

Of course, looking would have required someone to be there.

Had the camera panned around to take in the cavernous hall, it would have captured the bored looks of the three people sitting at one of the several hundred empty tables, all of them members of the service staff, there to clean up following the address.

Two's company. Three's a crowd.

Disappearing Act

A week after the night of dancing and partying in Muscle Shoals which had come to such an unfortunate ending, most of the volunteers were all milling about in front of the Habitat headquarters, waiting for the day's assignments. Clarence's car sat off to the side, looking no better than it had at the end of that disturbing evening.

A UPS truck pulled into the drive, and Clarence signed for four boxes of supplies. One in particular caught his attention.

"It's about time. I've been waiting for this. This has to go over to 26th Street. Who's up for taking a drive?"

No one else seemed very anxious, so Noah volunteered, and Joanna offered to join him. 26th Street was only a half-mile away, so they'd be back in a flash.

Clarence handed Noah the box and his car keys. But Joe was in a generous mood, or more to the point, was trying to impress a new girl he was standing next to with his generosity. She had just arrived yesterday.

"Take my wheels. Indulge yourself, love birds."

He tossed Noah the keys to his Porsche.

As they pulled away, Noah seemed a little embarrassed.

"Is it that obvious? We've been very discrete. At least I thought so."

"Who cares?"

They continued on the same street Habitat headquarters was on, and when they got a few blocks further, they passed five large unmarked vans heading in the opposite direction. The vehicles looked like typical delivery trucks but were rather out of place traveling in tandem in such a purely residential neighborhood.

Noah didn't pay them any mind but Joanna did a serious double take.

Not sure what to make of them, she picked up the thread of their conversation.

"Noah, you should know something. This is business. I like you. I like you a lot. But let's just keep it at that."

"Business. What's that supposed to mean? Why doesn't anyone tell me—"

"It's need to know. That's all."

Which left him more confused than before.

They pulled up at the 26th Street house. It was pretty close to being finished. There were two volunteers there, doing interior painting, hanging venetian blinds, putting the final touches on the place. Joanna quickly ran the box inside, jumped back in the car. They headed back, not saying anything, just enjoying the quiet of the spring morning.

When they were within a block of Habitat headquarters, Joanna looking intently ahead spotted something.

"Noah. Stop! Something's going on."

Noah hit the brakes and pulled over to the side.

They then watched a nightmare unfolding.

The five unmarked vans were parked in the area in front of the building, effectively blocking any access or escape.

About twenty military police, outfitted in full riot gear were hauling the volunteers into the vans. They were being extremely rough, pepper spraying them into submission.

Joe put up a good fight but three of the jackboots had him on the ground and were working him over. Clarence was unconscious. They didn't see what had happened to him but two of the paramilitary officers were lifting his limp body into one of the vans.

"Holy shit, Joanna! What should we—"

"There's nothing we can do. Wait until it's clear."

Finally, when everyone had been rounded up and stuffed into three of the vehicles, all five vans drove away in a neat military convoy.

Noah and Joanna just sat speechless for several more minutes. When it was certain that the raid was over and they wouldn't be coming back, Noah slipped the Porsch in gear and slowly pulled up to Habitat headquarters.

They got out and went into the front office.

Habitat's administrative supervisor was at her desk, slumped over and caught up in uncontrollable fits of crying. Noah and Joanna did their best to reassure and calm her.

"They're gone. It's going to be alright."

Finally, the lady got ahold of herself enough to utter a coherent sentence. She looked suspiciously at Joanna.

"They asked about you. Why did they ask about you? They knew your name."

Joanna grabbed Noah by the arm.

"Come on. Right now. We've got to get out of here."

Out of the office they ran. Each got their belongings from their rooms in the dorm house next door. They met back at the car in less than three minutes and were on their way. Joanna was behind the wheel. Noah was looking in all directions for any sign of suspicious vehicles or persons.

Soon, they were breathing a little easier, blending in with traffic on I-20 heading southwest toward Jackson, Mississippi.

The Gift of Giving

Maybe they were breathing easier, but they still had the paranoia of the hunted written on their faces.

It didn't help that they passed two military convoys going in the opposite direction. Obviously, the government hadn't deployed the infantry to look for them, but merely the presence of the grey-brown vehicles and soldiers decked out in their best camo, was a reminder of the disturbing ubiquity of government power and overreach.

Compounding the overall impression of turmoil, they passed a substantial number of abandoned vehicles on the side of the freeway, stripped of whatever could be removed, some then demolished for amusement or venting.

There was even a torched sheriff's patrol car.

On three occasions, they saw gangs of five to eight men — black and Hispanic — just standing or wandering on the shoulder without any discernable reason or direction. They were all dressed in work clothes but not doing anything. Certainly not working. Just standing around.

Joanna finally broke their shared reverie.

"IOU."

"You owe me what?"

"IOU is the 'what' and 'who' you were asking about."

"What does it stand for?"

"Internet organization underground. It grew out of Anonymous and Occupy."

"So what is it? Like a protest group?"

"IOU is an alternate world, Noah. A society within our society. It's everyone who's fed up with the bullshit. The lies, corruption, incompetence. The looting of our treasury, buying our politicians, the plundering of the environment, the endless wars. Especially the ripping off of the little guy, and the fraud our democracy has become."

"Can they fight it? Will they really make a difference?"

"Or die trying."

By mid-afternoon, they had gotten across Mississippi without incident, and now were approaching Shreveport, Louisiana.

There was a hitchhiker on the side of the road, a young black kid, late teens.

Joanna screeched to a stop maybe fifty yards beyond where he was standing.

At first he didn't believe he'd actually gotten a ride, then started to tentatively walk toward the car.

By the time he joined them, Joanna and Noah at her impatient urging had gotten all of their things out of the back of the Porsche.

"Hi. Are you headed—"

"Here you go. Have a nice day."

She tossed the kid the keys, then Joanna led Noah away. At first young man just stood there, incredulous that these two white folks had stopped and given him their car. He was just glad they hadn't shot him. Finally he shrugged and drove away.

As they walked down the shoulder of the highway, Noah looked as astonished as the black kid had. Joanna nudged him and smiled.

"Seemed like a nice young man."

"Sure, Joanna. Thirty seconds is plenty of time to evaluate the temperament and moral integrity of a complete stranger. Why did you give the car away?"

"Hopefully, for his sake, there was no tracking beacon on board. But if there was, he'll lead them someplace else. Where we're going, we can't take any chances."

I.O.U.

They left the freeway on foot via the next exit ramp. There was a truck stop there. After a greasy lunch that pushed the potential for cardiac arrest, Joanna used her charm to get them a lift with a farmer hauling a full load of supplies for the spring planting.

By sundown, they were hiking a secondary highway but still several miles from their destination.

Noah's legs were getting tired but his mind was going a mile-a-minute.

"IOU. I can't believe I never heard of this."

"Well, Noah. That's the whole idea. But you're hearing about it now."

"Jesus H. Christ, Joanna! Aren't you afraid? I'm afraid. I'm afraid now to show my face anywhere."

"Sure. Just like you, all of us are always on the run. Hiding. But there's one place they can't touch us."

"And where's that?"

She held up her phone.

"Here."

"You can talk? Communicate? Don't they monitor everything now?"

"It's pure genius! IOU has a special network which sits invisibly inside every form of data transmission. Sure, the agencies can intercept it, but it's just nonsense. Just noise. To the spy boys, my conversations on this phone sound like a fruit blender."

As they approached a thickly forested grove, they saw campfires. As they passed, they could see through the trees, a sizeable encampment of homeless people, maybe thirty or forty. There were even small children running around.

"How did this happen? I mean this secret IOU network. Someone had to invent it, right? Who put this together? Some team of hackers?"

"Team. That's funny you should say that. It was one guy. His name's Tim. I met him at a rave. Believe me, he is the last person you would suspect is the genius behind IOU's completely impenetrable security. He's very weird, but he loves to party. You know the expression, 'There is no I in team.' So Tim used to go around to everybody and say, 'There is no E in Tim.'"

"I don't get it."

"E, Noah. Ecstasy. MDMA. At the raves, Tim was always trying to get someone to freebie him some Ecstasy. Everyone just thought he was annoying and a complete loser. Inevitably someone would lay some E on him, or pour some 2C in his drink just to make him go away. They had no idea. This was the genius who pulled it off."

"One guy. This Tim fellow."

"The IOU network has billions of bits of communication data being exchanged all of the time and these brilliant government eggheads can't figure out what it says. They have whole floors of cryptologists and coders, systems security experts, cyber warfare and counterespionage gurus, the best internet systems analysts at the NSA, CIA, FBI and who knows where else working on it. None of them can make a dent. It's like trying to catch millions of flies in the Louisiana Superdome, blindfolded and in the dark, with chopsticks."

Fatigue was getting to both of them. They saw a fleabag motel just up the road. Just what the doctor ordered.

They checked in as Johnny Depp and Winona Rider.

Without even brushing their teeth or taking off their street clothes, they collapsed on the sagging double bed. The springs squeaked and rattled until they both finally lay completely still.

Noah had one last piece of business.

"So did you fuck this Tim guy?"

"Of course. Wouldn't you?"

"Only if he dressed up like a sheep."

"Noah, you're one in a million."

"Flies in the Superdome?"

"You jealous boy."

"Busted ..."

Buzz Central

Next morning, once they finally crawled out of bed, they wasted no time getting going. Turned out they were closer than Joanna realized. They turned up a country dirt road about two miles from the motel. They were out in the sticks, farm followed farm. Beautiful country, which somehow had escaped the ravages of corporate plunder and economic ruin that gripped the rest of the country.

"Noah, you need to understand it's no accident that I'm here with you. Because you blew up the bus—"

"Why doesn't anyone believe me? I didn't blow up the bus!"

"Whatever. It doesn't matter. The Feds think you did and you've been labeled a terrorist. Everyone thinks you're a high value personage. That's why I'm supposed to look after you."

"Here I thought it was true love."

Less than forty-five minutes later, they were standing at the entrance lane of a farm. A wood banner arched overhead.

None of Your Beeswax Bee Farm
"Honey – Nature's Confection"

The farm was huge and the entry lane wound nearly a quarter mile before coming to the actual buildings on the property. There was nothing much to see at first but after passing several copses of trees and a few ponds, Noah saw row upon row of apiculture boxes, neatly arranged and being tended by more than twenty workers.

They stepped on to the porch of a huge plantation-style mansion, which despite its columns and sprawling upper deck porch didn't look either pretentious or ostentatious. It was surrounded by thuja green giants, various azaleas, sky pencil hollies, and huge willows both white and green, which seem to cradle the enormous white structure in enormous billowing hands. All around the base of the house and in every direction were flowers and flowering bushes. Many were not yet in bloom but promised a floral display which would rival the Garden of Paradise.

Before they could ring the bell or knock, the door swung open. There stood Kevin, late 20s, tall, almost regal in his manner without being affected. Kevin, it turned out, was second-in-charge there, and took care of keeping everything running smoothly.

"Come in and meet the Queen."

Ah! Bees. Honey. Queen. Cute.

They stepped through the tall white doors and put their bags down, then were led up a grand staircase which curved elegantly around a crystal chandelier with more gems and tiny lamps than Noah could count. At the top, Kevin opened the door to a drawing room.

At the far end of the room lying on a gigantic stuffed pillow, with three young men at her side, was an enormous woman. White hair was piled volcanically like freshly erupting whip cream on her bulbous head, which also bore a tiara of brilliant blue gems. Her face was caked with makeup, lips looking like a hand grenade had gone off in her mouth, eyes thick with tar and metal flake spackling cement, the overall effect of which was like looking at a sumo version of Elvira, Mistress of the Dark. She was dressed — or perhaps tented was more accurate — in a shimmering black and silver sari. In one hand was a long silver cigarette holder with what looked like a cigarillo giving off a slender line of smoke, in the other a martini. It appeared that one of the young men was in the middle of reading from a hard-bound book, which he put down in his lap when they entered.

"Here are two more drones for you, Madame Queen. Noah and Joanna, meet the Queen."

"Welcome to my full-length animated feature, with dazzling artistry and special effects so real you will soon believe this is actually happening. Would you like a green apple martini?"

Noah and Joanna both declined and were given iced chrysanthemum tea.

What followed was a description of the official activities of the farm, the Queen's elaborate and detailed references laced with so much double entendre and innuendo, that it was a toss-up as to whether she was talking about honey production or ejaculations from legions of masturbating boys. Neither Joanna nor Noah were prudes but they were tremendously relieved when her pedagogical soliloquy drew to a close.

"Enough about the sweet succor of life that sustains and nurtures the real enterprise here. Kevin will tell you what you need to know. You will do what you need to do. And I will appreciate all that you contribute to vanquishing the evil which has insinuated itself like a poison into America and destroyed the dream."

Hmm! Maybe not the sweet matriarchal monarch she pretends to be.

She pulled out an old photograph. It was worn and showed the effects of too much handling and too many tears streaking its once satiny surface.

A wedding picture.

It was her. Slender, radiant, in love.

Beside her a handsome man with adoration in his eyes.

"They killed him. Vietnam. 1969."

Noah now could immediately see how old the Queen was. Mid to late 60s. The makeup and surreal bon vivant airs had initially fooled him.

Over four decades, she had mourned her loss. Over four decades she pursued her revenge.

Whatever madness had destroyed her life and transformed her into the giant deranged mutant whale that sprawled before them like some demented diva in a deranged Dionysian drama, was seeded by an unnecessary death in an unnecessary war. Her madness had metastasized into a methodology, a calculated siege intended to bring down those who sat in the imperial thrones of power and condemned America to more endless unnecessary wars, and more uncountable unnecessary deaths — deaths of other innocent pawns like her young husband who was sacrificed in a foolish game of power.

Noah and Joanna bid the Queen adieu. Kevin then gave them a tour.

There were a number of structures tucked away on the grounds. A well-equipped and very comfortable dorm housed the itinerants who split their collective energies working the honey and doing the heavy lifting of creating systemic political mayhem.

Under the main barn was Buzz Central, as everyone there jokingly called it. It was housed in an enormous underground cave, its interior finished in the finest style, with beautiful oak paneling, wall hangings, marble floors. It contained fourteen desks, with typically twice that many people sitting or milling about, a dozen top-of-the-line Apple G5 computers with associated monitors, printers, modems, and external hard drives. It could have been dark, dank and depressing, except it was well-lit and atmospherically controlled to protect the sensitive and highly sophisticated equipment.

A wide variety of contemporary and classical music always playing.

The room was divided in half. When coming down the steep entry stairs, the first thing a person encountered was a rustic old sign post like a trail marker, with arrows pointing in opposite directions for the two functional areas of the space. One side was called 'Information' and the other side 'Disinformation'.

The bevy of computer geeks, hangers-on, idea people, and thrilled spectators which populated Buzz Central 24 hours a day, shared in equal amounts a distrust of the system and a determination to bring it down. What the system consisted of — that is, who by name were the perpetrators of the injustices, who exactly were the criminal aggressors pillaging the country and destroying the American Dream — was always being hotly debated.

There were enough obvious targets, ones which so clearly pushed their own agendas at the expense of the majority of American citizens, the decision of which ones should be high on the "hit list" was pretty easy. The queue was already rather long and included the Federal Reserve, the major investment and commercial banks like Chase Manhattan, Goldman Sachs and Bank of America, the right wing media giants like Rupert Murdoch's News Corporation and Viacom, both the Democratic and Republican parties, and union-busting corporate megaliths and environmental abusers like Walmart, BP and the Koch Brothers.

Of course, everyone in the military-industrial complex was securely at the very top. Buzz Central was after all Madame Queen's operation, funded entirely by the money she made wholesaling honey. And it was the gigantic corporate beast consisting of the defense companies which made the killing machines of war in collusion with America's megalomaniac military leaders, collectively gripped by delusional imperial ambitions and Fourth Reichian fantasies, which had killed her husband. It was the imperialistic military-industrial complex which by definition put the spoils of conquest and the pursuit of profit ahead of people, and would stop at nothing, even if it meant the destruction of America and the killing of all of its innocent citizens, to achieve its psychotic visions of world rule.

Buzz Central was set up to block them any way it could. The Information section poured out to anyone they could get to listen, a steady stream of indictments and attacks against both individuals and organizations. The Disinformation section created rumors, spread lies, promoted confusion, engaged in character assassination, proposed elaborate conspiracy theories, did anything it could to keep the military-industrial complex on the defensive and disrupt it. The ends justified the means, so there was no code of ethics holding them back. It was a fun place to work.

The information dissemination was performed with style and erudition on several legitimate websites which they hosted themselves, using servers which had been configured to look like they were based in the People's Republic of China — menwithbigtoys.com, whatsthebuzz.tv, floatlikeabutterfly.org, thebigsting.net — plus video channels on YouTube and Vimeo, both of which had thousands of subscribers and millions of hits.

The disinformation dissemination crew used anything they could get its hands on, from legitimate media to chat boards and political blogs, even psycho sites, which with abundance of bad news on the economy and the general state of the country had lately been proliferating at an astounding pace. Their buzz of disinformation grated on the nerves, ate holes in the lining of the stomach, caused a lot of sleepless nights, and gradually gnawed away at protective layers of discipline and blind loyalty. It was as effective as an acid drip.

On their way out, Kevin introduced Noah and Joanna to one of their star players. Ralph was intelligent, intense, geeky, mischievous. His eyes betrayed his constant state of creative agitation. He was always cooking up some new outrageous prank.

"So, Ralph. What are you working on?"

"The Dot Gov Project. By next year, we're going to render the government a dysfunctional mess."

Noah couldn't help but let out a wry snicker.

"Doesn't seem like you have far to go."

"Good point."

CHAPTER SEVEN

Bee Keepers

Noah certainly learned his share from the cyber terrorists, but his favorite work was anything to do with the bees.

Every morning bright and early, he would suit up and head out to the apiaries. Either they would be setting new supers in the brood chambers, feeding the bees their pollen supplements, or just doing general maintenance to assure the overall integrity of the artificial hives.

One day he was in the middle of collecting honey, when one of the Queen's girly-boy attendants came running up.

"Quick! We need you! It's an emergency."

Noah was rushed to a large water oak tree behind the mansion house. The Queen was in an absolute tizzy, pointing up with her sausage-shaped fingers, waving her bulbous arms, grabbing her volcanically-coiffed hair in something bordering on despair.

Her favorite cat, Buzzby Berkeley, was stranded near the top of the tree, loudly acknowledging the desperation of his situation with long excruciating cries for help. He sounded like an ambulance in heat.

A ladder was already leaning against the huge trunk of the tree.

All eyes were now on Noah.

He wasn't sure what qualified him to perform this dangerous and arguably unnecessary task. Maybe they somehow thought his growing up in Missouri affiliated him with certain African tree monkeys. Whatever the logic, he knew what was expected.

He climbed the ladder and with a deftness that even surprised him was quickly near the top of the tree and within reach of Buzzby. A little sweet talk, a few vague promises of fresh tuna, capped with him singing a very out-of-tune rendition of Al Stewart's "Year of the Cat" and voilà! Frisky feline firmly embraced, he was making his way down the tree, receiving only superficial lacerations from the kitty's flailing claws.

As the drama unfolded with a happy resolution in sight, Joanna just laughed her ass off, and the Queen shouted praise and encouragement for his effort. By the time Noah reached the ground, Joanna was trying to catch her breath from the unexpected occasion of over-the-top hilarity, the attendants were entirely awestruck with near homoerotic fascination, and the Queen was comparing him to Albert Schweitzer and Nelson Mandela.

The reunion of the Queen and Buzzby was a melodramatic outpouring — at least on one side — so Noah went back to the apiary to give them the privacy they deserved. Joanna was working elsewhere, so he didn't get to talk to her for the rest of the day.

But later, as they always did, he and Joanna were eating together in the commons. The excitement of the day had Noah in a playful mood.

"I'm starting to be able to tell these bees apart. They actually have very distinct personalities."

"Noah. I'm leaving tomorrow."

His ebullience immediately turned to shock and sadness.

"I'll come with you."

"No. It's too dangerous. You're a marked man."

"So. Just like that. That's it?"

"That's it. You're a sweet boy. Stay that way. And stay out of trouble. But in case you get in a fix, take this."

She handed him a piece of paper. It had some writing on it. But he couldn't focus on it. Actually, he couldn't make out what it said through the tears.

The next day, Joanna was gone before Noah even got out of bed.

From the moment he realized she was out of his life — forever? would their paths ever cross again? — he felt empty, numb, semi-conscious.

He didn't want this to hit him as hard as it did. Noah had known the rules all along. It wasn't just because she was an IOU "operative". This was just the way it was. People living out here in the alt culture, outside the safe and regimented confines of regular society, didn't look at each other in terms of permanent relationships. There was a lot of sex but little romance. Nobody he had run into ever talked about trying to find that special someone. It was love the one you're with. Take it one day at a time.

But he had grown very fond of Joanna. Not in the same way as Naomi. Maybe in some respects more intensely, more explosively. Certainly that described their time in bed together.

Yet it was way beyond the sex. Joanna represented that world out there he had all his life been denied, that *opposite* of his Missouri hometown that he was seeking. Joanna represented a level of evolution, of competence, of intelligence, of worldliness, of awareness, that he had only imagined. For the first time in his life, here was someone who was *there*. He got to experience it first hand, every day for over two months now.

Now all that was gone. She was gone.

The next few days, as he went through his routine of daily chores, giving his time and energy to keeping alive the Queen's vision of toppling the empire, he felt listless, lost, anesthetized. He stayed away from the bees, which required too much focus and caution. Instead he did some much needed landscaping. The grounds were vast and keeping up with their cosmetic care often took a back seat to the excitement of Buzz Central and the meditative bliss of bees and honeycombs.

After a long day of tree trimming, lawn cutting, weeding, pruning and planting some new annuals around the front of the mansion, Noah was in his room taking off his work clothes, getting ready to shower.

Kevin knocked, then stuck his head in the door.

"Hey, Kevin! How are you?"

"Noah. We of course want you to feel at home here. But you know this is … a very secret, highly secure location."

"Sure. I completely understand."

"Then you shouldn't be getting personal mail here."

He then handed Noah a letter, addressed, stamped, delivered by the postal service. Noah could tell immediately. It was from his father.

"This is bad. Very bad. I don't know how—"

"Don't panic. We just have to be very careful."

Noah didn't read the letter. Nor did he sleep that night.

After a lot of thought, soul-searching, debate, he made a decision.

There really wasn't any choice. It was obvious what he had to do.

The difficulty was just accepting it. Even without Joanna around, he loved this place. He felt like he was thriving, learning so much. Everyone he met was so knowledgeable, interesting.

Next morning, he visited the Queen in her chambers.

"I'm leaving. I don't want to. But—"

"Are you sure?"

"I'm sure. Something is screwed up. Someone found me. It's best all around."

The Queen looked teary-eyed. Was she this way with everyone?

"Thank you for all you've done young man. Every bit helps. We've loved being your family, temporary as it always is. My boy, let me give you something to remember us by. It's a small gift but it comes from deep inside here."

She pointed at her heart.

One of her attendants handed Noah a gift-wrapped box.

The Queen got up, enveloped Noah in her massive arms, and gave him a hug as big as the world.

Noah would miss this strange lady.

He would miss the plantation.

He would miss the bees.

On the Road

With everything going on — which now included massive political demonstrations, some quite violent, one in New York City seriously threatening to undermine the entire corporate police state that America was becoming — Noah figured there were too many fires to put out for the G-men to seriously worry about him. He was only a smoldering match. The others were five-alarm conflagrations.

That didn't mean a lack of caution. Airports were out. Too much surveillance, too many ID checks, way too many cameras. Buses weren't exactly high on his list considering recent events in his life. But then again, what were the chances of getting on one again that happened to have a pig farmer carrying a duffel bag full of C-4? Hitchhiking? Probably not. Unless he decided to commit suicide. Of course, he could rent a car. But again, that was a risk. Showing his license. Using a credit card. He didn't know how precisely these things could be monitored, just what he saw in the movies.

Noah felt he needed to get going as soon as possible. He had no idea what his father wanted but was certain it was time to move on and get under the radar.

A kid named Phil who worked on the Disinformation side of Buzz Central came up with viable solution. Noah, understandably, at first was skeptical.

"You sure you're not making this up?"

It's called the Texas Eagle. That's how I got here from Chicago. But it keeps going. All the way to L.A.! You could become a star. You'd be perfect for a spinoff of *Brokeback Mountain*. It could be called *Sheep Dip Creek*."

Another hacker overheard them.

"Or *Dances With Wool*."

"How about *Scrotum of the Lambs*."

"What's with the sheep jokes? Is there something wrong with you guys?"

"We're geeks."

Noah checked it out. Sure enough. Amtrak ran straight through from Shreveport all the way to L.A. in a slightly sinuous line that only made 26 stops. He wasn't in a hurry. He could jump off at any or all of them! When else would he get the opportunity to visit such remarkable towns as Mineola and Cleburne, TX? Deming, NM and Benson, AZ? It also stopped in Dallas, San Antonio, El Paso, Tucson, and Palm Springs. This could be fun.

Next day he was sitting on the Texas Eagle heading west.

It was nicer than he ever could have imagined. For most of the trip, because he was doing short jumps, he just got a reserved coach seat. It had plenty of room to stretch out. He looked out the window or wandered. There was a lounge car and a dining car. Often when the scenery was too boring to even be called scenery, he read one of the several paperbacks he brought with him from None of Your Beeswax, novels ranging from pulp fiction to American classics. He passed them along to other passengers as he went.

A few nights, he sprang for the extra $100-150 to have a bed in the sleeper car. It was an unnecessary extravagance but it added some color to the adventure. Riding on a train, even in short spurts of two to four hours, was pretty tedious. Staying in motels night after night is as well. The sleeper car offered some variation.

What could Noah say about this little sampling of American life in the South and Southwest? On the positive side, the weather was great. Being late spring, it wasn't too hot until he got to Arizona. Very little rainfall. Where wild flowers and floral trees could grow, they were in full bloom. People were friendly enough. Being from Missouri he was still pretty rough around the edges. He certainly wasn't mistaken for one of those slick, self-important snobs from New England or them whiny types from the Midwest who should probably move to Canada where they belong. He made acquaintances easily and spent hours listening to people talk about themselves, their families, their dreams and setbacks.

But the novelty gradually wore off. After 22 days, the charming little desert towns and bleak stretches of southern New Mexico and Arizona started to all look the same. By the time he reached Palm Springs, California, Noah didn't even bother to get off. Too many cadavers driving golf carts for his present frame of mind.

He suddenly remembered the present from Madame Queen. He pulled it out of his duffel bag. It was a beautifully wrapped gift box containing southern style biscuits and surprise! Honey. There was a handwritten note inside.

Bee honest
Bee clean
Bee true to yourself
I am your Queen.

There was no doubt about it. The lady was certifiable. But in the grander scheme of things, she probably contributed more to the quality of human life than 99% of those who passed for sane. She was true to herself and what she believed in. She had a good message. Less war. More honey.

Who could have a problem with that?

He checked the train schedule. Four more hours and he'd be in L.A.

All he knew for sure about Los Angeles was that it was a place. Other than that it had a pretty mixed rap sheet. Some said it was Heaven. Some said it was Hell. Officially it was the home of the movie industry, stomping ground for a lot of pretty people who had the unique ability to repeat a set of words and phrases with passion and fresh conviction through 47 takes, while a camera recorded their every twitch and tremor and a lot of overweight people stood around wearing headphones or leaning on light stands.

There was predictably a dark side. Big income gaps, lots of racial and ethnic tension, high skin cancer rates, thriving drug trade, periodic riots, and it sat on a spiderweb of geological faults, meaning beyond the regularly occurring earthquakes, it would eventually break up like stale pie crust and disappear into the Pacific Ocean.

Not that any of that stopped over 14,000,000 people from calling it home.

Los Angeles. The City of Angels.

Noah liked angels.

He just hoped they liked him.

City of Angels

They called it the City of Angels.

Noah thought they should call it the City of Angles.

Everyone had an angle.

Everyone was cutting deals.

Everyone had just what you needed.

Everybody knew somebody who knew somebody.

L.A. was a town where you could trust no one and forgot how to trust yourself.

Getting around L.A. if you didn't own a car used to be impossible. Now it was just a gigantic pain in the ass. It was wall-to-wall motor vehicles and the distances were nearly incomprehensible. The Los Angeles metropolitan area stretched from one horizon to the other. Noah had never seen anything like it. If it kept growing, they were predicting the shimmering dusty blight that was the greater L.A. megalopolis would one day stretch from the Mexican border to Seattle. If there was a reason to set off a nuclear device in a major American city, this was it.

Noah got a room at a sleazy motel right off of Hollywood Boulevard. Except for a few luxury hotels, all of them were sleazy. The entire tourist trap, which included such landmarks as Hollywood and Vine, and Grauman's Chinese Theater, sure looked better in the photos. A lot better. Was there no truth in advertising anymore?

He did the typical stuff. The star walk on Hollywood Boulevard. Universal Studios. The Wax Museum. Madame Tussauds. He even hired a taxi and bought a Beverly Hills star map so he could look at the high walls and security gates of the rich and famous.

Lame.

The only thing approaching a high point — more like an upskirt panty shot than what Abraham Maslow would call a peak experience — was sitting in a café off Rodeo Drive in downtown Beverly Hills. He vaguely remembered visiting a web site about cosmetic surgery a couple years ago, and knew of the reputation of California glamour goddesses who spent mounds of cash fighting natural aging, as well as correcting deficits in their genetic endowments. But this was insane! He predictably saw enough 44 DDs to fill a stadium. But what was truly amazing was seeing the exact same face go by him and his $7.00 caramel latte at least seven times in 30 minutes. But not on the same woman. On seven different women. All had brow lifts which locked them into a perpetual state of stupefaction. All had bones glued in their cheeks giving them a cartoonish Thunderella, Queen Bitch of the Amazonian Conquerors look. They all had Demi Moore's nose. Their lips were blown up like sausages. When they smiled they looked like Jack Nicholson as the Joker. Their skin was pulled back so tight it looked like the shrink-wrapping for chicken breast fillets. They had so much Botox, a dime-store mannequin looked melodramatic by comparison.

Looking beyond the cosmetic surgery and the clothes ensembles, jewelry, watches, and shoes, that easily priced out at five and six figures, almost everyone who strolled by, had fixed, vacant eyes, afflicted with the pre-autopsy glaze of way too many anti-depressants and mood levelers.

Despite the horrific implications of this parade of neuroses, it was very entertaining. On the other hand, if this is where it got you, maybe fame, success and inconceivable wealth weren't all they were cracked up to be.

He had to get out of there. It was giving him the creeps.

He paid $8.50 for his one coffee, assuming $1.50 would be an adequate tip. Apparently it wasn't, in light of the hostile glare the waiter gave him as he stepped out into the extremely well-dressed pedestrian traffic.

Noah walked toward the bus stop on Santa Monica Boulevard, gazing down at the sidewalk, hoping to avoid seeing any more frankenbeauties.

Out of the corner of his eye, an L. A. Times headline in a curbside coin news rack caught his attention.

10,000 Predicted at Federal Building
Political Demonstration

Noah had to find out more. He dug in his pants pocket.

The vending machine swallowed four quarters, but wouldn't open.

Then some guy walked up, kicked the news rack, and it popped open. The man reached in, grabbed a paper and walked away.

Noah reached to get one.

"Those are 25 cents."

Noah turned around and there stood a Beverly Hills cop with Gucci sunglasses and his arms folded on his chest.

"But I already put four quarters in and the damn thing wouldn't open."

"It's 25 cents. Or do you want to talk about this downtown."

Noah reached in his pocket but was out of coins. He pulled out a dollar bill and held it toward the cop.

"Have you got change?"

The cop grabbed the dollar bill and put it in his shirt pocket. Then he bent down, took a newspaper, and handed it to Noah.

"Have a nice day."

As the cop sauntered away whistling the theme song for Starsky & Hutch, he read the front page story.

According to the article, there had been several demonstrations recently which had garnered very little media attention. That made sense to Noah. How could they in this town, unless Brad Pitt or some other megastar showed up? It went on to say that there had been a protest march just five days ago, where an unprovoked attack by the police had put four demonstrators in the hospital and had resulted in the arrest of 272 people who were doing nothing more than standing around holding signs and chanting slogans. A lot of people were outraged. Tomorrow at 12 noon, there would be a huge rally in front of the Federal Building on Wilshire Boulevard near Westwood. Police brutality would be added to the already formidable list of things being protested: Corruption in government, the corporate control of Congress, banking and Wall Street fraud against the American citizenry, the offshoring of jobs, the offshoring of money, the destruction of democracy, rule by the rich and powerful elite, money in politics, the rigging of elections using electronic voting machines, conflict of interest at all levels and in every branch of government, the bankrupting of the economy by the Federal Reserve, on and on. Since college students had been seriously affected by the economic woes of the country, the proximity of the demonstration to the UCLA campus seemed to guarantee a good turnout.

Going was a bit risky. Scores of news people, cameras, the FBI, the CIA, the ATF, and the usual sordid assortment of local undercover police would be there. But considering the size of the demonstration, Noah thought it was unlikely anyone would identify him. He would just get lost in the crowd.

Even so he decided to play it safe.

Noah got up bright and early next day and put on his ZZ Top mustache and beard, a beret, some purple overalls, black tank top, and cowboy boots. He looked like he was hawking Cornhuskers Lotion on the Shopping Channel.

He grabbed a day-old donut and rancid cup of coffee in the hotel lobby, billed as a 'Continental breakfast, no extra charge!' Having no idea exactly where the Federal Building was or how long it would take to get there, he was out the door before 10 am. It turned out to not be that far at all. Even with morning rush hour traffic, Noah arrived at the plaza where the demonstration would be staged more than an hour before things would get going.

All the news media outlets and TV stations had given it decent mention over the last couple days. No movie stars had overdosed or politicians secretly videoed soliciting sex from little boys, so this was the big item for the day. It promised to be a spectacle, prompting the L. A. police to be out in excessive force, helmeted and cloaked in thick padded riot suits, wielding huge batons and bulletproof acrylic shields.

Noah wandered among the scattered early arrivals. It was like watching the preparation for a football halftime show. Some just milled around, others were a bit more purposeful but not particularly rushed. The police staked out their territory off to the side of the plaza where they could best stage an assault on the crowd. They checked their equipment, adjusted the straps on their padding, exchanged tough guy talk. The media workhorses were inside their on-location transmitting trucks and vans in the process of ramping up and testing all the electronics, while reporters wandered about with cameramen taking random video footage.

Protesters and rally organizers continued to arrive. Some were alone or with just one or two other persons. Several were carting stacks of pre-made signs to distribute among the crowd. Nothing like a lot of inflammatory messages waving above a crowd to give it some credibility and punching power. The number of demonstrators steadily increased. More and more were talking and laughing in clusters, probably getting pumped up for whatever might unfold today. At this rate, it was not hard to imagine 10,000 people showing up.

Noah casually strolled over to one guy sitting on the cement with what was probably his girlfriend. Very hippie. They could have been Sonny & Cher celebrity impersonators from the really early years. The guy was sorting through several posters he had brought, taping long sticks to the back of the ones he selected.

He looked up at Noah and smiled.

In that very same moment, a gust of wind blew Noah's mustache and beard off.

The kid's face in quick succession became amused, curious, confused, astonished. For a brief moment, he stared at Noah like he had fallen into a hypnotic trance.

Noah turned and looked behind him thinking the guy must have seen a UFO or an incoming cruise missile. Nope. Just the dingy blue of the smog-filled Los Angeles sky.

When Noah turned back around, the kid was just pulling out a poster that said:

Here's your answer!

There were two photos on the poster as well. One was a generic explosion of some sort, all flames and debris flying about.

The other was Noah.

This couldn't be happening!

The kid studied the photo of Noah, then looked back up.

Before Noah could even react — he was still stunned at seeing his face on display, big and bold, unambiguously incriminating him as a terrorist — the kid was on his feet and rushing over to shake Noah's hand.

"Awesome, man! Friggin' awesome! I can't believe I'm getting to meet you."

Noah's mind was going a mile a minute. Was this was just some fluke? Or had he somehow become a poster child for the revolution?

It was a moot point. He couldn't stick around to find out.

"Thanks, dude. Good luck with … with the thing today. Gotta go."

"Gotcha. Place is gonna be crawlin'. Hey, don't forget your mustache and—"

Noah was halfway down the street. He was hurrying as quickly as he could without attracting undue attention. He spotted a bus stop. A city bus was just arriving. He got on. Didn't have the correct change. Stuffed a five in the receptacle and took a seat.

He felt some relief being on the bus but he slunk down low in the seat and kept his face turned away from the window. He really had to get away from there. Far far away. Away from cameras. Snoops. Spooks. Spies.

Noah got back to his room, put the chain on the door. A lot of good that would do.

This was unbelievable! So totally unbelievable! His head shot on a poster. Where did they even get that photo?

He spent the rest of the day brooding, pacing, jumping at every noise from outside.

Then he remembered.

Joanna, the evening before she left, had given him a small folded piece of paper. She said it was for him to use if he ever got in a jam.

He went through his bags. It had to be in one of the pocket compartments with his ID, credit cards, and emergency money.

There it was! Whatever personal flaws he might have, one thing he had going for him was that he was organized and methodical.

The slip of paper had a web server address and a password written on it.

http://217.345.111.042
narcissist000napalm

After putting on a Village People disguise — the construction worker but with a Sly Stone complex — he slipped out the door.

About three blocks away on Sunset Boulevard was an internet café. He made his way past a couple of overweight hookers, and entered. The place looked more like a halfway house for itinerants than a cyber café. All around him were some sad derelict types who sat or slept at the workstations, paying no mind to the computers.

The machine he got had an old 14” VGA monitor and was running Windows 95, but it would have to do.

He opened a browser, entered the URL and was prompted for the password.

The page immediately came up and consisted of a send form. It asked some very strange questions. Not his name or location or the nature of his business. Weird stuff.

How could a tail wag the dog?
Addition is to subtraction as ice is to…?
Does Martha Stewart write fiction or non-fiction?
True or false: the 80s spelled the extinction of proper diction.

He entered random answers in the provided boxes, filled in the Captcha box and hit the send button. Almost instantly it gave a phone number: 323-468-4767.

It was a local Hollywood number. Somehow they knew his location. That was supposed to be impossible.

Noah ran back to his room and called.

It went immediately to voice mail, which said: *'There's no E in Tim.'*

Then it hung up and he was listening to a dial tone.

This was confusing. He didn't even get to leave a message.

Noah sat down on the bed, grabbed the remote, and clicked on the TV.

The news had violent scenes of the demonstration earlier that day at the Federal Building plaza. Police were beating demonstrators, firing canisters of tear gas into the crowd, which were promptly hurled right back. It had turned out ugly.

The phone rang.

"Hello?"

"You really shouldn't go wandering around like that. There's still a lot of heat, you know. Your picture is everywhere."

"No shit. I gotta get out of here."

"We need 24 hours to put it together. Don't disappear on us."

"Got it."

It didn't quite take that long. An hour and nine minutes later his phone rang again. It was the receptionist.

"There's someone here to see you. He says its about an IOU. By the way, you can pay on your bill here anytime. The cashier is available 24 hours to take cash."

When he went downstairs, a guy in his mid 20s was waiting for him. His clothes were neat, his hair styled, he was nice looking, had a cordial smile, reassuring eyes — the kind of guy mothers wish their daughters would bring home.

"I'm Trevor. Get your stuff. Everything's been arranged."

"Where am I going?"

"I promise. You're going to like this!"

Burning Man

They drove straight through.

Eleven hours and 580 miles later, in the middle of a desert plain in northwestern Nevada, Trevor was pulling up to the entrance of one of the most unique celebrations of human creativity and ingenuity in history — the annual Burning Man Festival.

This was opening day and hundreds of cars, trucks and RVs were lined up at the gate. Trevor himself wasn't going to hang around.

"Now, don't forget. Four days here. Then you're at this place in Reno."

He handed Noah a slip of paper.

"How will I get there?"

"Ask anyone for a ride. This is all about peace and brotherly love. You'll be fine."

"Okay. Peace, brotherly love. Hitch a ride."

"Listen, Noah. Don't take offense. But in Reno? No hookers. Got it? The Feds love to use hookers."

"No hookers. Got it."

"And take this. It's IOU. Completely secure. Don't be afraid to use it."

Noah took it. Wow! Nice cell phone.

"Great! Thanks for everything. You're a life saver."

"Let's hope so."

Off Trevor went, back the way they came.

Burning Man had been going on for 25 years. It was a combination of a rave, an experiment in communal living, futuristic art, exploration of advanced technologies, ritual abandon, a laboratory for social democracy, radical self-rule and anarchy, a petri dish of natural order, and the biggest outdoor barbecue in history. Psychotropic drugs were everywhere, the hot desert climate encouraged frequent, spontaneous displays of flesh and sometimes complete nudity, wild costumes and weird tattoos were the order of the day, the music thump-thumped non-stop from giant sound systems everywhere, and Burners, as the attendees were called, danced anytime the rhythms took possession of their bodies.

Noah was amazed.

First, he was amazed that he had never heard of this mind-blowing event. It truly spoke to what a deep chasm of ignorance he had been living in all his life.

More immediately, he was amazed by the flood to his senses he was experiencing. It reminded him of the movie, *Wizard of Oz*, when Dorothy arrived in the enchanted land. Suddenly the movie went from black-and-white to dazzling color. That's what this felt like.

The truly majestic, awe-inspiring feature of Burning Man were the hundreds of sculptures, turning the sea of sand into a hallucinogenic dreamscape, especially at night. The enormous structures reached into the sky like technological prayers, beacons of light and color, inviting the rest of the Universe to join the party. It was as if the artists were only limited by their imagination. Anything was possible and everything was tried.

There were giant clusters of white spheres tethered to the ground and floating in the sky, undulating blooms of glowing jellyfish; a kinetic sound sculpture that propelled spinning jets in response to electronically-generated music spontaneously created by the audience; a seven-story hyperbolic frame supporting a flaming lotus flower to symbolize the interplay of male and female sexual energy; an enormous illuminated people-powered mechanical reptile; a gold and black Viking ship by day that morphed into a fire breathing dragon at night; a garden of rockets spun by ramjets formed by ropes of light containing propane-powered kinetic craft; 2-dimensional projections and desert paintings that created the illusion of vast 3-dimensional fantasy scapes; tall luminous poles which whipped around to create an illusion not unlike the Northern Lights; a multi-story garlic-shaped light resonator which reacted to the bodies of the people wandering in its internal labyrinth; a superconducting LED wall with over a thousand huge pixel plates that functioned as a light orchestra; a garden filled with carbon fiber flowers shooting long streams of fire actuated by ultrasonic range finders; enormous tornadoes of flame created by sheets of electromagnetically charged water vapor. Dramatic and breathtaking by day, the art projects at night were the stuff of dazzling dreams and consciousness-altering hallucinations.

As breathtaking as the giant displays of art were, as spectacular as the ceremonial burning of the towering effigy at the closing ceremonies, as mesmerizing as the dancing and the thunderous techno music that went on the entire time, Burning Man was really about community. It was about building a functioning, and some would claim, utopian community in the desert each year from scratch, then taking it back apart and leaving the vast expanse of sand and the surrounding environment exactly as they had found it when they had arrived.

The Burners claimed you would be hard pressed to find a gum wrapper or a bottle cap afterwards, though tens of thousands had just made the desert floor their home for eight days.

They also were extremely proud of their history of social harmony and safety. There was never any violence, and people were not just cooperative but often extraordinarily generous in sharing their food and supplies, often even themselves. Significantly, this made the event a celebration of the potential for peace on Earth and an auspicious future for the planet.

Nothing in his lackluster life had prepared Noah — even the weirdness of the past several months — for Burning Man.

He felt like a six volt flashlight hooked up to a 220 volt major appliance outlet. His mind was overloaded, his senses overwhelmed, his creative capacity hyper-inflated, his imagination hyper-stimulated, his libido hyper-charged. It felt like ten people all alive at the same time inside his till-now numbed-down, dumbed-down body.

It was a high.

It was a rush.

It was an explosive expansion of his universe.

Burning Man was a hydrogen bomb to Noah's fragile mind.

As a result, the four days were a blur. A *great* blur, as blurs go. But still a blur.

One incident, however, would later stand out. Though an astonishing coincidence, what unfolded in and of itself was innocent and hardly dramatic. But its later impact would be profound and deeply disturbing.

Noah was aimlessly wandering around in front of CoCoMo, Burning Man's variant of a "club", which had been improvised for the trancers who liked to trip the light fantastic in a more defined environment. Typically, burners broke into dancing whenever or wherever the impulse took hold across the sandy expanse of the festival grounds. But CoCoMo provided more of a closed environment, with massive speakers hung and stacked all around, lasers and lights flashing and swirling, everything right there in your face, moving and pulsing to the 128 BPM thump of the music. Trancers were twisting, twirling, bouncing, immersed in the abandon and freedom of their synchronized and syncopated rhythms.

Noah was off to the side, moving self-consciously, trying desperately to get himself to go for it.

Then ...

Directly behind him, he heard a male voice.

"Nice lobe stretchers. Tibetan meditation balls? Listen ... there is no E in Tim."

Noah whipped around. There he was. Dressed all disco, circa 1977. Andy Gibb polyester shirt. Ass-hugger stretch pants. Patent leather shoes. Sideburns. Soft feminine skin that had never seen the sun. Inverted bowl Flobee haircut. An incongruous leather string headband with beads. Smiling like he had forgotten how to stop smiling. Late 20s at best.

To get to him Noah pushed past two girls who were feverishly making out.

"I'm Noah. Some people call me the Bus Bomber. I ... I hope you don't mind my asking. But I have a feeling you are ... you are famous. Like when somebody owes somebody money ... *that* kind of famous."

"It's my pleasant duty to meet you, Noah. I am in certain privileged frames of reference referred to as the person to whom you are referring. Now I'm counting on you to keep our little secret but otherwise stay honest. Honesty is the fifth element. I forgot the other four. I should move on now to fulfill my sacramental search. I have concluded that you can't put the E in Tim. Bye for now, Noah, also known by some well-informed people as the Bus Bomber."

He turned and left. Noah heard the unique mantra one last time.

"Why hello, sweetheart. There is no E in Tim."

So that's genius in the flesh.

What a weirdo.

Cool.

The Little Engine That Could

The President loved playing the role of father figure to an entire nation of petulant children. He saw himself as the one person who with a deft choice of words, a rhetorical pat on the head, a soothing calm in his voice, was capable of giving comfort and reassurance to those who were the constant victims of everything which seemed to be going wrong — which seemed to be everything.

In tonight's televised address to the nation, he would truly have his chance to act out his paternalistic fantasies.

The program opened with a shot of the American flag behind what appeared to be the President's desk in the Oval Office. A voiceover simply announced, *"Ladies and gentlemen, the President of the United States of America."*

The camera then swung over and there was the President. He was in his pajamas, sitting on the floor, and was surrounded by a half a dozen children, ready to be tucked into bed. Two of the children were his own, the other four borrowed from somewhere, maybe some folks down the block from the White house. One appeared to be Hispanic, another Asian, another indeterminately brown, the last lily white Caucasian. It looked like a miniature United Nations.

On the President's lap was a book.

"I thought tonight that you, my fellow Americans, would like to join me as I read one of my favorite stories to my two children and a few of their friends who happened to stop by."

Aah! Kids are always dropping by the White House for some warm milk, maybe a game of Go Fish, or hide-and-seek. There sure were a lot of great hiding places there.

The President then proceeded to read the classic American kids story "The Little Engine That Could", right there in the intimate setting of the Oval Office, with an estimated 57,000,000 Americans joining in the bedtime fun.

After finishing the text of the storybook, he then gave a heartfelt but excruciating performance of the John Denver song by the same title. To say that he was tone deaf and lacked the most basic singing skills would be a vast understatement. But he forged ahead. At the end of the song, the President prodded the reluctant children to join him in singing the closing lines.

"Then up that great big mountain with the cars all full of toys
And soon they reached the waiting arms of little girls and boys
And though that ends the story it will do you lots of good
To take a lesson from the little engine that could
Just think you can
Just think you can
Just have that understood
And very soon you'll start to say
I always knew I could
I knew I could
I knew I could
Yeah!"

The First Lady, also in her jammies — a bedtime ensemble later reported to be a designer original created for her by Veronique Leroy and bargain priced at $57,000 — then came in and led the visibly bored children out of the room.

The President got up and strolled over to sit behind his huge desk. It was definitely surreal seeing him in blue cotton pajamas, sitting in the executive chair where decisions which affected the future of the entire world were made. But the President pushed ahead unaware, hence unfazed by, how ridiculous he looked.

> *"Sometimes when I can't sleep, when all of the problems facing our country right now are just too upsetting, I come down here just like this. I sit here and I think. I think about our country. I think about you. I think and I ask myself, 'What's best for America? What can I do to make things better?' Sometimes I think about our history. The stories of heroic men and women who built this great nation. Often I draw inspiration from stories just like the one I shared with you tonight. You know, if you think about it, isn't that about us? Isn't America the little engine that could? I'm just glad I'm the president and that I have the opportunity to make a difference. So darn glad. Really really glad. I want to take this special occasion and very special moment to thank every one of you. You are all very special to me. Special! So thank you. God bless America. And ... nighty night! Don't let the bedbugs bite!"*

Reaction to his address was surprisingly muted.
A respectful but eerie silence filled the air waves.
No one wanted to say what everybody was thinking.
The most powerful man in the world had apparently lost his mind.

CHAPTER EIGHT

Habeas Corpse

It was dead of night, the day before Burning Man would pack up for another year.

Tim was kneeling in a remote area of the desert. His hands and feet were bound and he was crying.

Two well-dressed but surly federal agents stood behind him. One had a Sig Sauer P226 pointed at the back of Tim's head.

"Court is in session. You have been accused of acts of treason against the United States of America. Do you have anything to say in your defense?"

Tim started sobbing convulsively. He choked. He bent forward and vomited.

"Aw! Wudja look at the little guy now. What a crybaby. Not such a big bad terrorist after all."

"We take your disgusting blubbering as a confession of guilt."

Tim tried to turn around. The one agent smacked him in the side of the head with the gun. Blood dripped down Tim's neck.

"Okay. Jury has met. The verdict is unanimous. Guilty as charged."

"Sentence?"

Blam!

Only the Lonely

After Burning Man, Reno was a letdown. A *huge* letdown.

Reno was a poor excuse for a city, where gamblers and tourists flocked to the downtown strip for gambling, bad stage shows, and copycat debauchery which feebly mimicked that of Las Vegas.

Noah had been there for only three days, but it felt like three months.

He was in another dump of a motel. He turned on the television. It was the ongoing parade of madness. CNN reported that Congress had just allocated $1.2 trillion in a bill proposing tearing down the Pentagon and replacing it with a Crucifix-shaped building.

Praise the Lord and pass the ammunition.

Suddenly, he felt famished. It was 2 pm and he hadn't eaten anything so far today.

There was a family restaurant a short hike away. The similarity between edible food and what they served there was purely a coincidence. But it was convenient.

He made his familiar trek to Hank's Chuck Wagon — Noah thought they should have called it Hank's Upchuck Wagon — and ordered the lunch special. Today it was onion soup and a bacon cheeseburger. Like all of their menu items it sounded good, but lost something in the implementation. Maybe the cook had gotten confused and accidentally switched a scouring pad for the beef patty. And he regretted not having a wheelbarrow with a frozen wheel bearing. The onion soup would have been the perfect lubricant.

He settled for only eating the complimentary saltines.

As he nibbled, a very slim but attractive young girl walked past his table. Then she stopped, turned around, and backtracked. She gave Noah a shy but pleasant smile.

"Hi. Can I join you? I don't know anyone here."

"Sure. Want to finish this dog food?"

"Ugh! No wonder everyone is so fat. I'm Cyan."

She sat down. She had lovely eyes, a pert feminine nose, beautiful hands and arms.

"I'm Noah. Cyan. That's different."

"My real name is Penelope. But I really hate it."

What a lovely mouth. It twisted a little when she talked. Watching her lips was more entertainment than Noah had had since Burning Man.

"Why Cyan?"

"I worked at an Office Depot for three months. It was the name of one of the color printer cartridges."

Cyan had just moved there from Bakersfield, California, a hell hole in its own right. Her parents were heavy drinkers, her father had been unemployed for over two years and regularly beat her. She said she was 19 and looking to get a new start somewhere. Noah certainly knew all about that. He felt a real bond with this sweet young lady, and not a little attraction.

Less than an hour later, they were walking into his motel room.

Less than thirty minutes after that, they had finished making love — incredibly hot, athletic, cathartic, explosive, rapturous sex, which left him spent and dreamy, floating in the billowy enchantment of post-coital euphoria.

Cyan got up and went into the bathroom.

When she came back out, she started to get dressed.

"Are you leaving? I thought you—"

"That's two hundred bucks."

Had he heard her right?

"You're a hooker?"

"You thought I was a schoolteacher?"

So much for bonding. At least spiritual bonding.

The dusty weariness of Reno settled back on him like a somnolent shroud, made more oppressive by the inescapable conclusion that he truly was a hopelessly gullible rube, who should probably go back to Missouri where he belonged.

He stayed in his room the rest of the afternoon, the sweet smell of Cyan's sex still lingering in the room and on his private parts.

Then he remembered Trevor's warning when he dropped Noah off at Burning Man.

There was no choice. He had to own up and find out what he needed to do.

Noah dialed through on the IOU secure phone. After a few switched connections, he was on with Trevor.

"She walks up to you in a restaurant, 30 minutes later you're doing the dirty deed. You had no idea she was a hooker. What did you think she was? A schoolteacher?"

"It won't happen again. I'm sorry. I feel so stupid."

"Look. There's a 99% chance she's just a working girl. But we can't take any chances. She knows where you are. We'll take care of this. Noah! Please keep the horse in the barn till we get back to you."

"Got it. Horse in the barn."

He stayed in all evening. Where was there to go? Slot machines, drunks, bad food, stupid floor shows and strip clubs were not his idea of a good time.

Television was almost as bad. This dump had no movie channel. He channel surfed. Several bombs had gone off in various parts of the country. Three congressman had been mailed envelopes containing what was suspected to be ricin, a highly toxic protein powder which can be fatal. There was a panel of international experts on Fox News. One blowhard who looked like a giant human lobster in an ill-fitting suit was carrying on like a rabid dog: *"America should just nuke all those godless socialist Scandinavian countries — Sweden, Denmark, Norway and France — and be done with it once and for all."*

Listening to this kind of idiotic blather made the distinction between conscious and unconscious a moot point. He wasn't quite sure exactly when he fell asleep.

Next morning, his restlessness got the best of him. He decided to usher into his life a dramatic paradigm shift. Instead of going to Hank's Chuck Wagon, he went to a dual purpose establishment three blocks further down called the Pump and Grind. It was a combo gas station and coffee house, where you could fill your tank with high octane fuel and fill your stomach with high octane caffeine.

This was certainly a step up from Hank's. Despite the obvious potential for error, the coffee here didn't taste like gasoline.

Two hours, three magazine, three cranberry apple muffins, and two lattes later, it was time to move on.

Noah had been cut off from the world for quite some time. He felt the urge to get online, maybe check his email, try to look at some credible news. About a half mile away on Carson-Reno Highway was a Best Buy, Reno's biggest electronics mega-outlet. It was actually fairly close to his motel and he had gone by it a couple times.

He walked into the monstrous big box store and headed straight for the computer department. He looked around and didn't spot a single sales person. Apparently they kept their prices low by having no one on the payroll.

Noah was really curious where he stood in the scheme of things.

He positioned himself in front of a totally tricked out Dell Inspiron 770, that had a fiber optic connection to the internet.

He skipped looking at his email for now and went right to Googling 'America's most wanted terrorists'.

Terrorism was apparently a very hot topic. Google returned 373,000,000 links. Noah clicked on http://www.atf.gov/, the official website for the Bureau of Alcohol, Tobacco, Firearms and Explosives — affectionately known as the ATF — which was dedicated to keeping the public suitably informed about its ongoing battles with some of America's most notorious killers, bombers, fanatics, and various enemies of the state.

A dedicated ATF page listed the ten most wanted terrorists in America.

Holy shit! His Andy Warhol 15-minutes was still going strong.

Noah was number eight. There was his photo, his bio, and a phone number for any do-gooders to call if they sighted this notorious outlaw.

What was he feeling? Dread or fear? Actually, healthy doses of both!

He quickly glanced around again. Still no one in sight. He closed the browser and for good measure, reached behind and shut the computer down cold by pulling the plug.

He walked quickly back to his hotel, feeling all eyes were on him.

Every time a car passed, he was sure they were pointing at him and whipping out their cell phones to bring in the helicopters and tanks.

He hurried along wishing he were a turtle, so he could retract his head from view. In spite of his extreme agitation — just a blink and a nod short of sheer panic — he thought about the bizarre, not to say entirely life-threatening position he was in.

Frankly, he didn't get it.

The eighth most wanted terrorist in America?

First of all, he was innocent. Hadn't anyone figured that out? Hadn't they caught whoever actually blew up the bus? Or was this lunatic still running around? Obviously *this* person was a truly dangerous character. Yet they were still conducting a full-blown manhunt for a harmless rube like him who had just needed to get to a toilet bowl so he could dry heave for a couple minutes.

Secondly, so much bizarre and truly violent stuff had gone down since then, how could he be the *eighth* most dangerous dude on the lam? Why, Noah couldn't even get charcoal lit at a barbecue, much less burn down buildings or blow up people. Check the record, morons. Even in the boring desiccated swamp that was Pulnick, he hadn't *ever* done anything more serious than turning in his homework late.

Lastly, why was he still running around loose? He was hardly clever or cagey. These agents must be dumber than a door bell. Of course, now that he got the loud wake-up call from the ATF site, he would try to be more careful.

As if he even knew how.

Message in a Bottle

When Noah got back to his room, there was a package leaning against his door. There was his name in black and white on the FedEx label. He brought it inside, locked his door and opened it. Inside was a beer bottle with a rag hanging out of it, and a note tucked inside. He immediately understood the rag in the bottle reference. It was in the style of a Molotov cocktail. Mercifully whoever sent this had left out the gasoline.

The note presented a challenge. He tried his best to shake it out of the bottle. He used his tooth brush to try to coax it out. Nothing worked. Finally, he put the bottle in a paper bag and smashed it on the edge of the bathroom sink, then recovered the note from the shards of broken glass.

Noah —

I know this is weird. Hope fuels trust. Trust is still blind.

What will this cost? It goes both ways. No worries. IOU.

How did this get to you? You used your Palmyra State Bank Visa card
to take the train to L.A. Feds have been watching Naomi all along (cool
girl who you <u>forgot</u> to mention to me ... hmm).

Can you be sure? You have a tiny flat mole the size of a pencil eraser just to the left of your coccyx.

Come to Detroit immediately. Stay at the Inn on Ferry Street. It's near Wayne State University. Careful at night.

I am with Lot 49. Ask around. You know the kinds of places. There are coffee houses all around there. Talk radical politics. Be careful. These guys are very very serious types.

Joanna

Was this for real? Was she really running around somewhere in Detroit?

He stayed in his room for the rest of the day. The note was all he could think about.

He had to get to Detroit. He had to find Joanna.

She was counting on him.

Wasn't she?

Go East, Young Man, Go East!

Next morning he split. Checked out of the motel and took all his stuff with him.

There were several car lots in Reno clustered on Kietzke Lane near Mill Street. Nissan. Honda. Dodge. Chevrolet. Hummer. They were within easy walking distance.

Of course, Noah didn't want a new car, just anything with four wheels that would make it the 2,180 miles to Detroit.

There was one small lot that specialized in *really used* cars, a hospice for autos that were in the winter years of their transportation lives. Otto's Pre-Owned Autos. The best car on the lot was worse than the worst car on any other lot in area. Perfect.

Noah spotted a 1978 Cadillac Seville in the corner. It was the kind of car he would normally refuse to even ride in, much less own. Filing cabinet grey, upholstery which probably matched the most popular models of wheelchairs, surely a gas hog of epic proportions. It was listing slightly toward the passenger side — grandma must have been packing a few extra pounds — and the left rear quarter panel was dented and rusting. For anyone not already convinced what a terrific find this was, the windshield had in big bold sloppy swathes of white paint: *A real gem! Priced to go at only $3000!*

A salesman, not much older than Abe Lincoln would now have been, hobbled over.

"You want to take her for a spin, pardner? Here's the keys."

"I'll take her."

"She's a real beauty, ain't she?"

"One slight problem."

"What's that?"

"The price."

"Well, we've got a little wiggle room on this. You seem like a nice young man."

"I am. My mother thinks so, anyway. Listen, sir. I don't mean to tell you your business. But with gas prices the way they are, you won't be able to give this away."

"I hear ya. This ain't no hybrid, that's for sure."

"So … here's my final offer. Take it or leave it."

Noah pulled $400 out of his wallet and held it out to the old man.

"You're joking, right?"

"Not anymore than you were when you priced this at $3000. But, sir, and I mean this with all due respect, I'm seriously doing you a favor here."

Now came the spluttering. The harumphing. Head shaking. Huffing and puffing.

"No way. No way, young man. I'd sooner cut off my balls than …"

With as much indignation as he could generate from his atrophied face, the old salesman, put on quite a show. Noah let the old guy carry on for several minutes. He didn't say a word. Noah almost felt sorry for him but this pile of junk was going to cost him a fortune to drive. Finally, the old man wore himself out. They went to the office and filled out the paperwork.

"I can run the title down to DMV for you, get this registered, put on your new license plate tags, if you want. Of course, I'll need a few extra—"

"I got it. I'm headed that way."

Right. Insurance? License plates? Sissy stuff. This was going to be a one shot deal. Directly to Detroit, then he'd drive this giant pile of tin off a cliff. Well, they probably didn't have cliffs in Detroit. Maybe he'd leave the keys in it in front of a liquor store. From what Noah had heard about the crime there, the vehicle would be gone before Noah could buy a bag of pretzels.

Within twenty minutes, he was barreling northeast on U.S. 80 and in 5½ hours he would cross the state line into Utah.

Noah had to admit. It was a pretty smooth ride, especially considering the car was almost fifty years old. The enormous gas-guzzling engine purred away like it had not a trouble in the world. Noah felt pretty confident this giant metal whale had some miles left in it, certainly enough to get to Detroit.

Unfortunately, he was way off the mark. Just coming up on North Platte, Nebraska he heard a metallic pop, followed by a mechanical groan. Noah looked in the rear view mirror and could see smoke pouring out, apparently from the underside of the old Caddy.

He made it to the next exit, lumbered into a service station — one which actually had a mechanic and not some pimply high school kid in a cash booth in the center aisle — and got the bad news. Unless Noah wanted to spend $4000 on a rebuilt engine, the metallic Moby Dick would be on its way to a scrap iron yard very soon. How sad. This Cadillac was probably actually built in Detroit during the time they were still building cars there. It would have been like an elephant make its last fateful journey to its sacred burial ground.

Frankly, it turned out to be a blessing. Gas prices were astronomical and Noah had already shelled out over $2100 just to make it this far. How could anyone afford to drive? Now that he thought about it, there were very few vehicles on the road.

He had made it slightly over half way to Detroit. What now?

He stepped off of the service station lot and stuck out his thumb. A truck which had just stopped there for some diesel pulled over.

That was the first of only three rides which got him to Detroit. This first driver — a real decent fellow who hauled biopharmaceuticals between two facilities owned by a Finnish company, one in Lincoln, Nebraska, and the other in Akron, Ohio — got him most of the way. He dropped Noah at a truck stop in Toledo, Ohio, talked to a couple other drivers there, and next thing Noah knew, he was in an 18-wheeler bound for Ann Arbor, Michigan.

Phenomenal luck continued to be with him. He stood on a freeway ramp for I-94 eastbound for Detroit for not more than twenty minutes, when an old Volkswagen bus pulled over to let him in. It was pea green, though most of the finish had been replaced by rust, and was covered in bumperstickers promoting the legalization of pot. The side door opened and the vehicle exhaled a huge cloud of marijuana smoke. Inside were six college students — all guys, late teens, early 20s — smiling, friendly, welcoming. Noah threw in his bags and crawled into the circle gathered in back around a waterpipe.

As if the gods were offering their divine guidance or at least had assigned a highly organized guardian angel to the task, these fellows were students at Wayne State University, had just visited some buddies at University of Michigan, and were on their way back to campus. And that was exactly where Noah was heading.

Forty-five minutes and a lot of high fives later, they dropped him off in front of the Inn on Ferry Street.

Down is Up

The prevailing mind set seemed to be, if we solve as many small problems as we can, the big problems will take care of themselves. This was under the circumstances totally backwards. Then again, backward was forward, in a world where down is up and left is right.

The simple truth was, there were no small problems.

But the people who should know better were in complete and total denial. Their take was, trying to make these big problems go away was by any measure annoying, impractical, and just too damn difficult.

This pointed to only one possible solution.

Critical thinking had to be replaced by wishful thinking.

With the reach and power of television and the internet, this was no problem.

The media was pressed into service, called upon to do their patriotic duty, and now stumbled over one another in the scramble to put a positive spin on everything.

Employment was plunging nationwide. This was heralded as ...

Job opportunities are expected to surge with increased availability of willing and able workers.

The stock market chart looked like the giant waterslide at Raging Waters. Media outlets specializing in business news and financial forecasting breezily predicted ...

Analysts are confident a buying frenzy will drive prices through the ceiling during the coming "bounce" in stocks.

Home mortgage defaults were at a historical high. The spin doctors stirred the magical sludge ...

Families freed of home ownership are discovering the freedom and flexibility of renting.

Inflation officially was zero but paradoxically prices on everything were up. Begging the question was much easier than trying to make sense of it ...

Buyers are focusing on quality rather than quantity as studies show that shoppers are getting smarter.

Poverty was increasing and people were starving. Pundits suddenly extolled the virtues of asceticism as the new chic of pop culture ...

Americans are turning away from materialism and now looking within as a widespread spiritual awakening sweeps the nation.

Public schools were closing and being dismantled. An Amish social psychologist was tracked down for some unbiased commentary ...

Home schooling is a proven method for bringing families closer and fostering the virtue of self-reliance.

In six months medical care and pharmaceuticals doubled in price. Fox News saw the bright side...

Over 85% of those polled are pleased with the shorter lines for health services at hospitals and clinics.

With oil at over $300 a barrel, gasoline was $57 a gallon. The Wall Street Journal saw the glass as half-full ...

Environmentally conscious Americans are now driving less.

Everything was being privatized and owned by banks and corporations. Great news for everyone! ...

Consolidation of economic control introduces more efficiency and reduces possibility of political or public corruption.

The U.S. military was now engaged in five concurrent wars. When mentioned — which was rather infrequently — these military campaigns were trumpeted ...

The dream of freedom and free market capitalism being delivered in a humvee to a world hungry for the American Way.

It was indeed an Orwellian wet dream. Of course, Orwell never specifically wrote about his wet dreams but people could imagine. Everything could readily be seen as it was, but what was said about it bubbled like a giddy laugh track over the surreal sitcom that had become American life. It was weightless pop muzak being played in an elevator accelerating in a fatal freefall plunge to certain annihilation.

The White House staff and the President himself, whether they read or heard this steady stream of Pollyannaish drivel from the media, or were themselves responsible for some or all of it, had apparently spent considerable effort to construct their own versions of reality, which only served to gratuitously expose the myopia and tunnel vision of the Executive branch on the pathetic state of things. The President addressed the nation quite regularly now, in fact a little too often, each time looking more and more like the kid caught with his hand in the cookie jar. On a recent Sunday evening, he had just given a barely noticed and widely ignored televised address to the nation, which had with a colossal lack of judgment been scheduled at the same time as Dancing With The Stars, the most popular program on TV. This guaranteed that no one except the cameramen and President's personal assistants who were physically present, would actually see and hear him. This turned out to be a blessing in disguise. He seemed to think he was doing a tent revival, rather than presenting a plan for a way out of the dark cave of dysfunction and despair in which America was trapped. He could have capped it off by having some wheelchair-bound victims rolled in for a little faith healing. Maybe he was saving that was for his next address.

> *"See folks, the Devil's in the details. But we ain't lettin' the Devil in the door. Nope. Not on my watch. Been there done that. Hallelujah! But that doesn't mean we ain't paying attention. You can cut the tension with a knife with all the attention we give this. Day and night. We haven't given up, we ain't gonna give up, you can take that to the bank, and put a quarter in the cup. Amen! I tell it like it is. When you elected me, I became part of your family. And where I come from, family takes care of family. My family had a Ford family station wagon. <u>That</u> was a great car! My dad used to work on it himself. He knew how to always keep it in top notch running condition. Every week, he used to tighten the screws on the license plate, polish the hub caps, clean the lint and candy wrappers out from under the seats. It always ran like a top."*

Got it. Quarter in the cup. Family. Start your engines. Hallelujah. Devil bad. President good.

People seemed to buy it. Or maybe they were just too numb to react. Or...

"OMG! Was that who I thought it was on Dancing With The Stars?"

Okay. Quick review.

Backward is forward. Down is up. Stupid is smart.

Need some clean underwear, Mr. Orwell?

CHAPTER NINE

The Motown Sound

Noah didn't believe a lot of what he read on the internet. So much of it was poorly informed, superficially researched, and almost never viewed with a critical eye or subjected to reasonable verification. While there was a great deal to be learned, it was always a crap shoot trying to figure out what had some basis in fact and what was just speculation.

When he read that Detroit was without question and beyond dispute the worst place in America and high in the running for the worst on the planet, he took it with a grain of salt.

It was one time he could have believed them.

Detroit had once been famous for what was called the Motown Sound. This was the infectious, intoxicating blend of R&B, rock 'n roll, soul, blues, negro spirituals and pop which filled the airwaves and concert venues of America for well over a decade. It included the music of Diana Ross & the Supremes, the Four Tops, Temptations, Marvin Gaye, Smokie Robinson & the Miracles, and countless other performers snatched from the ghettos of the city, groomed and polished with the production genius of Barry Gordy and the incredibly talented staff of Hitsville USA. Its offices and recording studio were located in the heart of Detroit on West Grand Boulevard, in what had once been a moderately upscale area.

There was another sound coming from Motown, during these years of glory and economic boom. It was the combined roar of the powerful, gas-guzzling V-8 engines which powered Detroit's main product and the cavernous factories which produced them. Most everyone who lived in the city or the surrounding suburbs worked for either Ford, Chrysler, or General Motors, or one of the tens of thousands of vendors which fed the Big Three everything they needed to pump out millions of their imposing boat-like automobiles, worshipped by Americans and citizens from every country in the world, devotees who snapped them up as fast as they rolled off the assembly line.

Unfortunately, by the 80s both the Motown Sound and the industrial roar of the automobile factories had been quieted to a whisper and a whimper, and Detroit never recovered.

A severe blow landed with little warning when in 1972 Barry Gordy, producer and writer for all of the most successful Motown acts, packed up his whole record label and moved it to Los Angeles. Though he always subsequently claimed that the primary reason was to position himself in the world-recognized capital of the entertainment business, to be center ring to duke it out with the other major labels, as well as to rub shoulder with captains of the film industry, perhaps he also had looked down the road and didn't like what he saw. Anticipating the decline and collapse of what had once been a great American city, he knew his fortunes would suffer if he remained in Detroit.

Long before the 80s, the Motor City was already having problems with its engine. The automobile industry started taking hits in the late 60s and early 70s. First there was the massive oil shortage, which drove gasoline prices through the roof. Detroit at the time was only making enormous, gas-guzzling behemoths which measured their fuel efficiency in gallons per mile instead of miles per gallon. Along came the Germans with the VW bug, the Italians with their Fiat, the French with their cute if unreliable Renault Dauphine. Then with the market share of the U.S. being chipped away by European manufacturers, arrived the Japanese with cars that not only actually worked, looked great, were phenomenally fuel efficient, and fun to drive, but had cool names like Toyota and Honda.

The Big Three kept on making cars. But the damage had been done. Their monopoly was a thing of the past. To survive the challenges of competitors from all over the world, adjustments would have to be made. Those adjustments largely involved closing all of their factories in and about Detroit and moving them to places where taxes were lower, labor was cheaper, and workers less empowered and demanding of fair treatment.

The tables turned and the fortune cookie crumbled.

In the late 60s, if anything there were too many jobs in Detroit and the result was there was a shortage of labor. The population of the city was approaching 2,000,000 and it was the sixth largest in the nation. When Noah was dropped at the Inn on Ferry Street by his stoned acquaintances in their smoke-mobile, estimates of unemployment varied between 28 and 50%. The city's population had dwindled to a mere 752,000.

Poverty was pervasive. Whole city blocks had become decaying piles of rubble, as formerly magnificent office buildings and hotels were now empty, overrun by rats, and strewn with trash, broken glass and crumbled plaster. Gigantic factories occupying huge chunks of the skyline which at one time were the engine of enormous national wealth, had become giant, empty, rusting carcasses, the archeological ruins of an abandoned empire. Detroit was its own Third World country within the country.

Amazingly, there were still a few pockets in the outlying suburbs of the greater Detroit metropolitan area where extreme concentrations of wealth supported the ostentatious lifestyles of the rich and oblivious.

Noah would certainly not be seeing any of this during his visit.

It only took him the short ride from the city limits to his hotel to codify his own thinking on the situation.

They should stop talking about the Motown Sound.

They should probably be talking about the Motown Smell.

The smell of gunpowder, industrial decay and urban rot.

The smell of abandonment and surrender.

The smell of neglect and carnage.

The smell of human misery.

Lot 49

The first thing Noah did after he checked into the Inn on Ferry Street was report in with IOU. Using the secure phone he had been given, he quickly got through. It was the familiar voice of whoever it was he always spoke to. Apparently he had been assigned as the primary contact for Noah.

"Where have you been?"

"Everything's fine. I got the message in a bottle."

"Message in a bottle? What are you talking about? Where are you?"

"Detroit."

"Nice. For what? Looking to buy some abandoned buildings?"

"I'm trying to find Joanna."

"Who's Joanna?"

"You know. The lady at Habitat."

"Joanna? I have no idea who you're talking about. Detroit, eh?"

"Not my first choice."

"Anyway, we were concerned. But since even we couldn't find you, you must be off everyone's radar. At least for now. So do what you have to do. But no hookers. Got it?"

"It never crossed my mind."

Next morning he hit the streets.

Noah eventually found what he was looking for.

After wasting two days hanging out in the more popular coffee shops near Wayne State University, places like Bear Claw and Tech Town, he came to an obvious conclusion. These cafés were just yuppie student hang outs, not hot beds of political revolutionary fervor.

Then he spotted a poster for a teach-in — they still had teach-ins? wasn't that a 60s thing? — sponsored by a Queer Studies campus organization. It wasn't exactly the kind of political event he had in mind, but it wouldn't be a Tupperware party. Lacking alternatives he decided to go. It was at 8 pm that very evening, at a place called Scramblers on Napoleon Street, a decaying strip of asphalt which turned out to be a mere service drive in the industrial area next to the Fisher Freeway. It was a dodgy area of town with many abandoned homes and run-down public housing projects.

It wasn't very far. Noah could have walked but took a taxi, in light of Joanna's warning about being careful at night.

Scramblers was on the second floor of a warehouse space. A hand-painted sign hung on a steel door which opened to a narrow stairwell smelling of urine and cheap wine. It was hard to say what exactly the establishment was. Not a bar, though people drank beer and wine out of bottles they brought themselves, not a restaurant, though they served some finger foods like fries with catsup and hard boiled eggs, not a coffee house, though they sold pots of hot water and packets of Nescafe instant and Cremora.

There was no teach-in. Or if there had been one scheduled, it was canceled.

But this was the kind of place he was looking for. It was a hovel for the disenfranchised, the left out, the left of left, the lunatic fringe. Punk and anarchy meets hip hop and guerilla warfare.

Considering the skin tone of everyone he saw on the streets as he rode there, surprisingly the place was mainly full of whites. A few Hispanics. A couple Asians. But no African-Americans.

And no females.

It was all dudes. And what a surly lot of dudes it was.

In a the dark expanse of a seedy warehouse space filled with cheap mismatched diner tables, wood and metal chairs in varying states of disrepair, the ceilings and walls painted an absorbent flat black, the entire room inadequately lit by four harsh bare bulbs hanging from the steel-beam rafters, there were about fifty guys. Smoking. Staring. Thinking or brooding. Not much conversation. Rage Against The Machine played almost inaudibly in the background.

Noah played with his fries and let his instant coffee get cold. Neither were fit for human consumption. He tried not to stare or even look around conspicuously, but it wasn't easy.

This was hands-down the scariest looking bunch of people he had ever seen.

In real life or in the movies.

It wasn't just their hair or clothes or piercings or tattoos, though each of these cosmetic elements combined to put everyone who they confronted on notice that these were strange and probably dangerous types standing before them.

It was the look of focused intransigence. It was the impatient edge to every movement as if every muscle was a tight-wound coil of steel ready to brutally unleash a torrent of malevolence. It was the uncompromising set of their jaws, the body language which smirked and growled and hinted at bad intentions, the unblinking eyes which brooked no negotiations. It was the calculating stare of absolute certainty, the cold exactitude and disdain of men who viewed the world through a rifle bore or down the length of a dagger.

These were men for whom discussion was long past and action long past due.

Noah wondered if he should stay or leave.

Within the exact same instant, three guys flipped their folding chairs around, sliding them right up against his table. They sat straddling them, leaning in within only a few inches of his face. The two on either side stared down at their hands which were tensely folded and rested on the lip of the table. The one directly across from him had long stringy curls hanging in his face, which clearly had been strangers to shampoo for quite some time. He looked filthy, though part of that impression resulted from three days of black stubble and an oily sheen to his skin. His teeth were grey with plaque and his breath smelled of cigarettes and rancid cooking oil.

"What do you want?"

Noah looked at each of them, then pointed at the plate of fries on the table.

"I'm not going to eat these. You want them? Go ahead."

The spokesman was not amused or in the least deterred.

"What the fuck are you doing here?"

Noah decided to go for broke.

"Lot 49."

"Did I hear you right?"

"I don't know. Did you? I said Lot 49."

They were on their feet. Noah was as well, though his feet technically weren't touching the ground at this point.

"I haven't paid for—"

"Don't worry about it. I'll put it on my tab."

There was no resisting. They weren't that big but were incredibly strong.

Three minutes later, Noah was in the back seat of a 1972 Chevy Nova. The physical arrangement hadn't changed. The same two who basically had carried him were on either side. He definitely wasn't going anywhere. Stringy curls was driving. Driving with little regard for traffic regulations or common courtesy. Maybe Detroit had different rules of the road. Maybe there were no rules.

Noah had no idea where he was. As if he had any concept of this awful city to begin with. They took all side streets and alleys. All he could say for sure was that things just kept getting worse. No matter how bad the streets and buildings looked now, a few blocks later they would plunge into a deeper level of deterioration and blight.

Fifteen minutes later they finally stopped in front of a warehouse. From the peeling paint on the building's high windowless façade, it had apparently at one time been commercial storage space.

He was taken into an office with plate glass viewing windows. There was nothing to view except piles and piles of debris in every direction.

His two handlers roughly pushed him into an old executive chair on wheels. They spun him around. He didn't know what to think. Around and around he went. He started to get dizzy. He began to think it was some sort of joke and started to laugh. Suddenly the chair stopped. Then a fist came flying directly into his face, catching him squarely on his left cheek.

The pain was incredible. His head was ringing. At the moment of impact there was a loud dull thud unlike anything he had ever heard before. There were flashes of light.

As his head started to clear, it slowly dawned on him that he had never, not even once, been hit before. Not really hit. Full and flush with a human fist, or any pugilistic weapon. Sure, he and his buddies had rough housed, wrestled, tossed each other about. But nothing like this.

He also discovered that being hit with a roundhouse right hook is not at all like it is in the movies, where the guy just shakes his head then looks mad and goes after his assailant. Actually, it's more like it is in cartoons, where there is the sound of a gong, the person sees stars and all sorts of weird shapes around him, and does the daffy dance of delirium with his tongue hanging out and a completely stupid look on his face. Then he either falls to the floor or starts crying.

Noah started crying.

"Lot 49, eh? I have a strong suspicion you're not a cop. No cop would be stupid enough to just come out and say it. But that begs the question of exactly how you know about Lot 49."

"I'm looking for Joanna."

"There's nobody by that name around that I know of."

"I worked with her in Alabama. She was arrested. Then I got a note from her."

"You got a note from Joanna. Did she pass it to you in history class?"

Stringy curls had been massaging his fist. Now he was clenching it again.

"Please. Please don't. I'm not here for—"

Wham!

The guy was good. He didn't hit Noah hard enough to kill him. He hit Noah just hard enough to make him wish he were dead.

Noah felt his face with his hand. He found it hard to believe his cheek was still there, that it had not been pulverized, leaving just a sunken hole of shattered teeth and bone all the way to his esophagus.

"Fuck! Fuck! Oh God! That hurts!"

"I'm just warming up. You better do some explaining. You better get to it right now!"

He shoved Noah and the chair rolled back until it hit a desk. The chair bounced hard, knocking him off balance. He fell forward onto his hands and knees, and immediately curled into a protective ball, at least to keep from being hit in the face again.

Then he thought of something.

"Has anyone here got a smart phone?"

Because his face was buried between his thighs, what he said came out muffled.

"What did you say?"

He felt someone kick him from the side with the bottom of their foot. He lifted his head just long enough to repeat it.

"Has anyone here got a smart phone?"

"Yeah. What of it?"

"Google February 16. Bus. Indianapolis."

He resumed cannonball position and waited for the anticipated flurry of blows.

"This better be good. We're not fucking around, you know. You've stepped in some deep shit here."

"Not once have I thought you were fucking around."

It was quiet for almost a minute. He cautiously looked up. All three were looking at an iPhone. Stringy curls had it in his left hand and was scrolling and tapping on the screen.

Stringy curls looked at the iPhone. Then he looked at Noah. He looked at the phone again.

"Is this you?"

"That's me."

"You're the guy who did this?"

"I'm trying to get away. I don't know who I'm running from but I'm running."

"We know who the fuck you're running from. Believe me. We know!"

Truce in place, they took Noah back to the car, this time letting him walk on his own, then drove him to his guest house. There were no apologies for bashing him in the face. Evidently, one had to expect a little rough and tumble among these incendiary sorts, these propagators of systemic change and political revolution.

Of course, Noah was making a leap of faith on that. It seemed like a safe bet. If Joanna was tied in, then they were definitely insurrectionists of some shape and size. This had to be the extreme outer fringe, however. IOU in need of anger management. Most everyone he had been rubbing up against until now were more about media, information, disinformation, propaganda, misdemeanor civil disobedience. They were boilerplate tune out, drop out, raise a little hell, hold up some signs, chant some annoying chants. Probably the only notable exception would have been Francine and company, whatever they were all about. They were more rude than violent.

These guys were cut from a different cloth and very hard to read. Usually these political types were non-stop rant and rave, or at least engaged in an ongoing dialogue about the system, corrupt politicians, corporate abuse, the movement, what had been tried and what should be tried, how next to hammer the existing order. But these three didn't say a word. They didn't talk to Noah. They didn't talk to one another. It was all business, very cut and dry. No small talk. No big talk. Only the most basic functional verbiage. Where are you staying? Are you alone? What time can you be ready? Bring

113

something to eat. We don't feed you. Don't fucking talk to anyone.

They agreed that Noah should be standing at the curb in front of the Inn on Ferry Street at precisely 12:30 pm tomorrow. They would swing by.

He was. They did.

They headed across town, generally in a southwesterly direction from what Noah sensed. At one point, they turned onto West Grand Boulevard. Trey — that was stringy curls given name — actually made a normal human comment. He pointed to one particular building they were driving by.

"That's the old Motown Records place. Hitsville U.S.A. That's about all this shit hole of a city is famous for."

The entire area looked like Berlin or Dresden must have looked the day Germany surrendered back in 1945. Apparently a big annual ritual here in Detroit was the torching of buildings on Devil's Night, the evening before Halloween. It looked like it.

Things only got worse as they plunged deeper into a mixed-use area which included many abandoned factories. The only relief were open lots where structures had crumbled and either been scavenged or cleared.

Trey turned into a drive and both Sal and Kenny — these were the two who had bookended him the evening before — jumped out and opened a swinging chain link gate. There was a building, which couldn't be seen from the road because the property was surrounded by high corrugated sheet metal. It was huge. Apparently it had been a steel forging operation and warehouse at one time.

They parked in a sprawling dirt lot behind the building. Noah noticed their Chevy Nova was by far the oldest, most run-down vehicle in sight. There were some very swanky cars and vans. Noah even spotted a few BMWs and at least one Mercedes Benz.

They approached a steel door with an intercom next to it. Trey punched the button.

"Lot 49."

"W-A-S-T-E."

The door buzzed and they entered.

Had Noah stepped onto the set of the Starship Enterprise and been greeted in person by Spock, he would not have been any more shocked.

In some ways, it did look like a space ship. Lot 49 was a very exotic night club which had been themed around interstellar travel and deep space exploration. Every single piece of furniture, accoutrement, even the uniforms worn by what appeared to be waiters and hostesses, were out of some futuristic science fiction movie. Only the ten or twelve people sitting at one large table and in the plush rounded cushion chairs next to it, had on regular street clothing. They were as harshly informal as the three who had brought him there. Despite their dress and bad boy attitude, they didn't appear to be out of place. How could they? It was their place.

Trey leaned over to Noah as they approached the table and whispered.

"We don't use names here. They will give you a designation."

One man appeared to be in charge. He must have been in his late 40s early 50s. He was AIDS-victim UNESCO famine-poster thin. He was clean shaven but apparently extremely uncoordinated, in light of the number of razor nicks on his neck and chin. His jet black hair — dyed with no attempt to disguise the fact — was precisely cut and fastidiously groomed, in the slick style of a 40s cinematic gangster.

Pale as wax paper, his skin interestingly had a healthy glow, as did his brilliantly blue eyes.

He gave Noah a piercing look as they approached.

"You are Chemtrail. Call me Element, if you must."

Noah was directed to sit down by another person at the table, who then gestured with his hand to the candy offerings in small crystal bowls sitting in the center. Noah at first thought they were tiny sugar candies, like Pez or Tic Tacs. Looking closer he realized they were pills. He felt Trey's hands on his shoulders as he leaned in whisper something.

"I would go easy if you are uninitiated." He pointed at each bowl. "Those are acid. Those ecstasy. Those are probably Valium or something like that."

Noah took a pass. That's all he needed now was drugs to completely disable his already addled brain.

He waited. Everyone was staring at one or the other of two enormous flat panel screens. One was playing a movie he vaguely recognized. It was *Charlie and the Chocolate Factory* with Johnny Depp. The sound was off. The other screen was filled with a live commodities chart. But it only followed one item. Gold. Inset in the lower right corner was a scrolling chat box.

Element tore his gaze from the screen and looked down. Noah now noticed there was a computer keyboard in his lap. He typed something. It appeared in the chat frame.

Element: Tell dickweed he's gonna get us all busted.
           Just stay with the original plan. Or I'm out.

G-Spot: I agree. Got it. Burial at sea.

Element turned to look at Noah. Then he turned back to the chart. The candle indicating the price of gold ticked up and down. A little up. A little down. It would jump a bit. Then inch back to where it was.

Element popped open another window. It looked like a spread sheet. Some of the boxes were blinking red or green. Usually alternating. Noah couldn't make any sense out of it. He saw the cursor hovering over a box. Apparently Element clicked it. An alert frame opened which offered 'Execute' or 'Cancel'. Execute. The alert frame closed. The price candle dropped halfway down the screen, hesitated, came back up slightly, then dropped another huge amount. The cadaverous Element tapped away again on the keyboard.

Element: Their assholes must be feeling the pain and I
           don't even have my dick in the whole way.

He then reached over to one of the bowls and ceremoniously took an orange pill between his index finger and thumb. With a dramatic flourish he tipped his head back and held the pill high over his head, then slowly brought it down and placed it under his tongue.

He looked at Noah as if to gauge the reaction.

If Noah had it correctly, that was the acid. Maybe he better conduct his business before the atomic bomb hit this guy's brain.

"I know you don't use names. But a woman sent me here. She promised she would be here. Maybe 30 or 31 years old. Beautiful. Looks a little like Charlize Theron."

Element just stared at Noah. The way you might look at a gum wrapper floating in a fish tank. No one else said anything. Half of them stared at the screen with the movie. A army of dozens of oompa loompas were dancing in formation and candies were swirling in an enormous psychedelically rainbowed vortex. It was a mind-boggling, dazzling show of computer imagery. No reaction. Not even a sigh.

Even those who had been watching what had just happened with the gold trade sat there like they were hypnotized, or had become one with the infinite vapor of nothingness.

What was with these people? These had to be the most conversationally challenged individuals in the entire world. There was more going on at a deaf-mute convention and those poor slobs were at a distinct disadvantage.

Noah looked around. Like the scene at Scramblers it was mainly dudes. The only women were the waitresses, or whatever they were. There were no drinks and no dishes of food anywhere in sight. Both the waitresses and their space-age male counterparts didn't seem to do much of anything. They were sitting at the bar, talking it up. Flirting. Noah checked them all out. Joanna definitely was not among them. She said she'd be here but Noah couldn't imagine she would be welcome in the tight circle of drugged out men he was sitting with. She would have to be a waitress. Maybe she worked here but on another shift.

Noah figured he had nothing to lose. Well maybe a broken jaw or cheek bone. Desperation got the better of judgment.

"Element. Sir. Mr. Element. Your Highness."

Element turned but it was clear he didn't see any humor in Noah's whimsical approach.

"Her name is Joanna. She's a terrorist. Like me. I have to find her."

Did he? He had to admit that at this point he wasn't sure what the hell he had to do. He certainly was not wholly committed to the kind of risks he was taking here. Who knew what these crazy fuckers were capable of?

Element looked back at the commodities screen. Then twice he slowly waved his hand in front of his own face at arm's length. Right. Looking for trails to see if the acid had kicked in. Then he replied in a bored monotone. No discernible irony.

"A terrorist. That's not good. We don't believe in terrorism here. As Karl Marx famously said, 'Capital is money, capital is commodities. By virtue of it being value, it has acquired the occult ability to add value to itself. It brings forth living offspring, or, at the least, lays golden eggs.' Eggs. Not bombs. He also said, 'Revolutions are the locomotives of history.' See where I'm coming from?"

"Got it. To make a locomotive, sometimes you have to break a few eggs."

There was the briefest momentary vacuum of dead silence.

Then Element finally actually showed some emotion. A flash of something alternating between disdain and disgust flushed his normally bloodless face. His brow furrowed and his saucer-sized pupils suddenly became ominous pinpricks. With a dismissing flick of his hand, the conversation was over.

Noah was hustled toward the exit, Sal and Kenny behind him, Trey in the lead.

In a bizarre counterpoint to the mortuary social graces of Element and his silent clones, and the prevailing sense that Noah wouldn't be any less welcome if he were in the advanced stages of leprosy, as they were leaving one of the waitresses rushed ahead and assumed a perky happy hostess pose next to the door. When they got there, she held it open for them and gave Noah her best Miss America smile.

"Thanks for coming to Lot 49! Please come again sometime."

It literally stopped him in his tracks, bringing him eye to eye with her. Their noses were practically touching. Her smile seemed epoxied in place and her perfect white teeth gleamed like a brand new microwaveable soup bowl. He inexplicably started to get a boner.

"What are the drink specials here?"

"Coffee, tea or LSD."

Right.

Prediction!

The trumpet-heavy fanfare of the show's theme song played, the logo swept across the screen, then dissolved showing the panel of pundits fidgeting as they got ready. Another episode of the weekly news editorial program, The McLaughlin Group, was off and running.

John McLaughlin: "Issue One! Things just keep getting weirder with this president. His recent appearance on national television reading from the toddler's tome *The Little Engine That Could*, may go down in history as one of the most bizarre events in presidential history."

Pat Buchanan: "He's scrambling. He's got no ideas. So he's trying to put on some sort of cartoon show to distract the American public."

Eleanor Clift: "This is an election year. He's got to play down the bad news — and there sure is a lot of that — and try to charm the voters."

John McLaughlin: "What's charming about looking like a full-tilt lunatic?"

Susan Ferrechio: "What gets me, and I think this is the question just about everyone inside the beltway is asking, is when is this president going to start campaigning? It's August. And this guy hasn't made a single campaign appearance. Sure, he'll get the nomination. But he needs to start getting his message out to the people."

Pat Buchanan: "This President is MIA. He's missing in action on every front. Why, I barely made it to the studio today. There's so much garbage piled up on the curbs."

Mort Zuckerman: "I saw patients in their beds lined up out in the street in front of George Washington University Hospital. I'm serious. Patients on the sidewalk. Some of them even had I-V bottles."

Eleanor Clift: "Maybe the President should read a bedtime story to them."

John McLaughlin: "Prediction! This president is no dummy. I say he's playing rope-a-dope and will pull something out at the last minute. Look for an October surprise. You heard it first, right here. Next up, boon or boondoggle. Florida governor wants a missile defense system for Disney World. That, right after a word from our sponsors."

The Good Samaritan

For four days Noah pointlessly hung out at and around his guest house. Based on nothing more substantial than his druthers, he entertained baseless fantasies that Trey and maybe even the reticent and emaciated Element might produce the missing Joanna. To kill time he visited both the Detroit Institute of Arts and the Museum of Contemporary Art. Not exactly much of a fan of art per se, he was quite impressed. Considering the abysmal state of the rest of the city, it was amazing that either of these two institutions survived. It seemed more likely that the structures would have been bombed and burned to the ground just to steal the bathroom fixtures.

He spent way too many hours caffeinating himself at Tech Town Two café. The girls were decent enough to look at. But for fucks sake! Detroit was an unfriendly town. These folks made the Rain Man look like a debonair socialite. They looked fairly normal but must have all been raised in steel shipping containers by Inquisition monks who had taken a vow of silence.

Late afternoon of the fourth day running, he sat scrunched at a corner table at Tech Town, trying not to look like he was loitering or casing the joint for a stick up. He had just polished off his third caramel latte and two low fat apple-cinnamon muffins and was getting up to leave. Suddenly, Trey came rushing through the door, walked directly over to his table and sat down.

"Hey! Trey! Here for the tasty but healthful low-in-cholesterol muffins?"

No response. Trey seemed fidgety. Noah tried to make conversation.

"Are we going back to Lot 49? Is that a night club or something?"

"At night it's a club. Exclusive membership. You wouldn't make the cut."

Okay. Let's make a guy feel like a worthless piece of shit while we're at it.

"Element wants to talk to you."

"What about? Is it about Joanna? That girl—"

"I have no idea. Normally we just deep six guys like you. I think the old man is getting soft. Too much acid."

It took less than thirty minutes to get to the club. Traffic jams for the motor city were things of the past. Most people couldn't afford a car. The city looked even more odious and barren than the first excursion through the wasteland route to Lot 49.

The staff was getting the place ready for the hordes of exclusive patrons which would be descending on the disco, assuming they didn't get shot on the way.

Element was alone, just staring at the screen with the active chart of gold futures.

He didn't bother to even look at Noah but left him standing there, unsure whether he should sit down.

"I don't know why I'm helping a pathetic pissant like you. A terrorist, no less. But we found your lady friend, Joanna Templeton."

Element minimized the gold trading chart window and opened up Internet Explorer, already displaying a YouTube page.

It was an MSNBC special report about a new push by the White House to counter terrorism. As if the President didn't have enough on his plate with the economic collapse and a 87% disapproval rating, he was taking a lot of heat from a number of congressional hitmen about the anarchy in the streets and the administration's alleged lethargy when it came to keeping the country safe. To counter the criticism, the President pointed to the capture of what it called a "high-value target", a young woman who represented a grave danger to the American public. There was video footage of her being taken into custody by federal marshals, handcuffed and manacled.

It was Joanna.

She was surrounded by agents, FBI and CIA, as they walked from the courthouse where she had just been arraigned. They were attempting to load her into the back of a black sedan, to cart her off to a high-security federal detention facility. Joanna had been denied bail and would be locked up until the completion of her trial.

She was struggling and clearly in a fit of rage. Noah didn't recall Joanna swearing at all. But she was letting loose such a continuous stream of expletives, when the news program bleeped them all out of her rant, it sounded like Morse code.

Over earlier footage of her being marched into the same court for her arraignment, a reporter excitedly announced that the trial promised to be a highly publicized and contentious one, then explained that she had been nabbed while working at a soup kitchen in Baltimore. She had cleverly covered her tracks by creating the impression that her work was purely humanitarian, that she was merely a volunteer doing social work and community service. Authorities were accusing her of being one of a handful of conspirators who had planned and were about to unleash a firestorm of violent acts against both government agencies and corporations, which she and her terrorist cell of fellow insurrectionists had deemed "enemies of the people".

To shrill outcries by human and legal rights groups claiming foul play and gross violation of her constitutional rights, Joanna would be kept in solitary confinement, allegedly to prevent her from coordinating through her network of violent collaborators, retaliatory attacks against the government.

Noah sat there both stunned and horrified.

They got Joanna.

They said she was about to unleash a firestorm of violence. She was so dangerous she was being kept in a hermetically sealed cage like they would have put Osama bin Laden if they hadn't recently aerated him will a lot of bullet holes.

What a pack of lies! Joanna didn't have a violent bone in her body. Noah knew what she was all about. She was not about blowing things up or hurting innocent people.

Element finally turned and looked at Noah.

"Okay, bomber of buses. Your business is done here. So I'd really appreciate it if you got the fuck out of Detroit. Trey? You know what to do."

Without any further fanfare, Element went back to work buggering the gold market.

Trey led Noah back to the car. They drove for some time in silence, returning the route they came. Apparently they weren't going to put a bullet in the back of Noah's head, at least not yet.

Trey finally did his approximation of a chuckle, which came out more as a grunt.

"That was priceless. 'I'd really appreciate it if you got the fuck out of Detroit.' Truly amazing. Element has taken a liking to you."

"I sure wouldn't want to see what he's like when he hates someone."

"That's right. You wouldn't."

"If we're such bosom buddies now, why is he so anxious to get rid of me?"

"He thinks you're dangerous."

"Me? Dangerous? Has he looked in a mirror lately?"

Trey pulled up in front of the Inn on Ferry Street.

"Tonight. Scramblers. I'll situate you. You know. Your stealth mode thing."

"Trey, I really appreciate it. Nice gesture. But you guys don't seem to be the magnanimous types. You want to situate me? I have a little difficulty believing any of you give a shit."

"We don't. We just want to get rid of you. As soon as possible. Before you fuck things up. There's a lot at stake here." He suddenly stopped. "We don't screw over the people on your end. That's all you need to know."

In his room, Noah tried to sort it out. He got nowhere. If these guys were somehow part of the counterculture, they had an odd way of showing it. They seemed more like common criminals. Or maybe uncommon criminals. They had some kind of high-tech scam going on, something to do with trading gold. Lot 49 was a front. But what a weird front! It was hard to imagine that anyone with money or influence — Trey did say they had a very exclusive membership — would go anywhere near that war zone where it was located, regardless of what was happening inside the place or how plush and wonderful it was.

Noah had zero confidence or trust in any of these guys. But what were his options? No Joanna. Stuck in Detroit. He had nowhere to turn. No plan. Even coming here was pretty much an impulse, though it was at the urging of someone he trusted. So who did send the message from Joanna?

Trying to make sense out of any of this made his head swim.

Noah had a pizza delivered, then watched television for an hour with the sound off. It was a collage of misery and hopelessness from sea to shining sea.

Trey swung by the hotel and they arrived at Scramblers a little after ten. They made their way over to a table where sat an olive-skin, rotund, middle-age man, peering with wide-eyed ebullience through John Lennon wire-rim glasses, wearing a Nehru jacket over a white silk kurta. He looked like the Laughing Buddha guest hosting on the Home Shopping Channel.

The Swami — as he with no obvious irony called himself — was extremely congenial and high-spirited. The way the man beamed at him, Noah wondered if he was getting a suntan.

"Namaste. Bless you. We are all one with the great cosmic oneness. And I am one with the revolution."

Noah managed to keep a straight face.

"Revolution? What revolution?"

"You humor me. You insurrectionists are so very funny. My new friend. My good friend ... Vermont is absolutely lovely this time of year. Do you know this?"

"I do now."

"Such beautiful country. You will love this place. A place of peace and splendor. Holiness and love. You'll be well-treated. The guest of honor, so to speak, with a good word from me."

"You'll put in a good word for me?"

"It goes without saying."

"Why?"

"You've got the right stuff, bomber boy!"

"I've got to lay low. I'm being hunted by—"

"I'm quite aware. Your safety is paramount. Trust the Swami. You'll be fine."

Noah looked at the odd man sitting across from him. He sensed no malevolence. No hidden agenda. The Swami maybe was a little kooky but seemed genuinely trying to help. Maybe it was part of his spiritual calling to come to the aid of fugitives from the oppressive police state America was fast becoming.

Noah decided. What did he have to lose? Vermont it would be.

That evening, Noah secured an Amtrak ticket online which would take him to Albany, New York, then identified the bus service which would complete his 600+ mile journey to Brattleboro, a rustic little town in the very southeastern corner of Vermont.

Next morning, the taxi was sitting at the curb when he bounded out the door of the Inn on Ferry Street, after a barely edible breakfast of margarine and strawberry jam on white toast. He left the omelet untouched in case someone needed a tire patch.

It took only six minutes to get to the Amtrak station. Noah could have walked.

The driver, an old black guy with short grey hair and a cabby cap, turned around and collected the fare, then handed Noah an envelope.

"Some guy came up while I was sittin' back there at the hotel. I'm supposed to give this to you."

"Who? Who gave you this?"

"Didn't ask."

"What did he look like?"

"He was a white guy."

"Okay. That narrows it down a bit. But what did he look like?"

"White. All you white folks look the same to me."

With a lot of dread and very little anticipation, he opened it and read.

> *Hey! Those Detroit Tigers really suck, eh?*
> *Oh! While I'm at it, thanks for everything.*
>
> *Wyatt Grayson Tass*

Behind Closed Doors

The President was again brainstorming with his group of nerdy young advisors. They all looked mortified.

"Mr. President, do you really want an honest answer to that?"

"I take my truth straight up, Carl. Go for it."

"No repercussions?"

"No repercussions."

"I'll still have my job?"

"Goddammit! I'm a big boy. I think I can handle it. Just spit it out!"

"According to our most recent polling data, 96% of voting-age Americans think you're a complete idiot."

"Hmm. I see ... so I have an image problem."

"That would be a vast understatement, sir."

"Well thank you, Carl, for your frankness and honesty. That wasn't so bad now, was it? By the way you're fired. Just kidding, Carl. Just kidding. Now listen up, everybody. You've heard it for yourselves. Now put those thinking caps on. I want some ideas! I'm counting on you."

With that, the monthly Brain Drain session came to a close.

The President's Chief of Staff was waiting in the hall. They went two doors down to a highly secured conference room for a very special meeting.

As soon as the President stepped in the room, the Director of Internal Security and Surveillance tapped his pipe into an ashtray and smirked.

"How was the draining of the brains this time around, Mr. President?"

"Like lancing a boil." The President glanced around and made eye contact with the Deputy Director of Budgetary Planning. "I hope we're not paying them more than minimum wage."

Most everybody chuckled or choked on a self-satisfied snort.

The Secretary of the Treasury put on his best 'my-shit-doesn't-stink-but-I'm-still-just-one-of-the-boys' face for his disingenuous contribution as a stand-up comic.

"They sure don't make geniuses the way they used to."

"They sure don't, Mr. Secretary, they sure don't. So gentlemen. What have we got? What's the word?"

The Director of Homeland Security took his cue.

"Fear. The word is fear. It never fails and it's recyclable."

Another round of throaty snickering burbled through the room.

"Mr. Director, I can always count on you to state the obvious. But I sense — and please correct me if I'm wrong — I sense the country is suffering fear fatigue. For sure, everybody's pissed off, some are even certifiable. But frankly, I'm not sensing much on the fear front."

The Secretary of Defense, the only total deadpan among the nine high ranking officials and close presidential confidants in the room, spoke like he was towing a humvee using a rope he had clamped between his teeth. He was startlingly loud and commanding for someone with lockjaw.

He nodded disdainfully toward the Director of Homeland Security.

"We played that card a little too often, thanks to the one-trick ponies over at DHS. That's why we have to go cosmic."

"Cosmic? What's that supposed to mean? Angels and ghosts. Metaphysical shit."

"No, Mr. President. I meant it in the literal sense. The cosmos is a great untapped resource. An alien invasion would be perfect. But there are way too many technical issues with that."

"What are you suggesting?"

The Secretary of Defense had an annoying habit of clenching and unclenching his fist. He held it out in front of him like he was methodically working an exercise ball.

The President's and the Secretary of Defense's eyes locked. Everyone else in the room became equally riveted, listening with total fascination to what their boy Arnold Defensenneger was saying.

"I'm talking about our own cosmic event. One that we invent and have complete control over. One that we own."

"One that we own."

"Something really big."

"An event we invent. For example?"

"It's been narrowed down to three which are technically feasible with current technology. Comet, asteroid, or black hole."

"It'll be convincing?"

"It'll look so real, people will shit their pants."

"Elegantly put."

The President took a moment to think.

"My gut says go asteroid."

"That's fine. It doesn't matter which. The plot is the same. Earth is doomed. You save the planet and the human race from total annihilation ..."

"I'm liking this."

"... and we're performing our patriotic duty in the process. This country is coming apart. Citizens are at one another's throats, isolated, angry, disunited. We will bring them together with a shared sense of fear, then a shared sense of pride. America will be united again. America will be strong again."

"And I'll get re-elected."

CHAPTER TEN

The Best Intentions

Things were so bad most everyone agreed it couldn't get any worse.

They were wrong.

It started on Monday August 26th when the stock market fell 2829 points.

Three days later the unemployment statistics came out. There had been a modest and hopeful signs of improvement every month for the prior three months. But the government's official rate of unemployment shot back up 9.7 points, putting it up over 21% — 21.6% to be exact. This shook the shaken financial markets, which already resembled a bag of limestone fragments from so much shaking.

It became a feedback loop, a death spiral. Business owners didn't see much point in hiring if no one had any money. And the fewer people who had jobs, the fewer had money, even for the basics of survival. As one owner of a lawn mower and gardening tools manufacturing plant in Cleveland put it: "If people can't even feed themselves, I'm not anticipating much of a demand for hedge trimmers." He had just laid off all of his 263 employees.

This was just the beginning. The gods of catastrophe were just getting warmed up.

Four days later, the unthinkable and presumed impossible happened. The USS Ronald Reagan and the USS Harry S. Truman — not one, but TWO of the most valuable aircraft carriers in the American naval fleet — were sunk, clearly by terrorists, though no specific insurgent group stepped forward to take credit. Since the instantaneous and simultaneous sinking of these seemingly invulnerable craft was inconceivable, there was no workable system in place to save the crews. Only a handful of crew members miraculously survived, meaning over 9,000 were at the bottom of the ocean somewhere between Australia and Japan, along with 180,000 tons of metal, 152 aircraft, and hundreds of millions of dollars of the most sophisticated electronic warfare, navigation, intelligence, counterintelligence, surveillance and computing equipment in the world.

Then on September 9th, the largest such failure in history shut down 96% of the electrical grid serving the eastern seaboard, plunging most of the original thirteen colonies and much of Florida, Tennessee, and Ohio into primeval chaos. Life was as it was when these territories were being settled back in the 17th century. At night, viewed from outer space, the blackout was so complete it looked like a third of the United States had vanished. This went on for four days. Everything was shut down. All air traffic cancelled. People didn't even drive their autos. Without external power only a bare minimum of emergency communications survived. Thus, effectively the whole region was shrouded in a news blackout, leaving much of America wondering about the fate of their fellow Americans on the East Coast.

If this wasn't bad enough, that same week enormous quantities of both beef and chicken were found to be contaminated with E. Coli and had to be recalled and destroyed. 1,493 tons of the red meat and 2,804 tons of poultry, mostly heading for fast food outlets throughout America, had picked up the bacteria at meat processing plants scattered across the South and Southwest. Incinerating it created a plume that looked like Mt. St. Helens had erupted again. The smell of barbecue that enveloped the planet would have caused noses of dogs on Mars to twitch.

This all looked like child's play compared to something that had been steadily building to a mega-crisis over the past few weeks, and culminated in totally freeze drying the consumer economy.

It was a phenomenon that impacted just about everything at every level in America.

Gold had just surpassed $22,000 per ounce. Since the U.S. by far possessed the largest gold reserves in the world, it was now theoretically the richest nation by a considerable margin. Its new currency was directly tied by law to gold. People could slam those new orange bills on the counter knowing that this was not some worthless piece of paper. It represented real wealth.

Thus it appeared that the move to the gold standard was genius, pure and simple.

Unfortunately, something occurred which the big brains of economic theory that had inaugurated the new policy had not anticipated.

Most of the major commodities on the international markets, regardless of where they were produced, had for decades been bought and sold in U.S. dollars, the acronym for which was USD. The USD was the de facto common currency of the entire world for all international financial transactions.

When the U.S. government adopted the new orange money, backed of course by the full faith and credit of America itself plus a shitload of gold, it confiscated and outlawed its original currency, the old green Federal Reserve notes. It completely abandoned the USD.

The rest of the world, however, did no such thing. 99% of money is virtual anyway, not a physical thing. Money mostly exists digitally as debits and credits in electronic transactions and as electronic entries on spreadsheets across the vast virtual economies of the world's banking system. Just because the USD was no longer being printed and no longer in use within America itself, it didn't go away. It continued to exist on the books and continued to be the preferred monetary unit of exchange for trillions of dollars of transactions each day.

A truly unanticipated and catastrophic thing then followed. In order to conduct its business, the U.S. literally had to buy on the international currency market its old abandoned U.S. dollars. This was not merely awkward. It was a monumental calamity! It became a swan dive into financial Armageddon. As economists and investors alike watched, the value of the USO against the USD plunged lower and lower with each new day of business. No one knew why. It just did.

The result was it was now officially trading on currency markets at over 5 to 1.

That meant that oil which was priced at $86 USD per barrel was costing American buyers almost $450 in orange money.

It was the same across the board. Wheat. Soybeans. Wool. Coffee. Steel. Everything!

The impact was swift and devastating.

Nobody could afford anything.

Except maybe the twelve or so items that were still actually manufactured here. Not that anyone could remember what they were.

Consumers were in shock. Or livid. Usually both.

A 6 ounce bag of generic drip coffee was $28. That was *on sale!* A loaf of bread for many people started showing up on their wish lists where a Mercedes Benz used to sit. Anything with chocolate in it and you needed an escort of armed guards to safely get it from the checkout counter to your car. Fill up the old gas tank and you were looking at a collateralized loan. Some new Nike's manufactured in Malaysia? Forget about it. It was more than anyone could afford just buying a roll of electrical tape to fix their old sneakers.

If this continued, people would be taking out second mortgages on their houses just to drive to the supermarket for a half bag of groceries.

Orange money?

Back to the gold standard?

It seemed like a good idea at the time.

The tragedy? In a modern economy there are no do overs.

The truly astounding thing was that the country didn't at this point erupt in revolution.

Then again …

Maybe no one could afford the bullets.

Green Tambourine

The nearly total breakdown of society was practically all the media talked about. In a tsunami of violent, bloody, tortuous, painful and frightening reportage, news about the details of the latest incidents, stories, statistics, diagnosis, prognosis, official reaction, unofficial reaction, public reaction, predictions on what horrifying thing could top the last horrifying thing, news of the newest horrifying thing, comparison of this horrifying thing to previous horrifying things, it was everywhere. Then it was posted all over the internet, linked and shared, reposted, on and on. The internet itself had practically come to a crawl from the overload of appalling accounts of disaster and dysfunction.

But in spite of all of that, Noah could see from the moment he arrived in the quiet, charming New England town of Brattleboro, tucked away as it was in semi-seclusion, relatively shielded from the massive brawl going on in the rest of America, things here were very different.

The pace in Vermont was markedly slower, more thoughtful, more introspective, certainly not given over to fashion and fad thinking, or frivolous chinwag, at least when it came to the things that really mattered. The bandwagon in Vermont was reserved for the band, so people didn't jump on and off every time the tune changed.

This was even more the norm at Green Tambourine, Noah's new temporary home.

Forty five years ago, Cynthia Magelin had been a member of the one-hit-wonder band the Lemonpipers, briefly quite popular for an infectious, if rather enigmatic pop song. She was the mandolin player. After the group's meteoric rise to fame, and equally meteoric fall to oblivion, Cynthia started an arts cooperative in her hometown of Brattleboro. She named it Green Tambourine after the hit song that had made her a notable, if fleeting beneficiary of fame and fortune. Her royalties were certainly enough to give her little art project a nice start. Sadly, as an organization promoting psychedelic and grass roots painting and sculpture, Green Tambourine never took off. So after a few unprofitable years, she shifted her focus to her lifelong love of stringed instruments. Onstage she played acoustic guitar and mandolin, but her serious musical study, which started when she was four and continued through college, was classical violin.

Cynthia loved everything about the violin, a romance which extended with almost equal affection for its siblings — viola, cello, and double bass. While her dream had been eventually to perform with a symphony orchestra, too many years passed and her musical chops had atrophied. By her mid-30s, it was out of the question. Instead she started to collect and refurbish violins. Often after restoring them, she donated them to local schools. She also did maintenance and repair on guitars, banjos, mandolins, lutes, zithers, ukuleles, dobros and harps, generating more than enough income to keep the doors open. She had a natural gift for the painstaking, delicate work required to transform the most beat up calamity into a beautiful and playable instrument.

Over the years her reputation as a connoisseur of quality stringed instruments and master craftsman at repairing and restoring them grew and eventually flourished. Green Tambourine now regularly received work from the best string musicians in the world. The Boston Symphony and New York Philharmonic would not consider having anyone else touch their instruments. She now had 17 employees, most of whom she had trained herself. Each had a specialty which he or she continued to perfect. Paul was the bridge man and was backlogged with requests from all over the world. Margo did tuning pegs. Casey worked on fine tuners and tailpieces. Ginger could be seen leaning over her eight month pregnant belly to sand and finish the finger boards. Gil and Dench shared the difficult task of taking apart the instruments and doing crucial structural repair and modifications to the innards. Dora did the purfing and any required aesthetic touches to the sound holes and scrolls.

The crowning moment to date occurred last year when two of the world's rarest and most prized violins arrived for some minor but necessary touch-ups. A *Stradivarius* valued at almost $2 million and a *del Gesù* made in the early 18th Century by Giuseppe Guarneri — which had just sold at a Sotheby's auction for $3.8 million — were hand-carried and accompanied by a very solemn contingent of armed guards who never once smiled the ten days they were there.

The prized instruments were repaired, polished and packed for their return journey.

Noah spent his first week there completely mesmerized.

What a unique and fascinating world this was.

Violins! He had never given them a second thought.

Cynthia was cordial and generous. Noah could not have felt more comfortable. Slowly, he was introduced to the range of duties and specialties being performed by the incredibly skilled craftspersons there, even given a few simple tasks which carried little risk of catastrophe on his part. He helped refinish a couple folk guitars and a dobro.

The staff was a much older crowd than Noah had ever experienced on a daily basis. The youngest was Louise at 35, the oldest Carmichael who was 72. Cynthia was 66.

It was also by far the most intelligent, well-informed, articulate, politically aware, philosophically sophisticated, and emotionally stable group of people he had ever encountered.

Noah was given a comfortable room on the third floor of the main house, a good old-fashioned farm dwelling shaped like a barn. He stayed with Cynthia and her live-in boyfriend Charlie, who with his perfect pitch and music-god level of aural acuity made him Green Tambourine's in-house tuning expert.

None of the rest of the staff lived there. It wasn't a commune or hippie community of artisans. They all had families and lived their small-town lives independently of Green Tambourine. This didn't mean they treated their work there as a mere job. They were devoted to Cynthia and the lifelong fulfillment of her dream. On her end, she had created the ideal work place. The workshops, though set up as partitioned rooms in a barn, were clean and comfortable in every possible way. Beautiful posters and art prints hung on the barn walls. Wonderful music of every variety was played softly over an excellent high-end stereo system. Selections of music rotated to accommodate the wide range of tastes and included jazz, folk, R&B, blues, rock and even pop. The single restriction was that the Lemon Pipers big namesake hit, "Green Tambourine", never be aired. It wasn't that Cynthia hated the song, it was merely she had played it onstage over two thousand times and just couldn't stomach listening to it again.

As if the place could have been more enchanting than it already was, there was another aspect to operations which made it the sweet sticky stuff of hometown charm.

Brattleboro, Vermont was the marmalade capital of New England. In addition to five main marmalade factories, it seemed like everyone there was bottling the stuff for their own private enjoyment. Over the years, an unspoken competition drove the race to not only make the best marmalade, but come up with the weirdest flavors. Of course, the cornerstones were orange and cranberry-orange. But also on the shelves around town were such oddities as tomato, mango chutney, jalapeno pepper, kale and kiwi, and fire-roasted marma-lava. It was anyone's guess what that last one was. Volcanic ash?

Cynthia prided herself in making some of the best traditional marmalades and one that had become her trademark, lemon-peel apple. Often Noah's contribution there was labeling the bottles, stocking the store, and helping Cynthia fill hundreds of internet orders for Green Tambourine Home-Style Marmalade.

Sweet topping for toast and breakfast rolls aside, the raison d'être and energizing core which commanded 90% of everyone's attention and 100% of their dedication, remained the string instruments. Noah was passed around the workshop, an itinerant in training, to pick up what he could of the special skills of each individual contributor.

He worked on bridges and tuning pegs, sanded and applied lacquer, filed the sound holes and fingerboards, carved the scrolls. He chiseled away inner bracings and helped glue new ones in place.

Everyone was so patient, so visibly enamored with and proud of their work, so excited to teach the new young man what they could, then give him a chance to do what he could. It was inspiring. But truthfully, every time Noah was set up to attempt some new task, it scared him to death. He would look at the beautiful instruments and easily imagine them splintering into a worthless pile of scrap as soon as he touched them.

Everyone was pleasantly supportive and always encouraged him just to try, just do his best, displaying much more confidence in him than Noah thought was warranted. He learned by doing, gradually felt increasingly self-assured, and overall experienced a greater sense of accomplishment than ever before in his life.

Each and every individual at Green Tambourine was interesting, but there was one gentleman who was a real character.

Brodie was the finish and chip repair guy. He was as funny as he was goofy looking. His beard was braided, his two top front teeth were gold capped — somehow he had managed to avoid them being confiscated by the government. He always wore big baggy overalls and a plaid flannel farmer shirt, even in the summer. He was famous for misspeaking, specifically choosing a similar sounding but wrong word for the intended meaning. It provided more than its share of laughs. The group called them Brodieisms and everybody had a favorite.

"If God intended fish to fry, He wouldn't have given them gills."

"Hey, could I bum one of those mint tar cigarettes?"

"Like they say: Life's just a chair of bowlies."

"It's as plain as the day on your face."

"I'm on a low carbon monoxide diet."

"That girl's got a posterior motive."

"I think clarity begins at home."

This kind of frivolity coupled with the intense and satisfying work repairing the musical instruments set the tone and made Green Tambourine as a very special place indeed. The pleasant purposefulness was in some ways remindful of working at Habitat and his time at None of Your Beeswax. But here it seemed less forced, simply more natural and wholesome.

What struck Noah as both fascinating and puzzling was that there didn't appear to be any political work going on here. It wasn't a front for anything. It was what it was. String instrument repair and delectable marmalade. This was quite a departure from every place he had been sent so far. Anything connected through IOU previously had had an intense insurrectionist bent, in spirit if not in action.

Without a doubt, these folks were liberals. Liberals leaning much further left than most mainstream liberals. There frequently were some very intense political discussions. But they just blended right in with the ongoing chatter — exchanges that covered a whole range of topics, philosophy, cosmology, ethics, world religions, dance, music, art. They certainly never explicitly talked about overthrowing the government. Generally the folks at Green Tambourine were more about the quality of life in America and what had to be done to rescue it, than punishing those who had messed it up. They were more about building up than tearing down.

Everyone definitely agreed that while their own lives there in Brattleboro were fantastic, they were among the dwindling exceptions. Most Americans had it hard and recent history had put onerous demands on their lives, creating a state of panic and paranoia throughout most of the country. Nevertheless, criticism of the government stopped far short of hostile acts of sabotage.

This left Noah confused about how he ended up here. After all, his being sent to Green Tambourine was the bastard child of drug-addled Lot 49 and the sordid and surly Scramblers. He still could make no sense out of Element and his band of lowlife thugs. Were they the dark outer fringe of IOU? Frankly, they seemed entirely apolitical, completely preoccupied with dropping acid and making money.

And what about the Swami? Where did he fit in? He claimed to be an advocate for the revolution, but Noah would just have to take his word on that. While sending Noah to Green Tambourine was a phenomenal and fortuitous gesture, unless he was missing something, this place had nothing to do with either IOU or revolution.

One day at lunch, Noah was relaxing in the kitchen eating a turkey sandwich he had just made for himself. Cynthia walked in. Smiling. She was always smiling.

"Hey, Cynthia. Excuse me for being so direct. But I don't get what this place has to do with revolution. You guys hardly seem to be mounting an insurrection."

"Revolution! Green Tambourine?"

"The Indian swami said he's one with the revolution. Then he sent me here."

Cynthia went from smiling to laughing.

"You mean Clark? He's not Indian."

"But he was all dressed up—"

"He's such a character. Clark is Italian. I think he's Italian. Anyway, he's from Idaho. I went to high school with him. We had this 60s band. Played at school dances."

"So you're not planning the overthrow of the government?"

"Look around you. Does this look like some terrorist camp? Clark called me and said you were in trouble. That a lot of people want to kill you."

"You take in complete strangers? Guys in the crosshairs?"

"Just the nice ones."

Fool on the Hill

Spit sputtered and sprayed from his bulbous pickled fish lips like melted butter from a clogged turkey baster, as Congressman Hayley Tullman Schutt, Dixiecrat from the "great state of Mississippi" wound up his five minutes of allotted time on the House floor during the continuing debate on a Democrats-sponsored bill to extend federal funding of education to troubled urban areas of the country. There were no more than 20 people in the chambers at the time but representative Schutt — 'Tully' as he was called by his friends — carried on like he had the ears of the entire nation cocked and hanging on his every word. Despite his enthusiasm, most of the hundred or so viewers of C-Span had used his speech as the perfect opportunity to take a bathroom break, check their email, or throw in another load of laundry.

"Late me ayusk you all this. Wuzzit dey been teachin' im dese gawdless schools anyways? Jes wut, huh? Whale eye-ul tail yuz jes wut! Wah it's wut cane mayuk a good mayun sick to hayuz stomuck, no layus."

Congressman Schutt went on as he always did, decrying the teaching of evolution, lack of Bible studies and prayer in public schools, and the inclusion of such atheistic anti-American subjects in school curriculums across the country as science, ethnic studies, world history, foreign languages, sex education, and the repair and maintenance of "dayum Jay-up co-erz" in auto mechanics classes.

He was perhaps the most ignorant, provincial, xenophobic, superstitious, narrow-minded person to ever hold public office at a federal level. But the voters had made their choice. Several times, in fact, in that he was serving his eighth consecutive term as a congressman.

As counterintuitive as it might seem, considering how thoroughly the 'duh factor' ruled his higher brain functions, he had through his own ruthless self-promotion and the arcane rules of seniority operating in Congress, recently won the prestigious and powerful position on the House Defense Appropriations Committee as its chairperson. This made him the key congressional player on all matters related to the military, its technologies, as well as research, development and deployment of its resources. Most importantly it gave him nearly unlimited access to the most secretive projects and initiatives related to the security of the nation.

He needed to wrap up today's political grandstanding quickly. Congressman Schutt had just before mounting the podium received a formal, extremely high priority request to report to the White House as soon as possible on a matter of utmost urgency.

"Mayuh Gawd blayuss 'mairkah."

As he stepped into the Oval Office, the President leaped to his feet and came around his huge desk to shake the legislator's hand like he was working a hydraulic car jack.

"Thank you, Congressman Schutt for coming on such short notice. Let's skip the small talk and get right down to business. My esteemed colleague, we are in some deep shit."

The President went on to talk about the current horrible state of the union, the evidence of social decay, the economic decline which had gutted the country's job market, how everything they had been doing seemed to backfire; how terrorists were lurking behind every door; how individual and national fortunes were under assault by a hostile world; and to add some special personalized cajolery to his rant, how the nation was becoming godless and neglecting the fundamental truths of the Bible.

Having said all of that, the President made it clear his real concern basically came down to the critical matter of the elections which were only three months away. He and all of the Democrats were going to face a real uphill battle if something dramatic didn't happen soon.

"Let me put it this way, congressman. From everything I'm being told by my staff of very able political analysts, it looks like we're going to get an ass-kicking of Biblical proportions."

But the POTUS — with the generous assistance of his highly creative staff — had a plan.

"So all I'm asking you, Congressman, is to listen to what I have to say, draw your own conclusions, and as one of the most important men in the nation, if not the free world, do what you have to do."

"Ah buh-leeve, Mr. Prayzdent, we playuh fo the sayum tame."

Yes and no. As the militant conservative that Schutt was, he was a Democrat in name only and voted more often than not with the Republicans. In fact as a southern

Democrat he was practically indistinguishable from the far right wing of the Republican Party.

The glaring exception was in matters of national security, where he was in perfect lockstep with anyone on either side of the aisle who wanted more guns and bombs, pushed for bigger and better wars, was inclined to deploy American troops and military know-how to solve any and all diplomatic conflicts, and was generally willing to show the rest of the world America was the bad ass in charge of the entire known universe.

"Congressman, this is one of those times in history when we need to step up to the plate."

The President then laid out his plan.

Sort of.

"I'm about to make an announcement that will fundamentally change the equation. I'm about to tell the American public that there is an asteroid the size of Omaha, Nebraska headed our way. This asteroid is so big that if — and that *is* the important word here, congressman — *if* this thing hits, it will destroy the world and kill every one.

"Yore ah sayun dat a big hunk ah rock is haydun our waya?"

"Not quite. I'm saying that I'm going to *announce* to the American public that a big hunk of rock is heading our way. I see this as a terrific opportunity. As you know, and largely because of your unwavering support for the development of our vast long-range missile and nuclear technology, we are at the end of the day the only nation capable of stopping such a big hunk of rock. *We* can get the job done. I'd say the entire world, and in particular the registered voters of this country would be pretty happy to hear that, wouldn't you?"

Then he winked.

The congressman saw the wink and nodded. Then he winked back.

The President winked and nodded again, leaned back in his chair and smiled.

The congressman winked again. And nodded.

Then *he* leaned back and broke out in an all-knowing grin.

Of course, Congressman Schutt had no idea what all the winking and nodding was about. But he sure as hell wasn't going to let on. Something was going down. There were things that were so hush hush, not even the President could say out loud what they were. The congressman himself had been in meetings like this before. Winking and nodding were all you could do without jeopardizing the security of the mission and the survival of the country.

Maybe he didn't know all of the details here. But one thing he did know: The President had performed his constitutional duty by confiding in him. Good strong government, especially in matters of such urgency and momentous historical impact, was about one hand shaking the other. It was about the men at the helm of state, the men who wielded the power vested in them by the people, men like the President and himself, doing what needed to be done.

By God in Heaven he would do it!

"Maystir Prezdint. You hayuv ma fool soo-poht. Ah tha-yunk you fer layten me know."

"God bless this great nation, congressman! We will prevail."

Every Wednesday evening was very special. It was a longstanding tradition to have the whole Green Tambourine crew gather in Cynthia's living room starting around six, for an evening of good food, fine wine, wonderful weed, and marvelous merriment.

Tonight the festivities would be augmented by what had been billed during the past two weeks by the White House PR staff as a historic announcement by the President, one which would impact every human being on the planet.

Most everyone in the country by now was extremely jaded to such grand hyperbole. The folks here were even more cynical than most. But the consensus was, what the hell? They would be together anyway, so they might just as well join millions of Americans watch the guy make a fool of himself. Whatever the big announcement was, it was sure to provide a comic nightcap to an evening of camaraderie and general silliness.

As was usual on Wednesdays, when everyone strolled in, they were greeted by a table piled with hot and cold dishes which by any measure were a gastronomical delight. Salads, fruits, fresh vegetables, mashed potatoes, chicken, roast beef, ham, dinner rolls, croissants, pies and puddings, and of course, several varieties of Cynthia's marmalades. To wash all this down was lemonade, iced tea, coffee, wine, and a several custom beers from local micro-breweries.

Once the chowing had run its course, and the imbibing began in earnest, Brodie and Gil took turns on acoustic guitar. Everyone sang along to rollicking renditions of Chuck Berry's "Roll Over Beethoven" and the Beatles' "I Wanna Hold Your Hand", then crooned to Pete Seeger's "This Land Is Your Land" and Elvis Presley's "Love Me Tender". Brodie's version of "Itsy Bitsy Teenie Weenie Yellow Polka Dot Bikini" with Casey and Ginger on fiddles got everyone up dancing and soon Cynthia and Louise were trying to teach Noah how to square dance.

When 8 o'clock approached, Cynthia yelled out over the music.

"Alright. Time to see what our prez has up his sleeve."

Carmichael grabbed the remote and clicked on the TV, as everyone settled themselves in the overstuffed chairs or on the floor facing the large flat-panel screen.

They waited, talked, laughed. The President's address was delayed a few minutes, without any explanation. There was just a night shot of the outside of the White House. A disco version of the "Star Spangled Banner" played softly in the background.

Noah made a quick trip to the bathroom, then rejoined the gang. As if they needed any encouragement, the wine and beer had loosened their tongues even more than usual, and the wise cracks were flying.

Casey: "Why are we watching this?"

Cynthia: "Because we're masochists."

Louise: "I wonder what story he's going to read tonight."

Carmichael: "I hear he's going to sing some Roy Orbison songs."

Ginger: "I'm sure this is very important. Like that time in the Rose Garden with the leadership of both houses of Congress, when he signed the bill that set a legal limit on the number of items in an express checkout lane at eight."

Gil: "Or the time he stood on the steps of the Supreme Court with the Postmaster General and announced that lickable postage stamps would now come in four flavors. Peppermint, tutti frutti, vanilla shake, and tequila sunrise."

Brodie: "That guy's a one-armed wallpaper hanger and his hunting dog is sniffing the glue."

Everybody: "What?"

Finally, the deep sonorous voice of the announcer declared, "Ladies and gentlemen, the President of the United States."

For many months now, in a lame and ineffective attempt to put a smiley face on the unfolding catastrophes and rampant chaos, in all his public appearances, the President always appeared upbeat and breezy. Understandably, considering the dismal state of the nation, this psychology totally backfired and he just looked frivolous, out of touch, merely creating the impression that the leader of the most powerful country in the world was a modern day Nero, fiddling away, callously or stupidly choosing to ignore the obvious fact that his Rome was turning to cinders all around him.

Tonight, however, the President looked solemn, bordering on macabre. He was almost scary.

"My fellow Americans and everyone joining me tonight all across the planet. I wish I could say I was coming to you tonight to give some breathtaking good news. Unfortunately, I bear perhaps the most somber message a person in my position has ever had to deliver to his fellow man.

Every year, there is a dazzling display in the evening skies around the beginning of November. Anyone looking up sees flashing trails of light streaking across the starry dome as tiny little meteorites, some only the size of the head of a pin, enter the atmosphere and burn up. We call this a meteor shower and there are several each year at various times. They are as harmless as they are entertaining, just the Earth sweeping in its orbit around the sun through some dusty regions of the solar system.

This year things are different. Drastically, frighteningly different. Using optical, radar and high-resolution infrared and ultraviolet imaging telescopes, astronomers at Mauna Kea in Hawaii and NASA data collection facilities monitoring earth-orbit astronomical satellites, have determined that a massive asteroid has joined the micro-particles in this region, posing an unparalleled threat, literally one of Biblical proportions, to this year's encounter. Our scientists have determined the location and course of this enormous object.

I don't how to put this gently or diplomatically. So I will just tell it like it is. The asteroid, almost exactly the size of Omaha, Nebraska has a trajectory which will put it directly in the path of the Earth in a little under two months. The date and point of impact have been determined. It will smash into our planet, in fact, into our very own nation, on November 3rd of this year. As it approaches and tracking devices get a better handle on the object, we will actually know to the minute, the exact time it will strike the surface.

The center of impact will be Knoxville, Tennessee, though to be so precise is meaningless, since most of the eastern half of the U.S. will be a crater of fused geological debris, the entire North American continent will be destroyed, and life on the planet for the next two hundred years will no longer be sustainable.

This object is predominantly made of iron and nickel. It is enormous but dark as space itself. Like many objects in our vast Universe, it has no internal source of illumination. Therefore, it won't be visible to the naked eye. Only the most-powerful space-based telescopes and special non-optical imaging instruments can see and track this mammoth chunk of rock. But it's there. And we are watching it as it proceeds on its collision course with our planet. What is at stake here is nothing less than the survival of the human race.

The best scientific minds of this great nation are meeting as I speak, to see what can be done to save the planet from this horrible catastrophe, or at least try to reduce the scope of its consequences. If it is any consolation, there are already proposals which seem plausible and modestly promising. But I'm a realist. I am not inclined to wishful thinking. As President, I owe it to you to never offer false hope or feel-good fantasies. Our lives and the future of all mankind are on the line here. I will always treat you with the dignity and respect you deserve, by telling you the truth, the whole truth, and nothing but the truth. Just know this. We are doing all that we possibly can. God be with us all. Good-night and God bless America!"

Gil muted the television, but everyone just continued to stare at the TV screen.
For the next few minutes, the room was filled with a deathly silence.
Finally Carmichael broke the spell …
"I wonder what's on HBO tonight."
Next day, Noah was taking a break from doing not much of anything, more often than not his typical daily work load, notwithstanding all of the praise and gratitude they always heaped on him for his excellent work. Cynthia had put out strawberry lemonade and a huge platter of English muffins with her famous lemon-peel apple marmalade. Noah was sitting under the workshop veranda when Brodie joined him.
"So, young man, what's your take on the comet thing?"
"Comet? Comet is my bathroom cleanser of choice. Golly. It disinfects while it cleans. Bathtub rings. Shit stickies. Hot damn, it's great in the kitchen too! Although caution is advised. Because of its intrinsic abrasiveness, it can dull the finish of even the hardest porcelain surface."
Bubbles of giggling set Brody's jelly belly into a good-natured roll. He was like a Jerry Garcia version of Yoda on nitrous oxide.
"You got me there. I guess it's an asterisk, right?"

"I think you mean asteroid."

"That's what I said. Well since you're not talkin', let me give you some Brodie instincts on the situation. I'm an old man, in case you couldn't tell."

"How old are you, Brodie?"

"I'm 62. Or is it 59? Up there somewhere. Anyway. I've always had a simple and straightforward credo. If everyone lived by this, we wouldn't be in the skim milk we're in right now."

"I'm a young guy. So I am always looking for good advice from someone like yourself who's been there and seen life from the belly up."

"You sure talk weird. Is this the way everyone your age expresses themselves?"

"I grew up in Missouri."

"You have my hard felt condalliances. So here it is. Ready? I always say … wear a raincoat if you're gonna piss into the wind."

Noah wanted to laugh. But maybe he was serious.

"I see. That's Socrates, right?"

Brodie looked at Noah in mock disbelief.

"Why, no! That's Testiclese."

Then Brodie started laughing so hard Noah feared his overalls might split down the middle.

Noah glanced around. Everyone was grinning ear-to-ear.

Aah! Another of Brodie's gotchas.

That summed up life and the good people there at Green Tambourine.

Good people. Concerned people. Caring people. People who might be horrified at what was becoming of their beloved country, worried that if the Earth did survive, what kind of life they were passing down to the next generation and the next generation after that. But people who remembered how to laugh.

Noah's only regret was that he had not grown up around anyone like this in his own community. They were everything that Pulnickians weren't. The folks at Green Tambourine were that special minority that lived in small cells sparsely scattered across the vast stretches contained by the nation's borders. They didn't make the headlines because they weren't outrageous, perverted, out of control, grotesque, violent, egomaniacal, ultra rich, or inclined to hysteria for its own sake.

They were the real thing. They were the hope. They were the promissory note which if the world came to its senses and chose to redeem, would deliver a better planet and a better variant of humankind.

A Yawn of Cosmic Proportions

The media was in a feeding frenzy. An asteroid destroying the earth and taking out the entire human race? Whoa! Talk about some serious shit! This was way better than a politician Twittering photos of his genitals or a runway model having calking compound injected to firm up her butt. The headlines leaped off the page.

President Says World Will End In Three Months!

Playbook To Close On Human Race!

Whole Planet Doomed!

The broadcast news stations were beside themselves.

Moments after the President finished his live address, reporters with their camera crew in tow were out and about everywhere to capture for live television the panic, the screaming, the weeping, the hysteria, the wrenching lunacy, to pump it all out live for viewing audiences to get their next fix of tittle-tattle shit-storm cracked-skull adrenalin. Microphone in hand, the scandal-mongers swarmed about like locusts, from parks to parking lots, from ticket lines to taxi stands, on sidewalks, in the middle of the street. They were on a coast-to-coast scavenger hunt for the anticipated mental breakdown of the American public. Much to their surprise and disappointment, they came up pretty empty handed.

A reporter in California was working the pedestrian mall in Santa Monica.

"What do you think about the President's announcement?"

"Whatever."

"How about you, young lady?"

"Same ol' same ol'."

"And you, sir."

"There's no business like show business."

"Madame?"

"Who's the president now?"

One reporter was stopping people in the street in front of Reading Terminal Market, downtown Philadelphia.

"Scientists say we will all be dead soon. Are you afraid of dying?"

"You should be. There's a bus heading right for you."

The simple fact was that the immediate and unequivocal reaction to the President's dramatic announcement about the asteroid was no reaction at all.

Apparently no one believed him.

Or if they did, they didn't give a damn.

Maybe folks were looking at the bright side.

They were totally fed up and the asteroid would put them out of their misery.

A small vocal minority who were either pathologically paranoid or *always* inclined to believe that the world was about to end — often both — seized on the opportunity to hysterically yell, 'WE TOLD YOU SO!'

But the vast majority who were against all odds still sane, just didn't want to hear it. They had had their fill of noise and nonsense. They either told the doomsday loonies to shut the fuck up or just cranked up the volume on their iPods and hummed along to Katy Perry.

No matter how you diced it, it was very very weird.

Day after day, everyone merely went about their business as usual.

Administration officials were completely baffled. They had braced themselves for the worst, expecting at least tectonic gnashing of teeth or volcanic outpourings of grief on a national scale, or in the worst case scenario, mass rioting and general mayhem, as people confronted their dramatically truncated mortality and the brief time remaining for them on the planet. But in terms of the asteroid, a calm denial prevailed.

To try to grease the wheels of trepidation and dread, the President even leaned on NASA to issue a press release to make sure everyone had heard him correctly.

PRESS RELEASE – September 8, 2016
National Aeronautics and Space Administration
(NASA), Washington DC

Scientists here at NASA in conjunction with respected astronomers and astrophysicists with expertise in keeping track of the natural and manmade objects which inhabit our solar system, and even more importantly those which traverse the region which the Earth occupies in orbiting the sun, have issued an official alert regarding a grave threat to America and the entire planet. They have checked and rechecked their highly sophisticated calculations and there is no doubt in this matter. An enormous asteroid almost the exact size of Omaha, Nebraska is headed directly for the Earth and will with 100% certainty impact our nation in one month and twenty six days. Experts tasked with monitoring the object have not fixed the exact time for this catastrophic collision, but it will occur the evening of Wednesday, November 3rd.

Still there was little reaction.

The nation continued to collectively break into a big yawn.

Maybe it was like a rubber band. The public's credulity had just been stretched too many times and just wasn't going to snap back anymore.

Or maybe it was like the President had observed when they first discussed the idea of the asteroid hoax. People were suffering fear fatigue.

Whatever the explanation, it was clear that the public no longer looked to political leaders or anyone in government for the truth. They now only depended on others they still trusted, like that nice man on the Home Shopping Channel with the great deals, or the people just like themselves in infomercials who found products they honestly liked, or the judges on *Dancing With The Stars* who weren't afraid to tell it like it is.

Thank goodness there were still some honest individuals around!

CHAPTER ELEVEN

The Empire Strikes Back

It was pure impulse.

Now a simple act which was as innocent as it was casual had produced a nightmare.

Noah had been in his room settling in for the night but felt a bit thirsty. He slipped quietly down the old staircase, careful not to wake Cynthia or her boyfriend.

On his way through the living room, heading toward the kitchen for a nice glass of fresh-squeezed orange juice, Noah had picked up the remote and clicked on the TV. Frankly he hated television and rarely watched, making this impulse even more random.

Now he stood there. Immobile. Paralyzed. In shock.

The TV was tuned to CNN. Wolf Blitzer was talking on the phone with some unnamed government official from the Department of Internal Security & Surveillance.

Wolf Blitzer: "You say this has been going on for some time."

DISS Official: "This is a huge and well-organized terrorist army. We had to keep this under wraps in order to assure a successful completion of the mission. But now that we've got the upper hand, I'm authorized to tell you a little about what's we've accomplished. We busted a lot of the satellite operations. One was some punks near our research facility at Area 51 in Nevada, led by a deranged former army colonel. We killed three PETA eco-terrorists in a fierce gun battle, who were bent on destroying a fur farm near Florence, South Dakota. We also rounded up some wackos who were planning on hijacking an ICBM in North Dakota to start World War III."

They cut to video footage of a siege on Quicksilver's house. Heavily armored and armed soldiers were firing machine guns, shooting tear gas canisters through the broken windows, storming inside and dragging the beaten occupants out, handcuffing them on the ground. At one point, Quicksilver can be seen being lifted unconscious, head drenched in blood, onto a gurney, then wheeled to a waiting military ambulance.

Wolf Blitzer: "These were hard-core domestic terrorists, then."

DISS Official: "Vicious to the core. No respect for property or privacy. We now have in custody cyber saboteurs who, if you can believe this, had as a front a bee farm."

On screen it showed the Queen and her "drones" being shoved and manhandled, then marched toward a prisoner transport bus. The Queen is crying so hard she can't walk, so three beefy soldiers are half-carrying, half-dragging her.

Wolf Blitzer: "We're looking at actual footage now of the ATF/FBI raid on that bee farm. You can see the huge computer facility they had underground. What kind of illegal activities were being carried out here?"

DISS Official: "Everything you can imagine having to do with computers. Breaking into bank accounts, stealing money, shutting down web sites, posting pornography on legitimate corporate web pages. Stealing credit cards. Attempting to compromise national security, unsuccessfully I might add, by infiltrating and sabotaging government computer networks. The list goes on and on."

Wolf Blitzer: "So fill us in now about a recent incident, one involving a suspect you have been trying to capture for several years. Perhaps the #1 cyber terrorist of the past decade."

DISS Official: "The suspect had been terminated. We don't know who killed him. We found his body laying in the desert, in Nevada."

Pain shot through Noah like he was being stabbed. Oh my god! No …

Wolf Blitzer: "Your agents just happened to be walking through a remote part of the Nevada desert and stumbled on the body?"

DISS Official: "You're a real comedian, Wolf. No, some local yocal found him. Maybe the guy was riding his burro or doing some snake hunting. He reported it to his county sheriff's office and they called us."

Noah's worst fears were being realized on screen. The eerie green glow of a night vision camera zoomed in on a body laying in the desert. There was a dark stain from the pool of blood that had seeped into the sand around the victim's head. His hair was matted and caked with slimy clots, his face twisted in the agony of a final cry of anguish, but there was no doubt about it. It was Tim.

Wolf Blitzer: "You then flew immediately out to investigate. You guys don't fool around. There must have been something which made this such a high priority."

DISS Official: "You could say that. This kid could've been of enormous value to us. He had only been dead for 24 hours. If he was who we believe him to be, he was the genius behind the most sophisticated domestic cyber terror system in the world. He was the top dog. We would have loved to pick his brain, but seeing how it's scattered all over the desert, that's not going to happen."

Noah was feeling nauseous. This man was sick. Really sick. He was not human. There was a coldness to his voice, a callousness that hinted at grim layers of cruelty, a chilling subtext to the smug words that slithered like venomous snakes from his mouth, a superior air that alluded to a dark evil within his soul, a black hole that had drained him of feeling and compassion for his fellow man.

Just the sound of this man's voice sucked the air out of Noah's lungs and choked him with a sense of dread and hopelessness.

Wolf Blitzer: "So what's next?"

DISS Official: "None of these anarchist punks are going to get away with it. None of it. Their days are numbered. Not weeks. Days. We're taking them down."

Wolf Blitzer: "I know this isn't your department. But aren't you concerned about the asteroid? Aren't you worried?"

DISS Official: "I don't get paid to worry. The best scientific minds in this country are working on the problem. That's all I can say."

Noah had heard enough. He turned off the television.

He was in complete and total shock.

Tim was dead.

For some reason, he took it very personally. It was strange. He had talked to him for what, thirty seconds at the festival. It had been over a month before that when he first learned about Tim's genius in making the IOU network invisible to the creeps in the CIA and NSA. He really hadn't given the guy another thought until he ran into him at Burning Man, or since.

Yet he was feeling a horrible gnawing grief. It was as if he had lost a close personal friend.

Some people are bigger than life. Their talent or presence or the magnitude of whatever it is they do creates a connection. Like with celebrities, movie stars, or icons like Albert Einstein and John F. Kennedy. Knowing how brilliant this eccentric young man Tim was, how his genius, enthusiasm, and dedication to what he believed in had changed the world. And now discovering how his voice and vision had been forever silenced with a bullet to his brain.

It was almost impossible to grasp.

He sat there for several minutes, immobile, too numb to think.

Then ...

Panic suddenly overcame paralysis.

He raced up the two flights of stairs, went into his room, grabbed the secure IOU phone from his backpack. Something was wrong. He kept punching numbers. Nothing. Only a simple, frightening message ...

No network connection available.

Noah kept to himself for the next two days. He told Cynthia he wasn't feeling well. He certainly wasn't making that up.

Like an endless loop, it played over and over in his head.

They got them all. Joanna. Tim. The Queen. Harmless old Quicksilver. Clarence. Joe. Tyson and the colonel. Francine. Leon and Al.

He cried until he ran out of tears.

Speed Dialing

The President was in the middle of talking with his Chief of Staff, about issuing a new executive order permitting cross dressing in federal buildings, national parks, and at all ATMs across the nation. His secretary buzzed in on the intercom.

"This is the seventh time he's called in the last ten minutes, Mr. President. I can't just keep—"

"Okay okay. Put him through."

"What the fuck are you doing? Is this for real? Or another one of your stunts?"

"What can I say?"

"You could say what's really happening, that's what! The heavens are kind of our area of expertise, if you know what I mean. My guys say there isn't any asteroid."

"Not to rub it in. It took your guys over 300 years figure out Galileo was right."

"I can see where this is going. But let me at least say, next time you've got news like this, maybe you could show a little courtesy and give us a heads up before you put the whole damn world in a hissy."

"In a hissy. Ha ha ha! I like that one. Where do you come up with this stuff?"

"I speak seven languages. What about you, Mr. Hotshot Hifalutin Leader of the Free World? English and Pig Latin? So, I'm outta here. Have your people call my people. Keep me in the loop. No more fucking surprises!"

"No more surprises. Till the next one anyway. Hey, how is Italy doing in soccer this year? Spain still kickin' your ass?"

"How should I know? I don't have time for that silliness. Oh yeah! I almost forgot. Thanks for that gold standard thing. We made a killing on that! We had all long positions when the gold futures shot through the roof. Anyway. Arrivederci! Don't worship any false gods."

"Don't take any wooden nickels. Thanks for calling."

On the other end, the Pope just shook his head as he hung up the phone.

"What an asshole."

A Sad Parting

Of course, when Noah came back to the workshop after two days, everyone noticed something was different. Ginger was the first to say something.

"Noah, is everything okay?"

"I'm not sure. Thanks for asking, but don't worry. I'll be alright."

Rather than make everyone else uncomfortable, he put on his best face, smiled, did what he could to be upbeat, attentive, wide-eyed and full of wonder, his old self.

But under the veneer of well-intended cordiality and nonchalance, it was obvious something was eating away at him. The lighthearted mask would disappear for a brief second, revealing dark anxiety, incipient fear.

Noah took a number of occasions to step outside, and just stood there staring off in the distance. He wasn't sure what he was looking for, or if he expected to see anything. But his unfocused gaze betrayed his awareness of some undefined threat, some menace, some negative presence.

Nights were worse. Under the veil of sleep, his guard was down. Often, he would bolt upright, prompted by no nightmare, no noise from inside or out, but be startled and instantly alert, listening, staring into the oily darkness, looking for he knew not what.

He was helpless in heading off these anxiety attacks. He had no clue as to their source. There was nothing in his present circumstance contributing to this acute sense of foreboding. He couldn't imagine that anyone — except the Swami and those he was now with — had any idea of his whereabouts. There were no strangers lurking around. Life at Green Tambourine was exactly as it was the day he arrived. Peaceful. Cheerful. Industrious. An island of serenity and sanity.

Then suddenly that changed.

One afternoon, almost two weeks from the night when he had seen the Wolf Blitzer interview, he was working with Dora. Actually, he was watching her do the purfing on an old but lovely violin. The work of etching and painting the delicate ornamental decoration on the backside of a violin required much too much artistic talent and experience for Noah to even attempt. But he handed her the required tools and brushes, making him marginally useful.

Noah heard a sound, faint but discernable, coming from outside. He couldn't quite make it out but whatever it was represented an anomaly. Typically nothing other than a rare passing automobile intruded on the uninterrupted chirping of birds and others of nature's small creature sounds.

He went out onto the porch. It was getting louder. He walked around the workshop into the large yard area in front of the main house, which offered a huge green welcome mat to anyone who came to visit, and a more open view.

He listened intently.

Rotors. It was the sound of rotors.

He peered into the cloudless sky.

Nothing.

Then he saw it. A helicopter.

But not just your boilerplate crop duster or airborne weathercast copter.

This was a big metallic hulk, an ominous, thundering military craft, gunmetal grey.

Noah ran to his room and took all of five minutes to pack. If he forgot anything, he couldn't worry about it now. There was no time.

By the time he bounded down the old staircase and out the door of the main house, everyone, sensing something was seriously wrong, had left their workstations and now stood in the yard. Cynthia headed over to intercept Noah, who was taking long quick strides toward the drive leading from the property.

"Noah! Where are you going?"

"Cynthia, I'm so sorry. But they're coming for me. I'm sure of it."

Carmichael caught up with them.

"Are you sure you're not being paranoid?"

"I'm a liability. I've got to get away from here. It's for your own good."

By now everyone else had edged forward in a semi-circle. Noah turned to them.

"Everybody. I can't begin to thank you. You've all been so kind. I'm going to miss every one of you. You're the best in the whole world."

Noah had to choke back the tears. He couldn't believe he it was ending this way.

But there was no time to be sentimental.

He half-cried, half-smiled, gave one last wave, turned.

Then down the driveway he went.

Off … somewhere.

No Mercy

Noah kept looking back over his shoulder.

The helicopter appeared to veer, then head at a right angle away from the farm, finally receding and disappearing in the distance. Within a few minutes, it was gone.

Though still anxious from anticipating the worst, Noah felt some measure of relief.

He was still convinced that he should leave. There was no excuse for subjecting any of the folks back at the farm to any risk. He couldn't take any chances.

By keeping a good pace, he had already made it down the long driveway and onto the lane which ran in front of the 30 acres of mostly wooded property that contained the several Green Tambourine buildings and barns.

It was unseasonably warm but Noah was shaded from the brutal sun by the trees which lined the gravel road he was on.

He slowed a bit as he walked up a long hill. On the other side of the rise was a paved county road, which he would take into town. His chances of hitchhiking would be better once he got closer to Brattleboro.

That's when he felt it.

A subsonic rumble, more a tremor than an audible sound, slowly suffused the ground, creeping up his ankles and legs.

Quickly it evolved into a guttural terrestrial swell, like the earth clearing its throat in preparation for an earthquake.

Suddenly at the crest of the hill appeared the first, then the second and third, then the fourth and fifth of a convoy of military vehicles. There were two humvees, a troop transporter, and two armored assault vehicles which looked like stubby tanks. Instead of artillery cannons, each of these was outfitted with a battering ram, turreted machine gun, and some sort of directional nozzle.

Dust plumed up behind them in huge swirling eddies. They were in a hurry to get somewhere quickly.

Noah's first reaction was to get out of sight. He dashed into a thicket of trees and shrubs beside the road, and ducked down behind some bushes.

The distance between him and the military vehicles quickly closed. He trembled at the thought of what carnage and horror these mere five vehicles could inflict on anyone who tried to stand in their way.

As soon as the humvee in the lead was so close Noah could see the singular focus and determination of the driver's face, he knew what he had to do.

He ran out from the bushes to the edge of the road, and started waving, jumping up and down, nearly putting himself in the path of the oncoming vehicles. Yelling!

"You want me? Here I am. Come and get me. Noah Tass. Wanted terrorist ..."

No one paid him any mind.

The vehicles never even slowed down.

Noah kept shouting, trying to get someone's attention.

When the last one passed, one of the armored assault vehicles, he started running after them. There was no way he could keep up. They were going way too fast.

He darted back into the copse of trees, out the other side, into a clearing which opened up on a harvested field. There was only one thing on his mind. He had to warn the folks at Green Tambourine. Taking a shortcut by running in a direct line across the field toward the farm might get him there just ahead of the military commandos.

He ran harder and faster than he had ever run in his life. Tears streaked his temples, his heart pumped like it would explode, his lungs felt like they were collapsing, but he eventually reached the thickly wooded edge of the property on the eastern perimeter. He fought his way through the dense forest, finally coming to a path which led directly to the back of the farm house.

Noah was too late.

It was clear that the assault team made no effort to engage Cynthia or anyone there, enjoin them to come out peacefully, inform them of the nature of their business.

They went in weapons blazing.

Noah ducked behind a small tool shed and watched, feeling more revulsion, more sickening disgust and outrage, more despair and hopelessness than he thought possible. A barbarity unfolded he could never have imagined humans capable of.

The farm house was already ablaze. Noah could see bodies riddled with bullets, lying still all over the lawn. Gil. Dora. Carmichael. Ginger. Poor Ginger and her baby. Louise and Dench. Paul and Margo.

Casey and Brodie at that very moment came scurrying out of the main farm house, choking, each holding a wet cloth over their mouths with one hand, the other hand held high in a clear act of surrender. They were obviously not armed. Their surrender was to their fate, as gunfire ripped holes in their torsos, lifting them in the air like meat puppets, then dropping them to the veranda floor for the last red droplets of life to ooze out of them.

One of the armored assault vehicles then rammed into the main work shop. Cynthia came running out, pleading. The other assault vehicle took aim and drenched her with a flaming liquid that clung to her and turned her into a human torch. She thrashed and spun, but only staggered a few feet before falling to the ground where her limbs stiffened and quickly turned to ash. Charlie, her live-in boyfriend of over twenty years ran from the side of the building toward her charred remains, face twisted in a scream disgorged from the anguished nucleus of his shredded soul. His grief and horror was quickly terminated by rapid short blasts from the machine guns of two nearby soldiers.

At least fifteen of the military police swarmed over the grounds, into the destroyed and burning buildings. Some kicked the fresh corpses to see if anyone was still alive.

The gunfire gradually subsided.

Mission accomplished.

They were all dead.

Battle of the Bulge

The three men in suits paced back and forth.

Looking frantically up and down the corridor.

Watching the main entrance.

They were desperate.

Stopping everyone they could.

Who would have thought it would be this difficult?

The President's Press Secretary and his two assistants were trying to recruit bodies for a press conference that was supposed to start in twenty minutes. The White House briefing room only held forty but at the rate they were going, it was going to look extremely empty.

It went without saying that some of this administrations policies were about as popular as tooth decay. But this was ridiculous. This was the President of the United States, unquestionably the most recognized and powerful political figure in the world. That should carry some sort of weight, confer a measure of star power.

But they were batting zero so far.

The Press Secretary was boiling mad.

"Goddamn reporters. All I get is 'Why would I go? Why should I waste my time!' Traitors. All of them are traitors."

One of the assistants stopped a passing tourist.

"Excuse me. Would you like to attend the President's press conference? It starts very shortly."

"Uh, thanks. But our tour bus is waiting outside."

The Press Secretary looked at his watch.

"Well, just keep at it. I've got to get things ready."

He rushed off, his air of self-importance perceptibly marred by the fear that for this particular media event, the President would be talking to himself and a CSPAN camera. After all, it was his job to keep the media ball rolling, or at least maintain the illusion that someone still took his boss seriously.

With only a few minutes before the press conference was supposed to begin, the two assistants managed to herd an older couple from Iowa, a custodian who was putting new plastic liners in the trash cans in front of the building, and a tall 30 something Arab fellow wearing a ghutra, into the White House Briefing Room.

The lady from Iowa was beside herself with excitement. This was their first trip to the nation's capital. She was a retired schoolteacher, he a self-employed plumber who had just sold his business to a Vietnamese neighbor in their hometown of Iowa City.

"This is so exciting! Isn't this exciting, Harold? Hmm. I thought there would be more people here."

"To hear this joker?"

"Oh, Harold. You're such a pill."

A high school girl was already in the room when they had entered and was sitting two seats away. She was busy texting on her cell phone. The lady turned to her.

"Are you from the Washington Post?"

"Actually, I go to Eleanor Roosevelt High School. I'm in the journalism club."

"That's wonderful, young lady! And now you get to interview the President."

Her husband rolled his eyes.

"Helen, it's a press conference."

Undaunted and still bubbling with excitement, the lady then turned around to the Arab man who was in the row behind them. He was wide-eyed and smiling, though he looked at her apprehensively.

"And you're not from here, are you? I'll bet you're one of those guys from … what's it called, Harold?"

"Al-Qaeda."

The high school girl looked up from her phone.

"Al Jazeera. He means Al Jazeera."

The lady re-phrased her question.

"Are you from Al Jazeera?"

The Arab just kept smiling, shrugging, working his eyebrows, staring a blank stare. He obviously didn't understand a word of English.

By the time the President strolled into the room with his Press Secretary close behind, the custodian — a black man in his early 50s dressed in his powder blue janitor uniform and sporting an inverted mop of electrified grey hair in the style of boxing promoter Don King — had made himself comfortable and was snoozing away.

The President stepped up to the podium, glanced briefly at his notes, then looked up with a grin that didn't stop at ear-to-ear, but seemed circle around the back of his head. While it appeared quite possible he was about to launch into a lively medley from *The Sound of Music*, he instead began to extoll the virtues of a new health initiative his administration was introducing to the American public.

> *"Lean and mean! That's the America we now see emerging. The latest statistics from our friends at the CDC in Atlanta have shown a dramatic reversal of the longstanding, disturbing trend of an America with too much jelly around the belly. But the war on fat, the battle of the bulge, has only begun. I am pleased to announce some great news in America's patriotic crusade against obesity. The First Lady, bless her heart, as a part of our new Just Say No To Flab strategy, will be leading the nation every morning in a fitness exercise regimen."*

The Press Secretary pulled the draping from a poster on a stand next to the podium. It said in big bold letters … **Just Say No To Flab!**

> *"Right here in the Rose Garden, weather permitting of course, at 9:00 am every day, she will head up a stretching and toning class, attended by individuals selected from our own neighborhood right here in Washington DC. This will be simulcast on participating television stations across the entire nation. So America, let's tone those abs, firm those butts, slim down that waistline. Pump up the fitness and bring down the weight. Together we can build a strong, hale and hearty citizen class, soldiering on into the greatest days of our history. Thank you."*

The President looked quite pleased with himself, nodded and smiled at the mostly empty chairs. It must be a darn good feeling to be president.

He stepped back from the podium and the Press Secretary came forward.

"The President will now take your questions."

Was someone going to wake the custodian in case he had some urgent matter to take up with the most powerful man in the world?

The Press Secretary then stepped back, the President again came forward.

What a strange ritual.

The high school girl stood up, didn't bother waiting to be acknowledged. It wasn't like she was battling a horde of excited reporters for the President's attention.

"Mr. President. What about the asteroid?"

"Hmm. The asteroid. Glad you asked that. Very glad. It seems to be on everyone's mind now, doesn't it?"

"Since it means the end of the world, yes. Everyone's talking about it. At least where I go to school, there's a lot of talk."

"Understandable. Very understandable. We're all worried. I just want you to know that. And I want you to tell the American people. We are worried too. Having said that, I can assure you we are doing all we can. Americans can do their part too. Think positively. Send out positive energy. Visualize a world without asteroids. That's it. That's what we all need to do. Together we can lick this asteroid problem. Thanks, everyone! Have a nice day and ... right. God bless America!"

On that reassuring note, the President left the room but not without glancing back over his shoulder to try to figure out who it was that asked the question. He leaned over to his Press Secretary.

"I don't recognize her. Who's she with? New York Times? Huffington Post? Maybe The Nation. Find out and pull that bitch's press credentials. And be sure to tell Homeland Security to keep an eye on her."

Troublemaker!

CHAPTER TWELVE

Roads Less Traveled

True, the military convoy of sadistic murderers had not stopped for him before going on to massacre everyone at Green Tambourine. But they probably had no idea who he was. They probably assumed he was just some bumpkin cheering on the big bad men in uniform.

More than ever in this absurd surrealistic journey of paranoia and misadventure, this lethal game of hide and seek, Noah knew he had to keep moving and stay out of sight. There was no room for error, no time to think. Every moment was a mine field.

At the same time, he could barely muster the clarity — or the energy — to organize a strategy for his own survival. He felt like he had been beaten within a breath of his life and left on the side of the road to die — numb, lifeless, devoid of hope.

Perhaps back in the beginning, after the shock wave of the bus explosion dissipated, he took comfort in the simple truth that he wasn't guilty of any wrongdoing, was buoyed by the naïve optimism that the real facts would come out and exonerate him, and was hypnotized by a suspension of belief, rendering him once removed from a true sense of what danger he was in. Because of the abstractness, the unreality of it all, back then he could just shrug, be more amused than seriously worried. His being labeled a terrorist felt like watching a bad reality show. Come on. Him a terrorist? How could anyone buy into this nonsense? It's just television. It's make believe. It's all so silly.

But now, after discovering what had happened to the colonel and those poor stupid kids at Area 51, to the PETA guys, crazy Al and Leon and Francine, to goofy, harmless Quicksilver, to the brilliant Tim — oh my god, poor Tim! — to Joanna, then finally seeing with his own eyes the cruel, senseless slaughter of decent people like the good folks at Green Tambourine, the bad reality show had suddenly become a bad reality. His bad reality. Mayhem and carnage in this show weren't the product of special effects. The actors weren't going to get up, brush themselves off, then go to the commissary for coffee and donuts. The truth of this reality show became crushingly evident to Noah.

These guys were out to kill him.

They had no conscience. They had no reservations.

Survival dictated that he had to keep moving and stay out of sight.

And that's what he did.

By darkness of night, shade of trees, cloak of anonymity, he put tens, then hundreds of miles between him and the incinerated pile of smoldering wood, destroyed buildings, and bullet-ridden, lifeless corpses that once was Green Tambourine.

In a dreamlike stupor, he did what he had to do. He was driven by survival instincts and a will to live that operated in some deep substrata of his brain,

149

submerged far below the unremitting torment, the drumbeat message of imminent mortality which now presided over his every breath: *Noah Tass, they're coming for you.*

Truck stops were his lifesaver. They were terrific. He had never appreciated them before. How could he? There were only a handful in all of Monroe County, Missouri, and he never had any reason to visit them.

Getting rides was easy enough. Noah would hang out in the restaurant or the wash rooms where the truckers got themselves ready for the next let leg of their haul, talk it up a bit, ask around who was heading his way. As long as they didn't suspect him of being a punk, pervert, or a troublemaker — as in a bus bombing insurrectionist! — they were amiable and receptive.

He made a good first impression. Young guy hitching his way around the country. Decent fellow. Friendly smile. Missouri boy. Not some faggy East Coast wuss.

Noah would throw his bags in the cab. Off they went.

He managed — at least for now — to stay off the radar of the federal goon squads. There were no enforcement types at the truck stops themselves, either local or federal. Though there were several check points on the roads along the way, small teams of military police who were scattered randomly across the country to discourage any uprisings and quell the anticipated panic over the asteroid, Noah sat high in the cab with the driver and sailed through them all without incident.

Conversations were easy. Male bonding at its most basic. Driving trucks. Sports. Pussy. Noah faked it well. Held up his end.

He didn't know where he was going. He was just going.

South through rural New York, Pennsylvania, into West Virginia.

The business of keeping moving, securing a place to lay his weary head, and the superficial but sufficiently engaging conversations kept his mind off the horrifying events of the past couple weeks.

After eleven days and countless rides, in a path which zigzagged across the map, taking him as far west as Zanesville, Ohio and then back to Cumberland, Maryland, he holed up in Morgantown, West Virginia at the Road Warrior Motel, which ranked as the worst dump he had seen thus far in his travels. He had his sights on Monogahela National Forest, where according to a trucker from Tennessee that Noah met in nearby Wheeling, there were people so lost "they're still wondering which way the Civil War is going."

Noah could fill them in.

We're all losing.

Gorgeous George

George Stephanopolous might have a surname even his best friends couldn't spell. But the guy never seemed to age. Boyishly handsome and accessibly articulate, he had one of the most popular Sunday morning news roundtable programs in America.

George Stepha...:	"Good morning. This week Cokie Roberts is with us, George Will, Sam Donaldson, Matthew Dowd, and joining us shortly by satellite linkup will be Secretary of Defense, Walter

Belvedere. The President three weeks ago dropped the biggest bombshell in human history on the world, the announcement that an asteroid the size of Omaha, Nebraska is on a collision course with the Earth. Day of doom is November 3rd. Then just yesterday, he appeared at the White House briefing room telling the nation that he's just issued Executive Order No. 213779, requiring all school age children to wear uniforms. What's going on here?"

George Will: "A very strong case can be made for the fact that the President has become completely unhinged. Recall the initial warning signs. His expletive-laced State of the Union Address, his reading to the nation of 'The Little Engine That Could'."

Cokie Roberts: "There certainly seems to be a disconnect. If we are to take him at his word, school uniforms and just about everything else will be a moot point if that asteroid hits the Earth."

George Stepha...: "Here's a graphic issued by the NSA Geophysical Mapping Bureau. This gives some idea what we're looking at here."

A graphic filled the screen depicting the asteroid hovering above Knoxville, TN where it was supposed to impact. It looked like an army tank poised over a box of breath mints.

George Stepha...: "I'd say that looks pretty bad."

Matthew Dowd: "But here's something else that's totally baffling. This stuff has been all over the news. Yet there's been virtually no reaction from the public. I mean, nothing. People are just going on about business as usual. From what I've seen no one seems fazed or the least bit frightened. Talk about a major disconnect."

George Will: "People have shut down. They're overloaded. This administration has no credibility. Even within the beltway, no one takes the President seriously. I'd bet most people don't even know he's up for re-election. The American people have hit the mute button."

Matthew Dowd: "Granted. The public has been numbed up by so much bad news and dumbed down by a lot of bad television for so long, they seem incapable of reacting."

George Stepha...: "Bad television. I hope you're not referring to this show."

Matthew Dowd: "No comment."

George Will:	"I'm inclined to think it hasn't registered yet. An asteroid this size? The magnitude of this calamity is too big to grasp. It's just an abstraction. It's not like the world ends every day."
George Stepha...:	"Let's go now to our special guest, Secretary of Defense, Walter Belvedere. What do you make of all this, Mr. Secretary? Why is the public so calm?"
Sec. of Defense:	"American citizens are smart. They're tuned in. But no, that's not good enough for you bloodthirsty vampires. You always have to sensationalize everything, keeping the public in a constant state of panic."
Cokie Roberts:	"Sensationalize? We're talking about the end of the world, the complete annihilation of the human species. How do you sensationalize that?"
George Will:	"Mr. Secretary, it doesn't do you or your president any good to attack us. We're just the messengers."
George Stepha...:	"We're running out of time. Let's cut to the chase. What is going on, Mr. Secretary? We hear nothing from the President. Are we doomed?"
Sec. of Defense:	"We're working the issue. These things take time. Listen up, you propagators of pessimism. If there's any way to knock this thing out of the sky, then we'll damn sure figure it out. So stop crying like a bunch of wussy-ass vapor sacks."

Reach for the Stars

Things got dicey for Noah for a couple of days.

From Morgantown, West Virginia he was sticking to secondary roads, starting with State Highway 7 heading toward Kingwood. It was all farm country, rustic and rolling.

Rides were scarce. He couldn't be choosy.

He even rode on a tractor with a local farmer for five miles.

Progress was extremely slow. People were by nature suspicious of strangers here. Noah stood at the side of the road with his thumb out, always ready with a courteous smile, a friendly wave. They would give him a good once over, then keep on going. One night, stuck between towns with only barns and some cattle in sight, he was forced to sleep off the side of the road in a gulley.

In the middle of a slumber that was more tossing and turning than actual rest, he was startled to hear the sound of a helicopter. It wasn't close enough for him to spot, but it's mere presence unleashed waves of anxious trembling through his whole body. Planes didn't even fly over this area, much less helicopters. The sound of the rotors were soon gone, even if the bitter taste of adrenalin remained on his tongue till the next morning.

Next day he made it to Elkins, West Virginia. What a beautiful area of the country. Gently rolling hills and lovely farms dotted with tiny little villages. This was an area of West Virginia which had been spared the ravages of strip mining and industrial blight, which knew no respect for natural beauty or the simple charm of unsullied country life.

Only a few miles down the road was something out of a science fiction movie. Only it was real science. Dozens of radio telescopes, including the huge 90 meter paraboloid dish at Green Bank, reached up into the heavens and beckoned the electromagnetic energy of the Universe to share the rich secrets of deep space with humble researchers here on Earth. The Green Bank structure, the largest land-based movable structure in the world, had discovered numerous astronomical wonders, which maybe had no immediate practical application, but were the breath of life for dreamers and cosmologists. These included several pulsars, a gigantic coil-shaped magnetic field in Orion, and a large hydrogen gas superbubble, just around the corner in terms of cosmological scale, only 137,000,000,000,000,000 miles away.

It was here, standing among the majestic real world products of scientific ingenuity that Noah came to an unavoidable conclusion, and accepted his inevitable fate.

They had it all.

They had the technology.

They had everything they needed.

They would come for him.

They would find him.

He didn't know how. But they would.

He didn't know what they wanted.

But they would come and get it.

When they were ready.

Panic!

It was only when people saw the asteroid on television that it became real to them.

A roving reporter happened to be in Times Square in that very moment, asking passing pedestrians what they thought about the asteroid.

As had become the drill, he was getting just shrugs and smart-ass comments.

"Same 'ol same 'ol."

"Come visit my neighborhood in the Bronx. It's already completely destroyed."

"Asteroid? What asteroid? Do you see an asteroid?"

"It's a charade. They're just trying to raise our taxes."

"Just more lies. The only time they stop lying to us is when they take a break to think up a new batch of lies. Excuse me. I'm late for my yoga class."

The reporter stared into the camera, addressing the anchor in the television studio.

"And that's what we've been getting all along, Carter. People can't be bothered. They don't have time. It's just not real."

Then something grabbed the roving reporter's attention.

"Wait! Something's going on."

He turned around to look at the gigantic Toshiba Vision Screen on the One Times Square Building, the largest flat-panel display in the Square. His cameraman quickly pointed the camera at it as well. There was a breaking news story from a national news bureau based in Washington DC. A banner scrolled at the bottom ...

Government scientists release the first video
footage of the approaching asteroid.

Everything and everybody in Times Square came to a stop.

As they stared at the image, people were dumbstruck.

It was an impressive chunk of rock alright, an incomprehensibly huge and heavily pitted planetoid of fused iron and nickel. Its gnarled and jagged surface made it look mad, mean and menacing. As it slowly tumbled through space on its calamitous journey toward Earth, the asteroid looked like the skull of the Elephant Man's head had become a planet and been tossed into the sun for annealing.

The scene in Times Square was duplicated tens of thousands of times all across America. People at home. In bars and taverns. Watching huge screens at sporting events. Just looking through the display window of an electronics or appliance store.

They just stared at the monstrous chunk of space debris. A worthless, lifeless, thus even more ominous destroyer of all civilization, all life on Earth.

Then as if everyone simultaneously heard a shot from the same starting pistol ...

Total panic broke out everywhere in America.

"We're all gonna die!"

A shrill chorus of screaming rose above population centers like a human siren. It was an orgy of pain which exited their throats like the ultrasonic scream of a jet engine. Fear had been cleared for takeoff. Piercing cries and eardrum-puncturing pleas for help were the new national anthem.

It was mass horror and herd hysteria unparalleled in human history.

Not that they could be expected to do anything different, over the next few days, media outlets continued to pour gasoline on the fires of fear, and fan the feverish flames of frenzy, by digging into hyperbole from the darkest pages of their Thesauruses. News anchors were tripping over their oily tongues trying make black blacker than black.

The graphic that NSA Geophysical Mapping Bureau had whipped up showing the asteroid hovering above Knoxville, Tennessee was emblazoned on television screens more than Kim Kardashian's cleavage — a historical milestone — accompanied usually by Maria Callas singing "Il dolce suono mi colpì di sua voce!", an aria which made people *want* the asteroid to destroy the planet.

The thing looked like the cosmic sledgehammer of total annihilation about to smash a tiny toy village. This graphic was then typically followed by an assortment of computer simulations showing the impact and immediate aftermath: The plunging of the asteroid into the Earth, which looked like a baseball taking out the center of a person's face leaving a giant sphincter hole where the nose and eyes had been; the melting of the northern hemisphere into a fused lump of cookie dough; the shrouding of the planet in a dust cloud that would last two hundred years; Earth looking like it had been dipped in a bucket of Agent Orange, with nothing growing on the surface and millions of people cannibalizing one another before finally starving to death.

People lost it.

Police, firemen, army reserves, and any public servants who had not themselves joined the rampaging hyena pack, were called to help quell the rioting and looting. It was a total exercise in futility. Panic had spread like a wall of flames in every direction. Real walls of flames could be seen in every direction in most cities, as building after building was set ablaze. The streets were filled with broken glass, flame-engulfed cars, burning buses, wild hoards of sooty, sometimes bloody individuals running in every direction, scrambling everywhere and nowhere at the same time.

It went on for three days, then temporarily burned itself out. Literally the fires went out because there was nothing left to burn. The looting stopped because so much had been looted, the stores were empty, so people were stealing from one another, then stealing it back again. It started to seem pointless.

A nervous, exhausted but anxious calm settled over the country.

The President came on television. At least he came on what televisions had not been smashed or secreted away onto piles of booty in the smoldering basements of buildings which now had no electricity.

> *"Now I know some of you out there are upset. I'm upset too. It's not everyday that we are forced to stare helplessly into the unforgiving face of the Grim Reaper. But as I have said in the past and will say until I breathe my last breath, this is America! And as long as there is an America, there is hope. Now I have been informed by the best scientific minds in the history of the world, that they are on the job and the ideas are flowing. Some damn good ideas! They're a little short on details but let me just sum it up by saying there are several very promising proposals to whip this asteroid problem. We've still got a couple weeks. I'd say we're on a solid track here. Now there is one other matter I need to address here. As you know, there were a few isolated instances of panic and vandalism over the past three days. Now I understand the frustration people are feeling, but this isn't a healthy way to express it. So let's show some spirit here. Let's show a little courtesy to your fellow Americans. When you get right down to it, we're just one big happy family, you know. So I'm going to make a special request. I'm going to ask that everyone, at least for the next couple weeks, just stay home. That's right. Stay in your homes, watch a little television. Make popcorn. We'll call it a national time out. Everyday from 6 pm to 6 am. Till we get these few isolated instances of misbehavior under control. Thank you for your cooperation. Stay strong. God bless America!"*

A few isolated instances?

How stupid did he take us for? If the instances were so isolated, why was the whole nation being grounded and sent to their rooms for twelve hours a day?

A superficial look at the results of a population driven by panic over the three days of madness and mayhem had produced some numbers, which if anything were on the conservative side.

In most urban areas, 40% of the commercial property had been destroyed. The majority of streets were so piled with trash and the smoldering remains of automobiles, buses and trucks, they were undrivable. At least 30% of the homes had been burglarized or torched. Only 35% of the remaining homes had electricity. It was estimated that nationally at least 120,000 people died in the rioting, either bludgeoned, shot or stabbed, or immolated in their homes or cars.

In rural areas the fatalism was more internalized. Over 3000 suicides were reported. That didn't include the 672 heads of households had killed their whole families and then taken their own lives.

Good luck if you were injured. There was going to be a very long wait among the hundreds of thousands thronging outside the emergency rooms across the nation.

It was going to take quite a while to clean up the mess and bury the dead.

But then again … why bother? What was the point?

"We're all gonna die!"

The reaction to the President's "time out" talk was not quite what he hoped for.

In fact, people were so pissed off at how utterly clueless and out of touch he was, the very next day they were back on the streets. For the next week, with no end in sight, this new round of violence made the initial one look like a badminton tournament.

Becky's Creek

Noah was in Valley Head, West Virginia. This was just inside the Becky's Creek Wildlife Management Area, directly west of Monongahela National Forest, and he had pretty much walked the entire way.

There had been only one other sighting of a helicopter. He had managed to duck into a gulch and get under some bushes and was sure he hadn't been spotted.

He came up on a rickety old building that had a wood sign hanging out front, claiming it was a boarding house. There was no office but he found the owner in a tool shed, which apparently was the old man's room. It had a cot, an old dresser of drawers, and a black-and-white television with rabbit ears sitting on a stool. The old man handed Noah a key, which was entirely unnecessary since the door to his room wasn't and couldn't be locked.

Exhaustion immediately overwhelmed him. He fell asleep in his clothes, without even bothering to unpack.

Next morning, when he came out of his room, there was a plate sitting there for him. Eggs, toast, some collard greens, hash brown potatoes. Noah wolfed it down like he hadn't eaten properly for the last two days, which in fact was the case.

He rinsed off the plate and silverware using a spigot he found next to his door and started to return it to the old man, when he spotted a pay phone attached to a wood pole, next to the driveway.

A pay phone! Now that's pretty special. Noah had seen pictures of them but never actually seen one in person.

Amazingly, it worked.

He tried to call Naomi.

An operator came on the line.

"May I help you?"

"Operator, I've been trying to dial a number. It's a long distance call to Missouri, but I'm getting nothing."

"I'm sorry, sir. But service for much of the nation is down. Please try your call again later."

Noah went around the building to the shed in back. The old man was sitting with his back to the door, riveted by whatever he was seeing on television.

"Thanks, sir. Here's your plate. Best meal I've had in weeks."

The old man turned around. He was a portrait of fear, and looked like he had been crying. He pointed at the old television set. Noah could now see what was upsetting him so much. There was the asteroid, tumbling through space like a hideous monster.

The old man's hand shook as he pointed at the television screen. He tried to speak, but nothing came out of his trembling lips. He made the sign of the cross and turned his back on Noah, continuing to just stare at the TV. His old arthritic shoulders sagged, and ever so faintly Noah heard deep from within the old man's throat the heartbreaking sound of a whimper.

Blowback

The rioting, looting, and chaos continued unabated.

The President convened an emergency meeting of his core advisors.

"Jesus Christ! I just wanted to scare them a bit. Not destroy the country."

"What do you suggest?"

"What do *I* suggest? This was your work of genius. What do *you* suggest?"

"Well, maybe you could tamp it down a bit. Give the country a little pep talk."

"Got it. Hey folks, the planet's about to hit by a wrecking ball. We're all going to die. No problem! Let's sing a song. Then I could pull out a banjo and do that tune, 'Don't Worry Be Happy'. Well, that was fun! So let's all buck up. It's gonna be alright."

"Well, sir. With all due respect, it *is* going to be alright. In the end, we're going to save the world. So maybe, I dunno, give them a heads up that we've got the situation under control."

"Have you ever tried to explain to stampeding buffaloes that they should just take a nice leisurely stroll and enjoy the scenery?"

"I'm not following, sir. You have experience with stampeding buffaloes?"

"No! But I have experience with thick advisers who are about to lose their cushy jobs. Give me something here. Give me something I can take to the public. Lots of technical jargon. Promising scientific shit. You know. You guys are always coming up with plausible gobbledygook. We'll start feeding some hope back into this sea of despair and futility we have created."

"That's good stuff, Mr. President! 'We have hope in this sea of despair and futility.' It has a real nice ring to it. Campaign slogan material there."

"Fuck you! Get to work."

They did.

Within 24 hours the President announced that effective immediately the entire nation would be under martial law. First off, the coming election would be postponed until further notice. Secondly, all public behavior was to be under strict supervision.

Anyone running or even walking too fast would be arrested. Groups of more than four people would be required to disperse. There was to be no shouting, chanting, whistling, hand signals, or break dancing. People could be stopped and strip searched without a warrant. Everyone to carry ID on them at all times, even in their homes.

Lastly, an ironclad dusk-to-dawn curfew would be enforced.

A psychologist from the Center For Disease Control was interviewed on Fox News and asked his views on the curfew: "If the world doesn't end on November 3rd, we can expect a huge spike in the birthrate in nine months."

CHAPTER THIRTEEN

Top Ten Reasons

That David Letterman. What a funny guy!

"Okay, folks. Here are the top ten reasons the asteroid will <u>not</u> destroy the world and kill everyone on the planet …

#10 – Kim Kardashian has not made the balloon payment yet on her silicone breast implants.

#9 – There are so many greaseballs in Knoxville, Tennessee the asteroid will just slide off the planet and keep going.

#8 – CBS has guaranteed me five more seasons. It's right in my contract.

#7 – The President has made the annihilation of Earth and the destruction of the human race an official campaign promise. We all know what happens with campaign promises.

#6 – The greatest scientific minds in the country have been working on this. They are sure they can finish the big trampoline by November 3rd.

#5 – Donald Trump has plans to turn the asteroid into an exclusive new casino and hotel called Trump's Gaudy Lump For The Common Chump.

#4 – Dick Cheney says they aren't through looking for Iraq's weapons of mass destruction on the asteroid.

#3 – Pfizer has announced they have developed a new ointment which totally relieves a person from any discomfort caused by asteroids. It's called Preparation A.

#2 – Rumor has it that riding in the trunk of the asteroid is over half million illegal immigrants. Knoxville is now crawling with INS officers.

#1 – The President and all members of congress are all going to stand at the foot of the Washington Monument, look up, and make a speech. The hot air will deflect the asteroid. The danger is the moon might get blown out of orbit."

It's hard to argue with that.

Rockets Red Glare

Overcoming gargantuan logistical challenges, four giant military rockets were launched within the same hour from Kennedy Space Center at Cape Canaveral, Florida.

Two Atlas 5s and two Delta 4s rose majestically on enormous red tongues of fire, skyscraper size blowtorches thrusting the towering ballistic cylinders into the powder blue sky over the Cape. It was the perfect day to save the world. The heavenly dome over Florida and the Atlantic seaboard was bright and optimistic, feather-brushed with only subtle wisps of translucent cirrus clouds.

The reporting of the launch at KTVX in Salt Lake City was pretty typical. It was as if a template had been handed out and replicated over hundreds of such television news programs across the nation. A grim-looking white male reporter stared uncomfortably at the viewing audience, giving minute-by-minute updates on the approaching asteroid. In the corner of the screen was an ominous doomsday countdown clock, ticking off the days and hours before Earth impact.

> *"With only four more days before Earth impact, and chaos and panic continuing throughout the nation, the White House has announced that four military rockets, each carrying enormous thermonuclear devices, have just been launched. This was the scene at Kennedy Space Center."*

The robotic voice of the communications officer droned on about launch system readiness. *"Comm data rate monitor virtual sub-system lock engaged, no anomalies detected, T minus one minute and counting..."* The camera scanned the VIP gallery, where the famous and important were talking, laughing, looking through opera glasses and binoculars.

Indeed, it was quite a soiree at the Cape, with the President, Secretary of Defense, Secretary of State, the head of NASA, joined by four and five star generals, religious leaders from many different Christian denominations, two Catholic Archbishops, one rabbi, an Imam from a mosque in Orlando, Tom Brokaw, Phil Donahue, Jon Bon Jovi, Barbara Walters, Arianna Huffington, Stephen Hawking, Brad Pitt, Angelina Jolie, and the President of the Teamsters Union.

It could have been a charity fundraising picnic promoting anti-bullying awareness in public schools. But they were actually there to offer prayers and hopeful words for the mission to save the only planet in our solar system to support intelligent life, or what passed for it.

As the camera pulled in for a tight close-up of Angelina Jolie, the local news anchor segued with a voice-over ...

> *"And here's the President's announcement."*

The program cut to the President sitting in the Oval Office.

"Just yesterday, four of America's most powerful military rockets were successfully launched on a course to intercept the asteroid. They are all carrying hydrogen bombs, the largest ever assembled, each with the destructive capacity of 450 megatons of TNT. Just one of these gigantic weapons is sufficient to destroy the asteroid. This is our best and only shot. In the event our efforts to destroy it fail, NASA scientists are now saying the impact event will occur between 9 and 9:30 pm EST. I thank our scientists for their hard work and dedication. Our prayers are with you for a successful outcome. For now, my fellow Americans, we can only wait and hope."

The grim KTVX newscaster wrapped up the dramatic segment.

"We have learned that the asteroid will be within striking distance of the hydrogen bombs about an hour before its predicted impact with the Earth. We'll have live video coverage from cameras onboard one of the missiles. God be with us."

This was the response to the gravest crisis in human history. Four shiny metallic hulks representing the muscle, might and technological ingenuity of our species, sent on a heavy-handed mission to greet the intruder from deep space, and send it packing.

It was interesting. No one challenged the specifics.

Yes, four beefy military missiles soared into the blue dome above Cape Kennedy. But 450 megatons?

The largest hydrogen bomb ever tested by any nuclear power was the Tsar Bomba, a Russian monster which was the equivalent of 57 megatons of TNT. The largest ever built by the U.S. was a modest 25 megatons.

450 megatons? It wasn't something you just whipped together from spare parts.

Whatever the actual size of the thermonuclear devices, they were certain to cause a very large boom in the sky.

And epitomize something America did very well.

Blowing things up.

Eyes Wide Shut

Peace of mind is relative.

Noah had peace of mind in Pulnick, for sure. But that was more the peace of mind of a coma victim.

Here in the backwoods of West Virginia, the calm silence had a vibrancy, an order. Away from the horrors of the city, and the horrors people were visiting on themselves and their country, it was hard to believe that America was in catastrophic collapse, and that in just a matter of days the whole ball of wax might come to a sudden and final end.

It was strange. Noah felt no particular anxiety. No sense of hopelessness or loss.

Whatever would happen would happen.

Whatever choices were there would be there.

Whatever we each chose to make of any of this was still our choice.

Whatever happened, there was one certainty in his life.

He had run out of clean underwear.

Noah took his socks, a t-shirt, and the offending undergarments, to a utility room attached to the tool shed where the old man lived. He found a bar of soap, filled the stainless steel sink with warm water, and started scrubbing.

After wringing everything out, he put them in a pile and turned to head back to his room. He figured he could lay the stuff out on the porch, they'd be dry in a few hours.

The old man met him at the door. The poor guy still looked so vulnerable, afraid.

"This was taped to my screen door. Came sometime this morning."

Noah looked at the envelope. Unbelievable!

He walked out of the utility room, wandered to the back of the property, sat down on a tree stump, and read the letter from his father.

Something to think about...

The Mayor of Pulnick was walking down Main Street. Suddenly he saw a steaming brown pile in the middle of the sidewalk. He bent over and stuck his index finger in it. He put it up to his nose. 'Sure smells like horseshit.' Then he rubbed it between his finger and thumb. 'Sure feels like horseshit.' He stuck his finger in his mouth. 'Yup. Sure tastes like horseshit.' He smiled his big mayor smile.

'Boy! Am I glad I didn't step in it!'

Wyatt Grayson Tass

That evening just as the sun went down behind the rolling hills of West Virginia, Noah and the old man sat on opposite sides of a nice campfire Noah got started with kindling and firewood collected from around the heavily treed property. They drank beer and exchanged stories, though Noah by far did most of the talking.

The old man had never been anywhere. He didn't say as much, but Noah could tell he had never been outside West Virginia and had probably spent 90% of his seventy plus years within a few miles of right here. Like most Americans, he had toured the country on the screen of his television.

Noah told him his whole story. He breezed over growing up in Missouri — not that much to tell there — but went into a lot of detail about the past few months. The bus, the stinky pig farmer, Indianapolis, Area 51, the Friendly Ghost Motel in Casper, the PETA wackos, the missile silos and Quicksilver, crazy Joe, Habitat in Tuscaloosa and the amazing Clarence, lovely Joanna (leaving out some of the more provocative aspects of their time together), the Queen and Buzz Central, Los Angeles, the Burning Man Festival, Reno and the young hooker (the old man's eyes got real big during that part), hitchhiking across America to Detroit, Lot 49 and the skeletal Element, the

Swami, the violins and marmalade at Green Tambourine, and finally how he ended up here, sitting in front of a campfire with his new friend.

Good grief! He didn't even know his name.

"What's your name?"

"Will. Will Travel."

"You mean, like ..."

"Have gun will travel. That's it!"

The old man let out a whoop and a belly laugh that belied the fact that the skinny old guy had no belly.

All through Noah's narration, the old man had made no secret of how much he was enjoying the company of his new young boarder. It was the first time Noah had seen him smile, and was a refreshing contrast to the fear which had gripped his old frame just a few days before, when he was confronting the prospect of annihilation courtesy of an asteroid.

"You've had quite an adventure, young man. I wish I had been so lucky. But the important question is always the same."

"Important question? There's only one?"

"Well, you're right. There's too many to think about. But there's one that I think pushes the other suckers out of the way."

"And what's that?"

"What have you learned?"

Noah, so full of stories, finding it so easy up till now, relaxing in the glow and easy warmth of the campfire, to fill the still night air with so many words, was at a loss.

"I guess I need to think about that."

And it was that very question he was thinking about an hour later, laying on the uncomfortable cot in his tiny room in Valley Head, West Virginia, in the protective embrace of Becky's Creek Wildlife Management Area, when he heard the helicopter land in the field across from the rickety old guest house.

At first the sound of the rotors was but a faint rattle from the distant reaches of the heavens, but slowly and steadily the sound mounted in intensity until by the time the aircraft touched down, the din nearly shook the old shack off its foundations.

Less than two minutes later, the thunderous crash of a boot kicked open his door and three federal enforcement agents from one of the alphabet agencies jammed into his room, taking up all of the available space of the tiny enclosure.

Noah looked into the barrel of an assault rifle. The guy pointing it at Noah's head was wearing a helmet and goggles, battle gear, and armor head-to-toe.

"The door was open."

"Just following orders."

"You never use the door knob?"

"Nope. We always kick the door in."

Noah's duffel bag and backpack were next to him, ready to go.

He picked them up, then calmly walked out.

Less than an hour-and-a-half later they were landing at Andrews AFB.

Not a single word was exchanged between him and his captors the entire flight. Noah still gave them high marks for hospitality. After all, they hadn't hooded or handcuffed him.

He was hustled over to a black Lexus waiting at the edge of the tarmac. Beside it stood two guys the size of water buffaloes dressed in suits the same color as water buffaloes, with impenetrable expressions, all business, just doing their job.

Noah had the back seat all to himself. There were no handles on the inside of the doors. The windows were darkly tinted all around.

As they cruised to wherever they were taking him, a scene unfolded for Noah he could not have ever imagined. It was out of *1984*. Though the weather was brisk, thousands upon thousands of people had gathered in the streets. They sat, stood, lay on the cold pavement or damp ground before giant LED video monitors. People had been pouring into the parks and public spaces where video walls had been set up by the government for people to view the greatest show on Earth, perhaps the last show ever, if things ended poorly.

Noah later learned that this scene was mirrored thousands of times over all across the country. In areas where winter weather didn't permit outdoor showings, people crowded into every available arena, stadium, theater and auditorium where again the government had provided the video link to what was occurring in outer space.

At one point close to the National Mall, the crowd was unruly. They were in the street, preventing any traffic from passing.

One of the troublemakers started pounding on the hood of the car. The agent riding shotgun quickly got out, pulled out his handgun and shot the guy in the face. Just to make sure his point was understood, he killed two others near by. The crowd backed off, in fact started running, and the car now had no problem making progress.

The water buffalos drove through a security check point, parked and Noah was taken into the service entrance of an imposing white marble building. He had no idea where he was. Somewhere downtown Washington DC, that's all he knew.

He was then escorted through several corridors, down an elevator, through more corridors and finally into a hall that dead-ended with a single door. While most of the way they had encountered no one, this whole area was teaming with military guards and what were probably secret service men.

They entered a medium-size conference room. It was full. Maybe thirty or so people, mostly seated. Chatting away. All men.

As he passed a wall-mounted clock, Noah noticed the time.

8:16 pm.

Last he had heard, the asteroid was expected to impact the Earth at exactly 9:28 pm, so it was now supposedly about halfway the distance to the moon away, racing the final 130,000 miles on its fateful mission of destruction.

Noah was directed to a chair at the very back of the room. There was a man sitting in the next seat.

"Glad you could make it. Not that you had a choice."

As soon as he heard him, it sent a chill through Noah and a paddlewheel started churning his stomach. He was sure he was going to be sick.

That voice.

This was the high-ranking official in the Internal Security and Surveillance section of the Department of Homeland Security. The one who on CNN had so crassly and cruelly dismissed the death of Tim, the genius behind IOU's uncrackable security.

Hatred painted Noah's throat.

"You were on CNN. On the phone with Wolf Blitzer. You killed—"

"So? You want my fuckin' autograph?"

Suddenly, everyone stood up. The President and the First Lady had just walked in. Both were smiling ear-to-ear. They seemed to already be on fairly intimate terms with everyone, so there was none of the typical presidential meet-and-greet shake-and-fake about his entrance. He just casually waved in one big sweeping motion at everyone in the room, then he and the First Lady took their seats front-and-center before the theater-size flat-screen video monitor which took up most of the front wall.

The President stretched, then leaned over and seemed to be sharing some private joke with the First Lady.

He turned around with a big grin.

"What's the movie tonight? Hope Jon Voight isn't in it."

Everyone laughed a little too hard.

The screen suddenly jumped to life.

It was a little eerie. There was no sound. Of course, there is no sound in outer space but it seemed like some sort of control center radio chatter, maybe a retired astronaut doing some narration, would have helped a lot. Noah wondered if people all over the country were getting this same silent treatment. It didn't seem likely. They probably got James Earl Jones.

The big nasty chunk of iron and nickel, dark and ominous, filled the entire screen.

Then the magnification slowly backed off and the asteroid receded into the starry backdrop of space. It became obvious that the vehicle transporting the camera was quite a good distance from the object.

Suddenly, there was a flash around the edges of the screen and everything shook. Almost immediately could be seen the huge plume of rocket thrusters filling the entire view. As the missile pulled away there was no doubt it was aimed directly for the asteroid, which itself was apparently approaching head-on the platform that bore the camera. The H-bomb laden missile fired navigational thrusters causing to swerve a bit. The maneuvering put it on the required trajectory, a direct collision with the enormous oncoming asteroid.

The missile accelerated quickly and within thirty seconds it was only the tiny tip of a butane torch against the vast black of space and the ominous metallic hunk that was the asteroid. Then it disappeared entirely.

Three seconds passed.

Suddenly in a flash that almost instantly filled the entire screen, a ball of hot solar flame expanded in a billowing cloud of vaporized asteroid and pure hydrogen fusion energy.

In less than a second, everything within hundreds of kilometers of the explosion was enveloped and dispersed into hot plasma. The shock wave of electromagnetic energy and heat overtook and presumably vaporized the camera. The screen went to electronic fuzzies.

That was it.

The President stood up.

"Well, isn't this one joyous occasion? We've saved the human race. All in a day's work, I say. Let's get a beer."

The First Lady joined him as they headed toward the door.

Then his Press Secretary stepped in and reminded the President that he would be making an address to the world.

"Everyone will want to hear a few words from the man who saved the planet. I have the text of your speech right here, Mr. President. It's already been loaded into the teleprompter. We played up the humility thing. No sense patting yourself on the back when everyone else is. You're certainly going to be the hero of the hour for a long time to come."

The Secretary handed him a single sheet of paper. The President winked.

"Should I start wearing blue tights with a red cape and an S on my chest?"

"You might want to spend some time in the gym first, Mr. President."

"Sometimes honesty is not the best policy."

All the President's Men

Noah was appalled.

"It was fake."

The high-ranking ISSS official next to him just smirked.

"How do you know?"

"Come on."

"Real is what people choose to believe."

"You guys conned the entire world. Aren't you special."

"There are a lot of pleased voters out there tonight. I just checked the news feed and it looks like there's a party going on nationwide unlike anything in history."

Noah glared at the man, seething with more anger and hatred than he had ever felt in his life.

"What do you want with me? Why am I here?"

"Come with me."

A few people still lingered on in the conference room.

The ISSS man got up and led Noah out the door. They walked in silence for several minutes. Through a number of corridors, up an elevator, another long corridor, then down a number of floors in a stairwell. Guards were posted on each landing. They saluted as they passed. Finally he opened a rather plain-looking door, though from the way it swung, it apparently was made of highly reinforced steel. There was no nameplate or identifying markings.

He led Noah into a magnificent office with a large executive desk on which sat two monitors and a keyboard. There were work tables around the perimeter covered with computers, monitors and electronic devices Noah couldn't identify. Beautiful paintings and sculptures were everywhere, creating a luxurious and pleasant ambience. The wall behind the plush executive chair was covered with Certificates of Commendation, Awards for Meritorious Service, and photos of the man shaking hands with former presidents, congressmen, generals, cabinet secretaries, and other notables.

Noah wasn't impressed.

"You still haven't answered my question. What do you want with me?"

"I thought we should finally meet face-to-face."

Face-to-face? Right. Like a cat toying with a mouse before it rips the head off.

"You seem to be too important to waste your time on someone like me."

"Do you understand what's been going on? What I do?"

"Apparently you kill innocent people."

The man gave Noah a twisted smile.

"Like you don't have blood on your hands."

"What's that supposed to mean?"

"You're lucky to be here. You were on a short list for termination. But then things flipped. You became valuable. You became the gift that kept on giving."

Was this man insane?

"What are you talking about?"

"We have some very very smart people working for us. But for some reason, a lot of times these guys can't put their hands in their pockets and locate their own dicks."

"And?"

"You took us places we needed to go. You were the best hunting dog money could buy. And you were free."

"What! You're saying I led you to—"

"Like a homing pigeon."

Noah lost it.

"You murderer! You killed Tim! You killed all my friends. None of those people deserved to die!"

The man stared with a cold steely dispassion that made Noah shudder.

"They were all terrorists. Traitors. That freaky tattooed animal girl destroyed property and people's livelihoods. Those idiots at Area 51 with that deranged burnout Colonel Kerr. He was discharged twenty six years ago as mentally unfit. The fat queen bee cow sabotaging the internet, breaking into people's bank accounts. That cunt with the violins, Cynthia. Now she's a work. Thought she was some kind of witch. That whole scene was like the Manson family. And that Joanna girl you screwed—"

"I knew them. They were all good people. They weren't—"

"Listen, young man. I care about this country. Everyone here deeply cares about this country. Which is why we can't leave it to you and your wacko friends, or even the typical imbeciles out there with their 2.4 children and their SUVs, to ruin. What we did — what we do — is beyond yours and 99.9% of the public's ability to grasp. But in the end, it all turns out for the better. In the end, *you* are the beneficiaries of our hard work, our vision. The President is always taking it in the ass. The man might be a political animal. He might even be considered a tool. But he serves a greater cause, a noble mission that keeps this country from turning into a compost heap."

"Those same words could have come out of the mouth of Goebbels. Him and his visionary buddy Adolph."

"Aah! 23-year-old Noah Tass. The expert. Grows up surrounded by a bunch of Bible-belt dimwits, gets a third-rate education. Now he's an expert on everything — sociology, history, politics."

"I know right from wrong! I know evil when I see it. I know—"

"You just don't get it, do you? There are no sides. At least there are no sides like you think of them. Good guys. Bad guys. There are just guys. Battling it out for one reason or another. That's the human race. That's history."

"So Pol Pot was just playing ping pong on the other team."

"Sometimes it looks like some causes are better or worse than others. Everybody paints their mission in noble colors. Drapes the flag over it, has God on their side. But there are always two, three, sometimes many more ways of looking at things. Take World War II. From Hitler's perspective, we were the bad guys. Germany had gotten totally fucked over with the Treaty of Versailles. He was doing what he thought he should do for his people, for the good of his *side*."

"You're a moral mercenary. A plug-and-play assassin for whoever has the deepest pockets. You are the ultimate whore!"

"So when that hippie anarchist chick, Joanna, was slick licking your dick, that was all for the good of mankind? I see! We misunderstood. You weren't getting fucked. You were performing a patriotic duty to your country, noble deeds for all mankind. Now the humanitarian can call me a whore."

"You would disembowel your own mother to win an argument."

"There is no argument. I'm telling you how things are. Accept them or piss your pants in frustration. I don't care. Nobody cares. Nobody cares about you."

"You used me! You fucking used me to track down what you ignorant, paranoid creeps randomly decide are terrorists. I know for a fact, not a single one of them was a terrorist. Or wanted to hurt anyone. Not even the Gestapo pigs you work for."

"I can assure you that if any of them were innocent, no harm would have come to them."

"Innocent? Are you joking? In your eyes no one is innocent anymore. This country is so fucked up."

"Well, you're right about that. But it's *people* who are fucked up. You saw how the public reacted when they heard about the asteroid. Like beasts in the jungle. They destroyed half of the country. Come on. Grow up, for chrissakes."

"The asteroid. The asteroid. The big fake. The con job. You knew people would lose it. You guys caused the riots. This is supposed to be a free country. Why should we put up with your lies and manipulations?"

"That's the price of freedom."

Noah looked at him like he was crazy.

"The price of freedom? From what you say, no one is free. Not even you. Certainly not you. You are a slave to your own delusions of grandeur. Of world control. You're a junkie. Going from one power fix to another. Fuck you! People want to make their own choices."

"People have no idea what they want. Unless we tell them."

"People want a decent life. They want to—"

"People want good television. That's what we gave them. That asteroid looked great! Can you argue with that? The best reality show this season. The best ever, goddammit!"

Noah's revulsion was total and he made no attempt to hide it.

He spit out his contempt for this man. His fate was probably sealed anyway. Here he was trapped in the bowels of some secure government building, no escape. What did it matter what he said.

"You and your elite corps of assassins sit here playing God, playing judge and jury, deciding who lives and who dies. You're just two-bit killers. Cheap thugs with Rolexes and shit for morals."

For the first time, the ISSS man raised his voice. Not quite yelling but visibly angry.

"Have some respect!"

"Respect? Because you have this fancy office, and some important sounding title. That doesn't change a thing. You're a murderer. You're a sick—"

Now the man yelled.

"Noah! I'm your father!"

His father?

His FATHER?

NO! NO! This is not happening! Oh god. Help me!

Noah couldn't breathe.

Please! This can't be real. This is a nightmare. I want to wake up. Make this all go away. Please! Please!

He bent over in tuck position and fought it. Fought the tears. Fought the urge to scream. Fought the urge to kill this vile human being claiming to be his father.

No! No! No!

His father came around the desk and stood over Noah. He rapped Noah on the back of his head with his knuckles, bent over, then let the stinging acid of his finely-tuned sarcasm coat his words.

"Don't look so happy, you little fuck!"

Noah refused to acknowledge him and just stared at the carpet.

His father then calmly walked over and stood before one of the original paintings across from his desk. It was an excellent rendering in acrylic, quite remindful of Edvard Munch's *The Scream*, but set against the rubble of some imaginary futuristic city.

He was more even-toned now. Introspective, almost plaintive.

"I'm 56. I could retire right now. I gave up everything for this. I've done my part, given my best years to my country—"

Noah stood up, whipped around, and pointed at his father.

"Exactly! Your best years. What's left now? The scraps? You want to share the scraps with the son you never had. That you abandoned. I'm not your son. You stopped being my father a long time ago."

Wyatt Grayson Tass, hands clasped behind his back, pompously erect and inflated with the vastness of his importance and indispensability, strolled like he had all the time in the world, back behind his desk.

He looked at Noah. There was a glint of amusement in his eye. He seemed to be thoroughly enjoying himself.

"You know, son, there's a sanctioned hit out on you. All signed and sealed. It's on hold for now. But that could change with a single keystroke."

For dramatic effect, he lightly tapped on his computer keyboard.

Noah just stared back.

"Right. The way you deal with everything. Play ball or die."

"I'm just trying to talk some—"

Noah screamed at the top of his lungs.

"Go ahead! Kill me! Kill me, you sick motherfucker!"

A stony silence filled the entire room.

Noah's father was no longer amused.

169

His face had hardened into an impenetrable mask.

It was impossible to fathom what he was thinking. Too many years in the business of stonewalling had turned Wyatt Grayson Tass to stone. Maybe it was just his eyes. But more likely, the petrification had worked its way down from the surface, through the soft tissue and sinew of his body, into the central chambers of his soul.

Noah studied the man, tried to analyze his expression, did his best to explore the stony face of the sperm donor who had brought him into this world. But it was like looking at a limestone statue that had just been dug up from ancient ruins.

Finally in a flat cadaverous monotone, his father replied.

"You're not worth the bullet."

Noah stood up, turned, and stepped toward the door. He had no idea if he was free to leave but he would try.

He opened it, stopped, looked back over his shoulder.

"I saw what you did. Your big lie. Aren't you afraid I'll tell?"

"No one will believe you."

The two buffaloes were waiting outside in the hall.

It took ten minutes for them to spelunk out of the convoluted underground facility. They went out a totally different way than they had entered the underground complex. When they finally exited one last steel-reinforced door and walked sixteen steps up to street level, Noah found himself at an intersection somewhere in the center of the capital of the most powerful nation in history.

His father at least had said one thing which proved to be true.

There was definitely a party going on.

Life on a Ferris Wheel

Woo-hoo! America felt good again.

And so did the rest of the world.

In an unparalleled expression of joy and appreciation, the parks and plazas, streets and boulevards, roads and alleys, bike paths and hiking trails, forests and fields, orchards and rice paddies the world over, were filled with people of every color, size and shape singing and dancing. Some were stoned, some were drunk, some just high on life and new hope.

The headlines over the next few days said it all.

U.S. Missile Destroys Asteroid!!
President Hailed As Greatest Man In History

Pope Says God Heard Our Prayers:
"The Holy Ghost guided H-bomb to target."

United Nations Building In New York
Painted Red, White and Blue

Saved Planet Becomes Investor Paradise
Stock Prices Skyrocket

Rock Stars Sign On For Woodstock III
To Celebrate New Age of Aquarius

America Again Proves It's #1!
USO Dollar Soars

Lady Gaga Releases New Song and Video:
"We Saw, We Went, We Kicked Some Assteroid!"

Understandably, Americans were particularly proud. Their guy had come through in the crunch. Forgotten, at least temporarily, were all of the political faux pas, ruinous policies, stumbles, bumbles, tribulations, backpedaling, waffling, and treacheries.

The next day after the world was saved, martial law was officially lifted. In the same press conference, it was announced that the postponed elections were now back on for the following Tuesday.

On election day, the President's approval rating was an unprecedented 99.6%. He was generously rewarded at the polls and won re-election by an impressive landslide. What a landslide it was! He got every single one of the 538 electoral college votes, and all but 5,402 of the popular vote. Those dissenting votes consisted of 642 people who apparently were still upset he hadn't banned the teaching of evolution in public schools, and 4,760 errors by the electronic voting machines. It came out months later in a highly under-reported story that the malfunctioning machines had been secretly programmed by a hockey-loving hacker to switch votes and give them to retired Canadian hockey star Wayne Gretsky. It was supposed to be a joke. Subtracting the voting fraud anomaly, the President had won 99.99% of the popular vote.

It had gone according to plan.

Fear had been replaced by relief.

Relief had instantly transformed into euphoria.

It was a time of unbelievable unity.

Incomprehensible fellowship.

Love of our fellow man.

America was #1!

Then ever so gradually, things returned to normal.

Or what would become the new normal. After all, normal is an ever-shifting and constantly evolving benchmark.

The mass solace and all-encompassing euphoria steadily dissipated, displaced by harsh reality.

True. The world was saved.

But it was still a messy world. Very messy. All of the myriad of problems were still there.

Complex problems.

Unsolvable problems.

In America there were still millions of unemployed people. With so many buildings destroyed in the rioting and looting, the ranks of the homeless had swelled to previously unimaginable numbers. Loose estimates put the total at over 25,000,000. Economic numbers, after a meteoric spike were starting to settle back down. The stock market, which had shot from its recent historic low of 3,153 to 33,998 three days after the big boom boom in the sky, was back down under 13,000. Everyday things were still unaffordably expensive for the average Joe, who had less money in his pocket than any previous time in history. TV still sucked, though people had been dumbed down for so long they couldn't quite put their finger on the problem. The number of people killing themselves after watching Thursday night network television was at an all time high.

The songs of ecstatic celebration eventually morphed into all too familiar shrill cacophony of whining. Blessings and beatitudes turned into bombast and bickering. Glad-handing became fist pounding. Fight clubs oddly enough were being resurrected and major cities boasted several on any given evening where a person could go and get their face bashed in just for the hell of it.

The honeymoon was over.

America returned to being the bitchy, anxious, frustrated, angry place it had been for so long, no one could remember a time when it was otherwise.

It became the usual feeding frenzy for the media. Always right there to whip up a good fight if it meant better ratings, pundits kept stirring the pot of vitriol. They had missed the old familiar angry mob and joyfully embraced their return — petty, sniveling, self-righteous, indignant, manipulative, hateful on the right; crybaby, hysterical, self-pitying, defensive, hesitant, moribund on the left; vituperative, schizophrenic, malignant, crass, nihilistic, menacing on the fringes. Reviewing the events of the past year, people again wanted to know how such horrible things could be happening to the greatest, richest, most powerful, personally-blessed-and-endorsed-by-God-Himself country in history.

Then the rumors started.

What may have been rib-ticklers exchanged between government insiders or even boiler plate civil servants always looking for the next can-you-believe-this-shit fodder to trade by the water cooler or happy hour toasts after work, soon crept into the national dialogue. First they showed up on the expected truth-digging web sites which were always on the lookout for official chicanery and malfeasance. Then they started getting some currency as major media outlets picked up on them. With all the feel good news following the destruction of the asteroid, media rock stars were ravenous for the juicy gristle of scandal to sink their fangs into. It was long overdue for them to assume their rightful place in the bloodlust spotlight, as the kings and queens of carnage that they were and probably always would be.

The juicy new rumor was that the whole asteroid thing had been a complete hoax, that the planet was never in danger because there never was an asteroid in the first place.

After the predictable initial rounds of posturing, puffery, and conjectural squabbling, two distinct camps formed.

On the left were those now convinced that this government and its charismatic but narcissistic and at times dull-witted President, was so ruthless and detached from reality, so thoroughly incapable of principled action, the entire bunch of criminal misfits had indeed concocted the whole thing as a last-ditch desperate attempt to stay in power. Cynicism had achieved a new summit.

The right took its usual position which regarded facts as bothersome and irrelevant: Even if there was convincing evidence to the contrary, the idea that the government would perpetrate a hoax of this magnitude just to win political points was just one more loony conspiracy theory. Like the one about the rich rigging the system so they could get richer. Anyone who questioned the veracity of the official story was obviously a traitor or a bonehead.

For now at least, nothing got resolved. The discussion — or more accurately, verbal cage fighting — continued for months as new "evidence", none of it remotely conclusive, and new arguments, none of them barely coherent much less convincing, continued to spew from the television and computer screens of increasingly disoriented and apathetic observers.

For several months, the real story would remain shrouded in the thick fog of speculation, the billowing vapor of bombast and bullshit, the sandstorm of soap opera and sophistry that was 24/7 news television.

And what else could be expected? In a world of Photoshop and digital action movies, truth and fiction are just indistinguishable terabytes of zeroes and ones. Spin is just the latest science in the spring collection of illusion and canned deception. Denial is the new steroid to pump up hope and trust in the system. Patriotism is the nitrous oxide for the divided and disenfranchised desperately craving the euphoria of being on a winning team. The President is the ultimate rock star superhero and we bang our heads on the stage where he bumps and grinds his version of reality so we don't have to deal with ours.

The world is a stage indeed — or more accurately a flat-panel display — and a constant stream of lies swirls about in a dazzling array, filling our heads with visions and holograms, soundbites and ideal worlds that never were and never will be. The music pumps from every direction, from our iPods and Surround Sound 5.1 multimedia systems, and we're always on television because there are cameras everywhere watching our every move, so we move and act and look like the revolving door of personalities we see on reality TV, in the movies, and on that pixelated screen, the backlit panel where unfolds the most unlikely and implausible plots. It's not daunting in the least. The laugh track tells us when to laugh and the music tells us when to cry or to feel something resembling a human emotion. And it's all so perfect and real because it's not but we can't tell the difference because we don't want to know and don't care. Truth is stranger than fiction? How could it be? They're the same thing.

Is there any way to sum it all up?

The simple fact was that by the end of year, the country's mood swing had gone down, up, over the top and come back full circle. It was a wash. This dramatic chapter of life's painstaking, heartbreaking, ennobling, humiliating, ultimately pointless journey was a Möbius strip. A slog on a treadmill. A bridge to nowhere. A spinning top.

A Ferris wheel.

Everything had changed.

But everything was still the same.

Godzilla Meets Bambi

Noah moved to New York City, found a room on the Lower East Side fit for a king if that king happened to be an insect or a rat, bounced around from one temporary job to the next, took up with a 19-year-old hot Puerto Rican tamala for a couple weeks, then decided it was time to settle down. The spicy Puerto Rican sex toy went bye-bye. Noah started to get earnest about life.

He loved the city and it took him about five seconds to convince Naomi that together they would thrive in the Big Apple.

Noah found a decent flat in Queens, put down a deposit. She made the long trek from Pulnick by bus, and they moved in a week later. Thus was cemented into Noah's new life the solid stuff of a serious relationship, that age-old business of building a private paradise together with a person mutually loved and respected.

Their reunion was consecrated — if that's the right word for an atheist couple — by Noah's being accepted to NYU's film school program. He would begin his studies Fall Term.

Naomi immediately found work stocking shelves at a deli on the Upper West Side. This was not a problem. Their flat in Queens was fifty yards from a subway stop that offered them a direct shot into the city. When not working, she studied art and modern dance at various studios scattered throughout Queens, Brooklyn and Manhattan, spent hours at the public library, and never stopped smiling.

In five months, they moved to a closet-sized flat on the extreme upper edge of the West Village bordering the meatpacking district. It was cramped to say the least, but the location was phenomenal.

When Noah finally started classes at NYU in September, he had a lot of catching up to do. He hadn't done classroom work since graduating high school six years ago.

Most of his schedule was filled with the typical basic required courses. He worked hard and did quite well for an undereducated rube from the armpit of America.

What amazed and thrilled him about the NYU program he was now enrolled in was that despite him being a freshman, they insisted he jump right in and start making films.

He turned in his first project at the end of the term, a short but highly inspired film.

The morning that his project would get its first public airing, a small public which consisted only of the other students in his class, Noah woke up early. He made himself a cup of spicy chai tea, started to sign on to the internet, but changed his mind and instead started watching the early morning news on WABC-TV. Naomi came out stretching and yawning, and joined him halfway through the broadcast.

It was the breaking news update on a story that had been unfolding for a while.

> *"We have just learned that two high level administration officials, Secretary of Defense Walter Belvedere and Director of Internal Security Wyatt Grayson Tass, resigned today amidst new allegations. Anonymous sources have told us to expect more such resignations in the next few days. Also, several members of Congress have reviewed the evidence and now claim they have indisputable proof that the asteroid scare, announced just weeks before the last election, which put the whole world in a state of shock and turmoil, was a fabrication and a hoax. The President and his staff are accused of planning and implementing the entire doomsday scenario purely for political advantage. The time frame for the start of the official impeachment hearings will be announced Monday."*

Naomi put her arm around Noah and ran her delicate hand across his cheek. "How does that make you feel?"

"Hungry. Very hungry!"

They made breakfast together. Noah's favorite. Soft-boiled eggs, English muffins with homemade jelly — he loved Naomi's orange peel marmalade — and strawberries with fresh cream. One more cup of chai and he was good to go.

Naomi walked him to the door.

"Good luck today, Noah. I'm sure it'll go great. I've got jazz dance tonight, so I'll be home late."

It took him twenty minutes to walk from their tiny apartment on Hudson and Jane, through Washington Square, finally to the arts learning center where he had class.

He plopped himself down ten minutes early, first to arrive.

Professor Theodore Lucas knew his stuff and Noah had learned a lot. But he was a rather pompous fellow, his own biggest fan, never at a loss for a condescending word, offering commentary which was often more self-aggrandizing than constructive.

"So let's pick up where we left off. For those of you who were at Starbucks last class, we're looking at the short films each of you have submitted as your final course project. This next one is from our friend from the cow-tipping grasslands of Missouri, not far from where Mark Twain lived most of his life. Let's hope some of Mr. Twain's legendary talent somehow rubbed off on this inauspicious would-be filmmaker."

The lights dimmed and Noah's film started.

It was a crude animation. The opening shot was the enormous leg and foot of Godzilla in a forest. Ominous music is playing. There are four twig-like limbs sticking out from under the giant reptilian foot, presumably those of poor little Bambi who has been crushed under the humungous weight of the monster. But the legs start to wiggle. Then they actually withdraw completely under the foot. Suddenly we are under the foot in a close-up of Bambi and can see that he isn't dead at all. He is crouched low in a slight indentation in the ground beneath the massive scaly paw. Though shaken, Bambi is fine. He now raises one of his tiny paws and starts tickling Godzilla's foot. We hear the first burbling hints of a deep throaty giggle. Bambi then lays on his back and uses all four of his pointy little limbs to tickle the monster. We begin to hear the huge thunderous roar of Godzilla laughing. Now there is a long shot which takes in the entirety of the towering superlizard. He has reared back his oversized head and is laughing uncontrollably. He lifts up the tickled foot and tries to grab it with his front paws. They flail away but they are too short to reach the foot. He begins to lose his balance. Still laughing hysterically he starts to fall. He struggles but it is too late for him to recover and his gigantic body goes over backwards. As he crashes to the ground, his head hits the jagged edge of a mountain range. It splits open. In a massive avalanche his bloody brains spill out and bury a nearby village. Now there is a close-up of Bambi crawling out of the hole, shaking himself off. He smiles, then bounds off into the low scrub of the forest. Butterflies and birds fill the screen as the pleasant sound of gentle flute music and birds playfully chirping swells under the closing credits.

Godzilla Meets Bambi
Produced and directed
by Noah Tass

The End

The lights came back on. The other students looked around at one another, looking for some clue as to how they should react.

Professor Lucas paced back and forth a bit, trying to appear lost in thought, a smirk betraying the fatuousness of his facade.

"Hmm. Interesting. Mr. Tass, what do you have to say?"

"Well, sir. It's an allegory."

"An allegory. Okay. We know what we've seen. But perhaps you were meaning to reach much deeper. Maybe an extended allegory with mythological sub-themes drawn from the classical Greeks. Or Romans? Possibly even a Biblical theme. David and Goliath?"

"Actually, just Bambi and Godzilla."

"Rocky Balboa and Apollo Creed?"

"I'll stick with Bambi and Godzilla."

"Not exactly the stuff of legends."

"Bambi has a sizable youth fan base. Godzilla is big in Japan."

"Godzilla is big wherever he goes."

There was polite snickering, which Lucas didn't hear because he himself found his joke so wildly amusing. He downsized his shit eating grin to patronizing amusement, then continued.

"An allegory of what, Mr. Tass?"

"Life itself, sir."

"Aha! Life itself! Interesting. Interesting. Anyone else here want to comment?"

Like the lemmings they were, and more to the point, wishing to avoid incurring spiteful vilification of their own short films when they were shown, Noah's fellow students combined to create an echo machine.

"Interesting."

"Yes. Interesting."

"Kind of interesting!"

"I'd say...uh...interesting."

"It was most definitely interesting."

"It was interesting how interesting it was."

There was a song in the early 60s.

> "What's life?
> It's a magazine
> How much does it cost?
> It costs 20 cents
> I only got a nickel
> That's life"

Life?
Interesting indeed.

More Books by John Rachel

If you were dazzled by what you just read, please check out these other fine novels by this author and political blogger.

"The Man Who Loved Too Much"
Trilogy

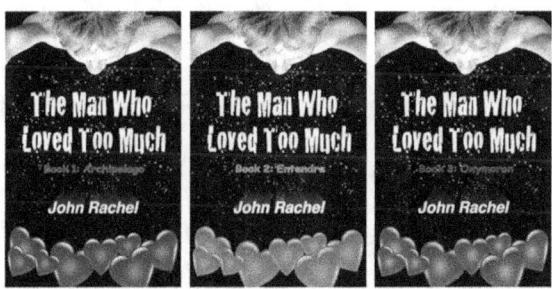

Billy Green is bright, enigmatic, and lost. He spent his first 28 years trying to figure out who he is and where he fits in. His life has been a wild, unpredictable quest to attach himself to some reality he can grasp and live with. He grew up in an abysmal suburb of Detroit, escaped to university life at Cornell, got married and divorced before being thrown headlong and entirely unprepared into the insanity and social chaos of New York City.

Book 1: Archipelago
Amazon (Kindle): amzn.to/1tyIRiw
Amazon (Print): amzn.to/1z8F8aD
Barnes & Noble: bit.ly/ZDnQVO
Apple iBook: bit.ly/1ycItFD
Smashwords: bit.ly/1w62HOX

Book 2: Entendre
Amazon (Kindle): amzn.to/18x1ZnS
Amazon (Print): amzn.to/1xfmjp3
Barnes & Noble: bit.ly/18OGY85
Apple iBook: apple.co/1bkFQe7
Smashwords: bit.ly/1AMUCPz

Book 3: Oxymoron
Amazon (Kindle): amzn.to/1LJnMc
Amazon (Print): amzn.to/1NZPU9Y
Barnes & Noble: bit.ly/1fvzxXD
Apple iBook: apple.co/1DfoG9g
Smashwords: bit.ly/1LJnRgJ

"An Unlikely Truth"

In this political drama, a bright, young, idealistic, Green Party candidate in his bid for the congressional seat of a conservative district in Ohio, teams with a beautiful, fiery African-American intern to combat the slick deceptions and ruthless tactics of a sweet-talking right wing incumbent.

Amazon (Kindle): amzn.to/1jetpiY
Amazon (Print): amzn.to/1lddvsp
Barnes & Noble: bit.ly/1l5FmuG
Apple iBook: bit.ly/1gT2O7w
Smashwords: bit.ly/1fIU3Mq

"Candidate Contracts: Taking Back Our Democracy"

**Candidate Contracts:
Taking Back Our
Democracy**

*A Step-By-Step Plan for
Radical Electoral Reform
and 3rd Party Empowerment!*

by
John Rachel

Prepare to understand contemporary politics as never before! Prepare to see the future of American democracy! This manifesto offers a detailed, step-by-step plan for cleaning up the corruption in Washington DC. This is electoral reform so radical that in one master stroke, it puts America on the path to a healthy economy and directly addresses its #1 and #2 challenges: the suicidal march to war and the destructive impact of a historically high level of wealth inequality.

Amazon (Kindle): amzn.to/1QJRiNZ
Amazon (Print): amzn.to/1Cuq0du
Barnes & Noble: bit.ly/1GpTTLq
Apple iBook: apple.co/1BXnPcy
Smashwords: bit.ly/1B4DQCp
Kobo: bit.ly/1QETE64

Coming Soon

[2016 and beyond]

"Sex, Lies and Coffee Beans"

"Love Connection"

"The Last Giraffe"

"13 - 13 - 13"

"Happy Happy Dreaming Girl"

"The Naked American"

"St. Jerome's Home For The Sexually Insane"

About The Author

John Rachel has a B.A. in Philosophy, has traveled extensively, been a songwriter and music producer, and is a bipolar humanist. He has spent his life trying to resolve the intrinsic clash between the metaphysical purity of Buddhism and the overwhelming appeal of narcissism.

Since 2008, when he first embarked on his career as a novelist, he has had eight fiction and two non-fiction books published. These range from three satires and a coming-of-age trilogy, to a political drama and most recently a crime thriller. The two non-fiction works were also political, his attempt to address the crisis of democracy and pandemic corruption in the governing institutions of America.

Never knowing when enough is enough, the hyperthyroid Rachel continues to be very busy. He has three more novels in the pipeline for publication in 2016: *Sex, Lies and Coffee Beans*, a spoof on the self-help crazes of the 80s and 90s; *Love Connection*, a drug-trafficking thriller set in Japan; and finally *The Last Giraffe*, an anthropological drama involving both the worship and devouring of giraffes, which unfolds in 19th Century sub-Saharan Africa. Several major publishers have declared that they will do everything in their power to make sure these books never see the light of day.

Moreover, he recently increased his output of incendiary political blogs, sure to alienate the remaining few remnants of his meager literary following.

John Rachel's last permanent residence in America was Portland, Oregon where he had a state-of-the-art ProTools recording studio, music production house, a radio promotion and music publishing company. He still writes music and, much to the annoyance of his neighbors in the traditional rural Japanese town where he now lives, attempts to sing his original songs.

• • •

You can follow John Rachel's adventures
and developing world view at:
jdrachel.com

• • •

Since the open mind recognizes no borders, you are also
invited to join us in the ongoing dialogue about
literature and the writing arts at:
literaryvagabond.com

Author John Rachel

Legal Notices and Disclaimers

Blinders Keepers is an original novel which is protected under international copyright law and registered with the U. S. Library of Congress © John D Rachel, 2013 (1ˢᵗ Edition), and 2015 (2ⁿᵈ Edition).

Blinders Keepers is entirely a work of fiction. Names, characters, places, brands, media, and incidents are either the product of the author's imagination or are used fictitiously. Specifically the membership of Cynthia Magelin in the 60s pop band the Lemonpipers is purely made up. Other references to celebrities and nationally-known figures and their roles in the story are likewise fictional. This includes but is not limited to the following recognized news show icons: Rachel Maddow, Ed Schultz, Wolf Blitzer, Christian Amanpour, George Will, John McLaughlin, Pat Buchanan, Eleanor Clift, Susan Ferrechio, Mort Zuckerman, George Stephanopolous, Cokie Roberts, Matthew Dowd. No participation by such individuals in the writing of this novel or their endorsement of its point of view and message is claimed or otherwise implied.

The author acknowledges the trademarked status and trademark owners of various products referenced in this work of fiction, which have been used without permission. The publication/use of these trademarks is not authorized, associated with, or sponsored by the trademark owners, but appear as common features in the story as they are common features in modern everyday life. No product endorsements are meant or implied by their use.

Two excerpts of *Blinders Keepers* have appeared as short stories in online and print publications. "The Little Engine That Could" appeared in the August 2012 issue of the Canadian magazine Ascent Aspirations, and "Crazy Is The New Desperate" appeared in the American magazine The Vein in September 2012.

The author also quoted song lyrics in the story: "Me and Bobby McGee" © 1969 by Combine Music Corporation, performed by Roger Miller and Janis Joplin, words and music by Kris Kristopherson and Fred Foster; "The Little Engine That Could" © 1997 by EMI Music, performed by John Denver, words and music by Warren Foster and Billy May; "That's Life" © 1962 performed by Gabriel & the Angels.

www.ingramcontent.com/pod-product-compliance
Lightning Source LLC
Chambersburg PA
CBHW070028260626
47159CB00005B/1982